Just Me

By

Graysen Morgen

Triplicity Publishing

2012

Just Me © 2012 Graysen Morgen

Triplicity Publishing, LLC

ISBN-13: 978-1477410745

ISBN-10: 1477410740

All rights reserved. No part of this publication may be reproduced, distributed, or transmitted in any form without permission.

This is a work of fiction. Names, characters, places, and incidents are the product of the author's imagination and are used fictitiously. Any resemblance to actual persons, living or dead, business establishments, events, or locales is entirely coincidental.

Printed in the United States of America

First Edition – 2012

Cover Design: Triplicity Publishing, LLC

Interior Design: Triplicity Publishing, LLC

Also by Graysen Morgen

Falling Snow

Fate vs. Destiny

Love, Loss, Revenge

Natural Instinct

Secluded Heart

Submerged

Acknowledgements

Special thanks to Lee Fitzsimmons, the person who spends countless hours correcting my mistakes.

Dedication

To my loving partner, you inspire me in so many ways. If it wasn't for your encouragement, I wouldn't be doing what makes me happy.

Just Me
Chapter 1

The sleek and powerful looking black Lotus sports car careened into one of the many available spots in the tiny parking lot of the *Snow Drift* ski lodge, at the base of Red Mountain in Aspen, Colorado. The driver of the car stepped out, ran a hand through her short blond hair and confidently wandered into the lodge. A horseshoe shaped bar was in a large room off to the left side of the lodge entrance. Wood paneling covered the walls, a gigantic fireplace was opposite the bar and a large mahogany counter ran across the back wall, complete with three computer terminals, and two well-dressed staff members. The blond sat at an available stool at the end of the bar. The perfect position for a cat on the prowl, she could see the only doorway of the bar as well as every surrounding table. A classic Aerosmith song played softly in the background.

"What'll it be?" The young man with thinning brown hair and a chewed up pencil behind his ear, threw the white dishtowel over the shoulder of his tight black tee shirt and rolled his eyes at his newest patron. Her steel blue eyes were ice cold as she answered him.

"Soco on the rocks."

The richest person in the state and she orders Southern Comfort. The bartender shook his head and poured the contents of her drink. He slid the glass down to her instead of walking back to the corner where she sat. She cocked her head to the side and gave him an eat shit grin as she grabbed the glass and tipped it up, emptying its contents in one shot. She tossed a ten on the bar and walked over to the shapely little blond sitting opposite from her, also sitting alone.

~ ~ ~

The sex was the same as it always was, quick, nameless, and strange. The egotistic blond never looked into the bar as she exited the lodge at one a.m. The first snowfall threatened to fall on the ground in the dark silence of the night. She could smell the flurries dissipating in the air. The black sports car mastered the twists and turns as she made her way back up the mountain. Finally, the tree line cleared and majestic Tudor style two story mansion came into view. The white pillars stood out from the giant wooden double front door. The estate appeared to be an architectural monument from the late eighteen hundreds. The black Lotus stopped at the beginning of the winding driveway in front of a large double gate with *Wiley Estate* scribed across the middle. A suntanned arm reached out to input the code and the massive wrought iron gates slowly opened as the car moved through them, a minute later the driveway ended in front of the mansion, circled around a large fountain and proceeded back down the same road leading to the gates. The sports car followed the driveway off to the side that led to a bulky garage that structurally matched the elegant house sitting next to it. She parked her Lotus next to the black Land Rover on the other side of a black Bentley, and punched in the code to close the garage door. Then, she strode towards the French doors on the side of the house leading into the spacious and very modern looking kitchen. As soon as she stepped inside a slightly taller man dressed in a tuxedo style, butler's ensemble with salt and pepper hair, a matching thin mustache, and light brown eyes, came around the corner to face the small blond. Her steel blue eyes didn't work on him and she knew it.

"I'm not in the mood, Giles." She recoiled and headed for the staircase in the main living area of the house. The man shook his head.

"Miss Wiley, you must come to terms, preferably sooner than later." He spoke with a hint of an English accent. Giles had always reminded her of Michael Cain from the movies. He acted more and more like Alfred, Batman's butler, instead of her own. She could swear she was Bruce Wayne herself sometimes. When she was younger she rode around on his shoulders and played games with him when he was left to babysit the young Wiley heir while her parents appeared at various dinner parties and events.

She stopped mid stride, halfway up the marbled rotund staircase. "My life is none of your business." She declared as she continued up the stairs. Once she was at the top she strode down the hallway, not stopping to look at the various family photo's or art paintings hanging on the walls. Instead she went straight to her bedroom, completely opposite from the Master bedroom at the other end of the hall. *If you know what's good for you old man, you'll leave me alone.*

She ran both hands through her short hair and tossed her keys on the dresser. Twenty minutes later, she'd showered off the remnants from her carnal encounter with the curvy blond at the bar. Now she sat on the small sofa drinking a glass of Remy Martin and stared at her bed on the other side of the room. Sleep would not claim her for hours. This was something she faced every night until she was washed away in a drunken stupor and then she would literally pass out. For the past three months, this inebriated state was the only way she could sleep at all.

Chapter 2
Three months and two weeks earlier

Leland Wiley, sole proprietor of Wiley Steel, an enormous steel company that was continuing to lead the Steel Industry almost a hundred years running. The business was started by his grandfather in the late eighteen hundreds and had been passed down to his father Ian Wiley, then to himself. Leland was very handsome, fairly muscular with dark brown hair and steel blue eyes. His wife Lorraine Wiley stood a few inches shorter than eye level with her five foot ten husband, her bright green eyes and flowing platinum blond hair made her look as gorgeous as a movie star. To most people the Wiley's were the picture perfect couple. Their young daughter, and sole heir to the Wiley fortune and corporation, Ian Leland Wiley was a mixture of both parents. She was her mother's height with a swimmers muscular body like her father. She had her mothers tan skin and bright blond hair, but her eyes were an identical copy of her father's heart stopping steel blue.

Ian had received her Master's in Engineering and her Bachelor's at the same time in Business Management from Colorado State University. She knew one day the family business would be handed down to her, the sole heir, as was her father, and his father. Leland and Lorraine threw a colossal bash for their daughter; most of the business executives and family friends were there at the Wiley Estate. Two weeks later Ian walked across the stage at her graduation ceremony, both of her parent's cried. They felt they were the proudest parents in the entire arena. Giles stayed behind to keep the house running, vowing he didn't need to see her on the stage, he knew the young Wiley shined as brightly as her father and was the center of attention in any crowd.

After the ceremony Leland and Lorraine decided to take the late train back to Aspen. Leland always insisted they take the train anytime they traveled. By all means, it was his family's steel that not only built the locomotive and passenger cars, but it was also holding the track together and he was proud to put it to use. Ian was planning on returning in the morning. She had a few small gatherings to attend to with friends.

~ ~ ~

Her cell phone rang in the middle of the night. Ian fumbled around the dark room for the obnoxious object.

"Hello?" The sleepy voice answered.

"Miss Wiley?"

"Giles? What the hell it's two a.m.!" She lazily wiped the sleep from her eyes.

"Miss Wiley turn on your TV."

"What?" She crossed the tiny room in the dark reaching for the remote. As soon as the picture came in to view in the large box she dropped the phone.

"Miss Wiley…please…Miss Wiley are you there…hello?" The screaming was heard for blocks. Tears streamed down her face as she continued screeching at the top of her lungs.

Just Me

"No!! Please god no! ...NO!!!"

The friend that Ian had spent the night with came tearing through the living room to the couch that Ian was supposed to be sleeping on instead she was across the room on her knees screaming at god in front of the TV. A picture of mangled train fragments and a blazing fire covered the screen. *Oh god no!* "Ian….Ian honey…" Ian didn't acknowledge her presence or the words coming from her friend.

"Hello?"

"Miss Wiley?"

"No, this is Shannon. What happened?"

"Ah Miss Meyers, Mr. and Mrs. Wiley were on the train that derailed early this morning, I'm afraid they did not make it."

"Oh my god, I'm so sorry."

"Where is Miss Wiley?"

"She's in a ball on the floor screaming. I can't…I don't know what to do."

"Please get her things in order. I'm on the way to get her."

Chapter 3
Present Day

Ian was in a ball in the middle of the king sized bed. The knock on the door didn't faze her as she continued in her slumber.

"Miss Wiley?" Giles shook his headed, noting it was pointless to try and wake the nocturnal woman before ten, especially after she drank herself to sleep around four a.m. He was sure she woke up and drank more in the early hours of the morning until she was once again passed out. *She will kill herself at this rate if she continues.*

~ ~ ~

Ian finally graced the house with her presence at noon. She had bags under her eyes that made her appear much older than her ripe age of twenty six.

"May I get you anything, Miss Wiley?" Giles stood with his hands by his side waiting for her reply knowing she'd say no, then, change her mind when her stomach growled.

Ugh! Leave me alone! She sat at the kitchen table. "I'll have a Mimosa and a piece of wheat toast."

"Young Wiley, alcohol and a dry piece of toast

Just Me

aren't going to give you enough energy to start your day. I've already made you a glass of chocolate milk and a stack of banana nut pancakes." He walked over to the table and set the glass and the plate down in front of her. She moved so that he could lay the cloth napkin in her lap. "Would you care for this morning's paper?"

"Nope."

"Wiley Steel has a small article in the business section."

"That's nice." She ate without paying attention to him as he began clearing the kitchen. He'd already washed the dishes from breakfast and was now putting them away. Since Giles brought her back home three months ago they had remained in the same holding pattern. She would stay out all night with god knows who, doing god knows what, then drink herself into oblivion to sleep. She'd stumble down the stairs hung over asking for a Mimosa and some kind of piece of toast. He'd deny he heard her, instead feeding her the nutrition that her body desperately needed.

The board members of Wiley Steel called her everyday. She refused to take the calls. To her, life ended three months ago. Why should she have to carry the burden of the company on her back at barely twenty six years old. She wasn't ready, she was nowhere near ready, her father had only been fifty-two and her mother wasn't even fifty yet.

"The season has started. We got a few inches of powder last night." She ignored him as usual. "Maybe you should think about taking your…fathers SUV instead of that racecar you drive, if you need to go into town."

"My car's fine. It's not snowing bad enough for four wheel drive."

"Suit yourself. You know they only clear Red Mountain Road, not Wiley Drive." He said sarcastically. *Fine, go snowplowing in your sports car dummy.* He thought as he watched her drive off.

Just Me
Chapter 4
Three weeks later

"Cassidy come on, we're gonna be late. You didn't have to bring your entire closet. We're only gonna be there for four days." Wendi shouted down to the hall to her best friend as she studied her own red hair in the mirror.

"I know, calm down, I'm just making sure I didn't forget anything. Geez Wendi." Cassidy poked her head around the corner. "Okay! I'm ready." She stood there with the largest suitcase any of them had ever seen. The woman smiled sheepishly, her jet black hair fell lazily to her shoulders as she ran her hand through it nervously. Her gray eyes shone almost baby blue in the recessed lighting of her apartment. She was fit and trim, with curves in the right places.

Wendi turned to the third girl standing in the room. "She is going to make some woman very miserable one day."

"No shit! And we're the straight ones!" The other woman said as she stood up, straightening out the wrinkle in her jeans. Her sandy colored hair was pulled back in a ponytail.

"Would you two leave me alone? We're not even there yet and you guys are picking on me."

"What are best friends for?" Wendi smiled. "Come on Trina lets help Cinderella load her suitcase in the truck."

~ ~ ~

Two and a half hours later the three women arrived at their destination. They parked in the last remaining spot of the recently plowed parking lot. All three women gathered their luggage and headed inside the four-story log cabin style building. The young man at the counter was dressed in a subtle business suit. His brown hair matched his eyes.

"Hello ladies, welcome to the *Snow Drift* ski lodge located at the base of Red Mountain." All three ladies laughed. He sounded like a robot reciting the brochure that had been mailed to them.

"We need to check in." Cassidy tried to calm her laughter long enough to get their rooms. He took their names and typed a few keys on the computer sitting behind the large mahogany counter that separated them.

"Okay, here you go. Take the stairs to the third floor. You're in room numbers 301, 302, and 303. Enjoy your stay, you should find the itinerary in your rooms. The lift starts running at dawn which is about six thirty a.m. and stops at dusk, that's about seven p.m."

"Cool, thanks." Cassidy took the room keys and grabbed her suitcase. Trina and Wendi followed her up the stairs. Cassidy stopped at the first room and handed two of the keys to her best friends.

"I still can't believe we have to all have separate rooms." Trina said as she took the key. Wendi had already opened her door and immediately realized why they weren't staying together.

"Look at the size of these tiny rooms, barely

enough room to walk from the bed to the bathroom. I guess they really want you to spend your time in the hole-in-the-wall bar down there." Wendi spat as she tossed her suitcase on the bed. Cassidy went to the last room, the numbers above the peephole read 303. She decided the entire room including the bathroom was as big as the living room in her apartment. Her bedroom at her apartment was fairly decent sized, as was the kitchen. But, this tiny ski lodge room was the size of a closet. The walls were all crème colored with a rust colored bedspread that went along with the rust and crème colored pictures on the wall. A quarter of a desk was squished into the corner. She found the pamphlets for the ski rentals, bar, and next-door restaurant lying on the desk by the phone. *At least there's a phone. Not like I have anyone to call.* The TV was in the armoire dresser across from the bed, under the TV shelf she found four tiny drawers. Going by the size of her suitcase, she wasn't going to waste time unpacking it, her array of clothing and toiletry items would never fit. The hardwood floor creaked in the hallway. She could hear the clip-clop of heavy boots that stopped at her door.

"Hey Cass, open up!" She tossed her dark hair out of her face and scooted across the bed to get to the door since her suitcase was blocking the walkway between the bed and the dresser.

"What?" She said as she flung the door open.

"Did you see this? Check it out...the restaurant next door serves breakfast, lunch, and dinner."

"Great, I bet it says–"

"*Home Cookin', just like mamma use to make!* That's what it says in the flyer, the pictures look like it has decent food."

"So I take it we're eating dinner at *Home Cookin'*?"

"Yeah, I'll go get Trina, she went to check out the bar."

"Already?"

"I doubt she's drinking. Besides we'll be tying one on tonight! Woo hoo!" She walked out of the room leaving Cassidy there shaking her head. *And yet another adventure begins!*

Just Me
Chapter 5

Ian dressed in jeans and a tight black long sleeve shirt under her brown leather jacket. She opted for her black Doc Marten shoes, considering it was lightly snowing, or so she thought. The blond stepped out of the kitchen and into the night, she was surprised when her foot sunk down an inch in soft white snow. *God damn it!* She went back inside contemplating Giles' idea. *I can't.* The older man walked into the kitchen and came up behind her.

"It's snowing."

"You think so! Don't say I told you so, Giles. I swear I'm not in the mood."

"Maybe you should take this as a sign and stay in tonight." He nodded his head in assurance.

She ignored his words and walked past him, at the end of the hall she stopped outside of the closed door. She ran a hand threw her blond hair and took a deep breath. When she opened the door to her father's study she swore she could see him sitting at the desk smiling at her as usual. She shook the memory aside and snatched the keys off of the desk, pulling the door shut behind her quickly.

When she opened the door to the overpriced SUV she smiled, her father had always had her extravagant taste in toys. She could smell the faint trace of his cologne when she sat in the seat. She slid it forward a notch and backed out of the garage.

~ ~ ~

"Come on ladies, let's check out the bar!" Wendi linked arms with her best friends and led them into the tiny room. All of the tables were full so they headed towards the bar. None of them were aware of the mischievous blond sitting across from them.

"What can I get for you ladies?" *The hunky looking bartender fills out his tight black tee shirt nicely* Trina thought as she smiled an ordered a glass of wine. Wendi elbowed her and winked at the guy. She also ordered a glass of wine. He walked away to fill their order.

Cassidy had stopped at the restroom before sitting down and was now stuck on the end of the threesome. "Did you guys order for me?"

"No, we were too busy trying to put the flames out. Did you see the bartender? Girl!" Wendi mock fanned herself.

"Uh no, thank you though I'll take your word for it." Cassidy shook her head.

"What can I get for ya?" Cassidy agreed with her friends, he was definitely a fine specimen, for a man anyway. Just then she noticed a woman with short blond hair sitting across the bar staring at her.

"Uh...I'll have what she's having."

She nodded towards Ian. The bartender rolled his eyes and poured the drink. When he returned she grabbed the glass and raised it up and nodded at the blond before she took the first sip. *Holy shit!* Trina saw the look on her friends face then sniffed her glass now half full of rust

Just Me

colored liquid and ice.

"Cass what the hell are you drinking?"

"I don't know, it's pretty good though." She swirled the liquor around in the glass and took another smaller sip.

"Here's to a weekend of fun ladies!" Wendi clinked her wine glass to Trina's and Cassidy joined in. "Oh and I definitely got dibs on the bartender." She smiled at Trina.

"My god you two sound like you're in high school."

"Oh get the stick out of your butt Cass. Lighten up and have some fun, that's what we're here for."

Have fun...I'd like to have a little fun with that blond...she's undressing me with her eyes, I can feel it. "I'll be right back." Cassidy grabbed her drink and walked over to the secluded woman.

"Hi." Ian nodded at her. "What do you call this?" Cassidy lifted her glass.

"Southern Comfort. It's Bourbon." Ian turned her head just enough to flash her sapphire eyes at her with a tiny wink.

Cassidy was enjoying the playful conversation. *Her eyes are gorgeous!* "What's your name?"

"I don't have one." Ian spoke surely.

"It can't be that bad." Cassidy sat on the stool that was closer to the other woman than originally anticipated. Ian leaned towards her, her lips dangerously close to brushing against Cassidy's ear, her finger tips grazed the back of Cassidy's hand.

"Does it matter?" She held her position.

The breath caught in Cassidy's chest. *Breathe damn it, breathe!* "Maybe...I don't want to be a notch in your belt." Cassidy was still holding her breath.

"That's too bad." Ian spoke just above a whisper and this time she touched her lips to Cassidy's ear, before backing away from her. She downed her second drink in one gulp as she tossed a twenty on the counter, then quietly and confidently walked out of the bar.

My god who is she? Cassidy walked back over to her friends and sat back down.

"Uh you wanna explain that *slutasaurus*?!" Wendi spoke first with her red eyebrows raised as high as they'd go. Trina had her head cocked to the side unmistakably waiting for an answer.

"What? I can't talk to someone? You two are sitting here pining for the bartender!"

"We weren't making out with him! A total stranger!" Trina chimed in.

"I wasn't making out with anyone, calm down. You're embarrassing yourselves." *And me!* She was sure her skin was hot pink, she could feel the warmth and it wasn't from embarrassment.

"It sure looked like you two got a little closer than strangers. What were you saying to each other anyway?"

"She has gorgeous blue eyes!"

"You were discussing her eyes? That was an intense conversation for eyes Cass."

"No, she wanted me to leave with her or at least that's how it sounded."

"No way!"

"Yeah, I...hell I probably should've went–" She smiled.

"Uh no, you wanna get killed?"

"By a woman?"

"You never know, she could be crazy! Maybe she

Just Me

has a husband at home and they like it rough so she goes tramping to bring someone home."

"Please, you two are something else. She's definitely a *bad girl* though, that's for sure."

"You look like you're in heat, girlfriend, Trina we need to get her outside before she catches fire!"

"Shut up!" She slapped the redhead's arm. "I am tired though, lets call it a night. We have a long day ahead of us."

~ ~ ~

At noon Giles finally saw the familiar sad face as Ian made her way into the kitchen, she was dressed in wool pants and a thermal turtleneck. She sat at the table like always.

"Can I get you anything, Miss Wiley?" He waited.

"Mimosa and a piece of wheat toast." He shook his head and returned to the table with a plate of chocolate chip muffins and a tall glass of chocolate milk. She was too tired and he knew she wouldn't argue with him, that would be pointless and they both knew it. So she ate four muffins and downed the milk.

"Are you going skiing today young Wiley?" He was hoping her spirits were turning around.

"No, I'm taking the snowmobile out."

Oh no! The last time she rode that thing she almost killed herself, just like her sports car she had to drive it with the pedal to the floor. There was no such thing as a speed limit to Ian Wiley. "Please be careful, you know how soft the fresh powder is this time of year."

"I'll be fine Giles." She stood up and put on her baby blue ski jacket and sunglasses. Her boots were by the door. She couldn't help thinking about the brunette in the bar. Rarely did a woman turn her down. In fact, this one hadn't really done so either. Ian always made it a point to back away when her barrier was being crossed. Exchanging anything other than nameless, meaningless, uninhibited casual sex, was crossing the barrier. Still, the brunette intrigued her.

~ ~ ~

"Okay ladies, these are the controls." The handsome blond guy with mirror lens sunglasses explained the snowmobiles to the three women standing in front of him. Trina was practically falling on him. "Does everyone have it?"

"Oh I got it all right. You can ride me, I mean ride with me just to make sure if you want." Trina ran her hand down his jacket-covered forearm.

Oh give me a break! I talk to a woman for two minutes, but you can paw all over some poor guy! He politely backed away and made it a point to smile at Cassidy who stood out of his face on the other side of the sled. As soon as he walked away Trina turned around.

"You! Ugh!" She stomped over to her own sled. "It figures they always fall for the lesbian of the group, stupid men!" She started the snowmobile and took off. Wendi and Cassidy were right behind her. The rental place gave them walkie-talkies so that they could talk to each other without getting too close. That idea seemed to cause fewer accidents since they began using them last season. They had the sleds for three hours and then they were suppose to go skiing if their bodies didn't give out.

They rode around the different trails watching

Just Me

various animals and down hill skiers go by.

"I think there's a snowboarding hill around here somewhere, let me check the map." Trina spoke into the radio.

"Here, I got it, let's go watch them, I think those are so cool, but I'm too chicken shit to do it." Wendi added.

~ ~ ~

Ian strapped her snowboard to her back and rode out to what she thought was a secluded part of the mountain. She parked the sled on the side and trudged up the hill until she was satisfied with the distance. She strapped her boots to her board and turned towards the bottom of the hill. She flew through the snow like there was no tomorrow the first time she went down. At the bottom she unhooked the board and again walked back up to the top of the hill. She could see a few other people snowboarding close by. *Don't they know this is private property!* She figured it wasn't worth her time to go scream at them, instead she decided to make her trips down the mountain a little more daring.

~ ~ ~

The three stooges stopped on the side of the hill closer to the other boarders that were going down the small slope. Both of them were male. Trina and Wendi were in heaven. Cassidy rolled her eyes and turned her head and noticed the person on the other side of the hill carving and twisting as the snow flew threw the air. *Nice!* "Look at that guys..." She pointed both of her friends in the other direction. One of the guys on the hill next to them stopped close to the sleds.

"Hi, what's up?" He smiled at Cassidy.

"Can you do those tricks? That looks really hard." He shrugged his shoulders.

"It's not that hard." He went to the top and decided to mimic the other boarder. He made it almost halfway, then busted his butt and fell flat on his face in the snow. Cassidy laughed, Wendi and Trina jumped up to go help him. When the second guy saw him fall he raced down the hill on his board.

"What the hell were you doing? Are you okay?" The dark haired guy was shaking his head.

"Yeah, fine, I almost had it, man!"

"I know, I saw you." He turned to the women and stuck his glove covered hand out. "I'm Charlie, this is Derek."

"Nice to meet you guys." Trina and Wendi were engrossed in conversation with the two men.

"Excuse me?" Cassidy looked at all of them and waited, she was still infatuated with the boarder on the other hill.

"Oh I'm sorry, this is Cassidy." Trina cringed from the embarrassment of not introducing their friend.

"Hi, uh…do you guys know that person?" She pointed at the hill.

Charlie answered sarcastically. "More than likely that's Ian Wiley, she owns these hills. I'm actually surprised she hasn't come over to yell at us."

"Wiley…Ian Wiley…as in…."

"Yeah Wiley Steel, yada yada yada…"

"Wow." Cassidy couldn't see anything but a figure in light blue riding a white and black snowboard.

Just Me

She couldn't even see the hair color because of the stocking cap covering the small head. "She's really good."

"Who cares." He turned his attention back to the other two ladies. Since it was their last night on the mountain they decided to invite the guys to dinner with them. Cassidy rolled her eyes. *I had the chance to hook up and didn't because of you two twits. Now you're going to hook up and ditch me, oh that figures!*

"Oh shit! Girls we need to have the snowmobiles back in like fifteen minutes."

"Holy shit! Hey do you guys know a quick way back to the rental place?"

"Yeah, watch out for Cruella Deville over there," He turned towards the other hill, but Ian was gone. "Never mind she's gone. Go down that hill and hang a left, that trail should lead right past her house and down to the lodge.

"Cool!" Cassidy was excited about seeing the house.

The girls took off with Cassidy leading them. As soon as they turned the corner they saw the trees open up with the most beautiful structure sitting in the middle about a mile away behind a large iron gate. *So that's where you live, no wonder you never come to the plant. Actually, I never met your father either...*Her train of thought was diminished when a snowmobile raced past them and cut off to the side of the property. *That's her! God I wish I could see her, I bet she's either old, straight, or like thirteen. Better yet, she's probably really ugly, with a mustache! Serves her right.* Cassidy grinned at her perception.

Dinner came and went, Charlie and Derek were both locals, growing up in Aspen, but now they lived in Denver. Cassidy spent the entire dinner thinking about the obscure blond from the bar the night before.

"Hey, let's go over to the bar." Trina suggested. Cassidy was the first one to stand.

"That's a good idea." As soon as they walked in she saw the blond sitting at the end alone, the same rust colored liquid on the rocks in the glass in front of her. *She's here!* Cassidy walked up next to her and ordered a drink.

"Change your mind?" The soft voice spoke.

"Gotta name yet?"

"Doesn't matter." She finished her glass and stood up. Cassidy was surprised to see the woman was a few inches taller than herself.

Cassidy winked. The woman smiled, her ocean blue eyes twinkled. She reached out and grazed the back of her fingers over Cassidy's soft cheek before walking out of the bar. *Ugh! I've failed twice with this woman. Why the hell am I so drawn to her? All she wants to do is have nameless, meaningless, no strings attached sex with me. And what do I do? I chicken out! Twice! She's gorgeous, I'm so stupid!* "Ugh!" Cassidy sighed and slid onto the warm stool that the mysterious woman had been occupying.

"What can I get for ya?" It was the same guy from the night before. She could tell there was definitely some thick air between him and the blond. Maybe ex-lovers. *Ew no!* "Uh, I'll have a glass of Southe...uh...So...Bour...hmm..."

Just Me

"Southern Comfort...Bourbon?"

"Yes! That's it yeah...on the rocks, sorry." He rolled his eyes and walked away, returning with the glass of rust liquid on ice. Cassidy downed the glass and slid into the booth with friends and the new found guys.

"I'm a little tired, I think I'm going to head up and start packing." Cassidy ran her hand threw her shoulder length jet-black hair. Her gray eyes looked almost black in the dim lighting. Trina looked at Wendi and shrugged.

"We should go up too, I mean we do have to get up early and drive back."

"No you guys stay here, have fun. I'll see you in the morning." Cassidy smiled and winked before she turned to go out into the lobby. *Oh mystery woman of mine, I wish I knew what room you were in. I might just give up on your name for one night of heated passion. Give up Cassidy? You're too late for that now. You're the one who backed out...twice.*

Graysen Morgen
Chapter 6
Three weeks later

"Miss Wiley the board is on the phone. You really should talk to them. This sounds important."

The salt and pepper haired man nervously ran his finger over his thin mustache. *Oh open the door you spoiled brat!* He decided to try the knob; to his surprise it was unlocked. *Please let her be dressed, and god please let her be alone.* He walked in and found the heap of blankets and sheets in the middle of the bed. *Hmm...* He spoke into the phone, telling them she was busy at the moment and would return their call.

He went over to the large bay window and slung the drapes open, letting sunshine fill the large room. That's when he noticed the empty bottle of Remy Martin on the little table by the couch. *At least you're getting slammed like you have money. This must be at least a thousand dollar bottle of Cognac. You've definitely got your daddy's taste, young Wiley. He'd kept this in...ah that's probably where you got it, his private stash in his study. You little sneak.* He started to pull the covers back when she stirred, a small blond haired head popped out from under the covers, her eyebrows were fused together and her eyes were almost black.

"What the hell are you doing in my room, Giles?"

"Uh...Miss Wiley, it's time for you to get up. You *had* an important phone call."

Just Me

She didn't move. Her head was the only thing he could see. *Thank god.*

"Who was it?" She said through gritted teeth.

"The board."

"Giles, how many times have I told you, the board is not important to me? They can all go to hell."

God give me ...wait...Mr. Wiley, please give me the strength to get this kid in line. She's ruining her life. That's it, he finally figured it out. "How would your father feel if he heard you say that?"

"Leave my father out of this. Giles, I'm warning you."

"Ian Wiley, you are wasting your life away for something that you couldn't control. You should be ashamed at the way you've been living these past four months."

"GILES!" She yelled.

"Listen to me, your father, grandfather, and great grandfather left you a legacy to run. It's time for you to get up off of your bottom and do what's in your blood. You're a Wiley for god's sake! Act like it!"

"You're fired!" She tossed the covers back and stood up. Giles thanked the lord she was at least covered in the right places. Tiny feminine boxer shorts and a tiny tee shirt was all she wore, nothing underneath either piece. She got into the old man's face. "You're fired you old bastard!" She was screaming at him.

"This is for your own good. Think about what you're doing Ian Leland, think about your parents, what would they say to you if they saw you like this? Your father would roll over in his grave!" She hauled off and nailed him square in the nose with her fist as a tear escaped her eye. Blood poured from his nostril. He put his hand up to his nose and tilted his head back to stop the bleeding. Luckily, she didn't break it. *Little shit!* "At least talk to someone, Miss Wiley. Counseling never hurt anyone. You're killing yourself like this." He turned towards her bedroom door. "I'll be gone in an hour."

She took a deep breath. *What the hell just happened?* "No...don't..." She drew in another breath and wiped the tears from her cheeks. "Stay, Giles, there's no reason for you to go."

"You fired me, Miss Wiley." He turned back towards her, he knew she was crying. *That's a start.* The young woman had been in a state of shock when he found her in that apartment on the Colorado State University campus. She was curled up in a ball, still in her tee shirt and shorts, her short hair looked like a rats nest and her eyes were black. She looked like she belonged in a mental institution. He knew he had better get her back to the Estate and let the Board handle the press. If anyone saw her like this they'd surely lock her up to keep her from hurting herself.

He took care of her around the clock for the first few weeks, until she finally spoke. She never cried after that first night when she had just found out, instead she pushed it all away and completely forgot who she was. Now, Giles was doing his best to fight the demons that she was hiding from. *She needs a Psychiatrist. She needs to talk to someone, anyone. Poor young Wiley, I can't begin to imagine what you're going through. The thoughts running through your mind are driving you mentally crazy.*

"I...didn't mean it...can you please give me some space, Giles?" She looked down at her half naked attire. He caught on and excused himself. An hour later she

Just Me

appeared at the table.

"You look like you're feeling better, Miss Wiley."

"Don't push it. I'm still pissed at you." She didn't look at him.

"May I get you anything?" He waited.

"Mimosa and a piece of cinnamon toast." He shook his head. *Progress is slow, patience is a virtue. Giles.* He returned to the table with a large glass of chocolate milk and a plate of waffles. He knew he wouldn't see her for the rest of the day; therefore, he always made sure she ate heartily at breakfast. That was the one meal he knew she was eating. As soon as she finished her plate he cleared the table.

"How am I supposed to do it?"

"Excuse me Miss Wiley, what was that?" He walked back over to the table.

"I don't know what to do Giles."

"What do you mean?" He was almost in shock. *She's not only conversing with me, but asking me questions. This is good, very good.*

"Sit, I hate it when you stand over me, I'm not ten anymore." He obliged and sat in the dining room chair on her right. "How could he leave me with this? I have no idea what I'm doing."

"He wouldn't have left it if you weren't ready, young Wiley. You know that."

"I've barely had anything to do with Wiley Steel. I was too busy with school."

"Yes and now you have those fancy degrees. Put them to use. You're very smart, Miss Wiley, your father knew that." He reached out and covered her hand with his. *Okay, so this is working.*

"I'm scared, Giles." Her blue eyes couldn't hold

the tears anymore as they slid down her cheek faster than she could wipe them. "I miss them so much. How could they just leave me?"

"Aww, young Wiley, they didn't leave you on purpose, these things happen. That's part of life." She leaned over and put her sobbing head on his shoulder. Her tears soaked into his tuxedo jacket.

"It's just not fair…it sho…" She sniffled. "It should've been me."

"No, you're wrong. You needed to be here to run this legacy. You're the heir, the only heir."

"Giles, I…" She cried harder. "I was suppose to be with them…I stayed back to go to a party with Shannon."

"That's the way these things work. It's destiny my dear." She continued to cry for another hour. The older man did everything he could to console her.

~ ~ ~

As the next two weeks slowly went by, Ian spent more time talking to Giles and trying to work through her problems. She figured it was time to contact the board and become a *Wiley*.

"Hi, may I speak to Frasier Higginbotham please." Ian's hand shook nervously as she held the receiver. Fraser was her father's assistant. Deep down he wished he was a Wiley so that he could run her father out of office. She knew he despised her for being the sole heir. The young woman on the other end of the line was turning into a nuisance.

"Ma'am may I ask who's calling and take a message for him?"

"This is Ian Wiley. I suggest you let me talk to him."

"Oh my, please hold on one minute, Miss Wiley."

"Frasier Higginbotham."

"Frasier, It's Ian Wiley."

He cleared his throat nervously. "Miss Wiley, let me start by saying how sorry I am about your parents."

"Thank you." *I'm sure you are 'rat bastard'.* He had always given her a bad taste. She never relayed it to her father to keep from insulting him since this guy was his assistant.

"What can I do for you?"

"Well, I want to personally thank you for keeping things in line for the past four months, I had many things that I needed to take care of and now I'll be returning to the Corporate Office to take over for my father Monday morning."

"So soon? Are you sure you don't need more time?"

No you're not going to sell or buy out my family's company you dickhead, your goose is in the oven and I just turned the temperature up! "No, things are fine. I'll see you Monday. Oh and Frasier? Make sure my fathers, rather my, office is clean." She hung up the phone and slapped her hands together. Giles sat right next to her in the study. She looked over at the framed picture of her and her father in front of the Wiley Steel plant when she was about nine.

"That sounded like it went well."

"He's pis …I mean he's shaking in his boots." She smiled.

Chapter 7

"Shall we go *Wiley Style* this morning, Giles?"

He knew exactly what the woman was referring to. The snow was thick on the ground, but Giles had already prepared for Ian Wiley's return to Wiley Steel as the head of the company. He had the street crew plow and salt the driveway and the Bentley was gassed up and ready to go.

"What, no Mimosa and toast this morning Miss Wiley?"

"Of course Giles. You know I want a Mimosa and a dry piece of toast everyday. What makes today special?" She smiled.

He brought her breakfast of chocolate milk and French toast to her. She quickly ate and went back upstairs to change. Twenty minutes later Ian Wiley was standing at the foot of the staircase ready to take on the world. She was dressed in a black pants suit with a canary yellow blouse under the jacket. Her hair seemed to glow next to it and her eyes shined. Giles thought he felt a tear roll down his cheek.

Oh, Ian Leland, your father would be so proud of you right now, Leland. You and Lorraine raised her to be one hell of a woman. "Shall we?" He nodded towards the door.

The Bentley was jet black with black leather

Just Me

interior and limo tinted windows. Giles held the door as Ian bent her head and slid into the back seat. The older man straightened his tux and walked around to the driver's side.

"Hey Giles, I know I don't have to ask, but can you…uh keep your cell phone handy today?"

"As always, Miss Wiley." He smiled in the rearview mirror when she looked up at him.

~ ~ ~

Everyone was excited to see the new President of Wiley Steel as she strode into the building. She had forgotten how elegant the building was. Railroad pictures and other various project pictures covered the gold walls next to the marbled white and gray tile floor. She'd seen the pictures numerous times of her grandfather and great grandfather in black and white in the hallway leading to her office. The door had a small sign that said *President, I.L. Wiley.* As she walked through the hall, anyone near her stepped back to give way to her, as if in her father's honor they seemed proud to have her there. That is, everyone except Frasier Higginbotham, who seemed to dig a thorn into her side anytime he was around.

The desk was deep mahogany wood with a large black leather chair behind it. Matching mahogany book shelves and file drawers covered two of the walls and framed pictures covered the others. She felt a sense of pride as she sat behind that desk. She took a long, deep breath to relax and let it all come into reality. *She* was the *one and only Wiley.*

"I want to see the books, give me all of the codes and passwords to the computer program, then call a meeting with the rest of the board. Make it..." She looked down at the silver Rolex on her arm. "Two p.m."

"Yes ma'am." Frasier nervously chewed his thick brown mustache.

Ian sat at her fathers, now her, desk and read spreadsheet after spreadsheet. "No wonder the boards been calling me. We can't seem to close a deal. We've missed one, two, three, four attempts in three different localities. What the hell?" She continued on.

The intercom buzzed on the phone. She leaned forward and pressed the button.

"Yes?"

"Miss Wiley, the board is waiting for you in the conference room."

"Oh yes, I'll be right there. Thank you."

When she walked into the conference room everyone immediately stood up. The blond smiled from ear to ear assertively.

"Please, everyone have a seat. You'll have to refresh my memory. I don't remember if I have met all of you. I was only in and out of here a short time with my...father." Frasier rolled his eyes. She swore she'd punch him in the nose before the day was over. *How did my dad put up with your ass you scumbag, piece of...*

"Miss Wiley, I'm William Goody, Director of Railway Transit." He smiled kindly and she returned the gesture. His black hair shined brightly under the florescent lights.

"I'm Carey Stewart, Director of Metro Transit." Ian nodded at the blond haired man. The last person in the room looked familiar. She figured she'd probably seem him with her father a time or two.

"I seem to be last." The corner of his mouth tried

Just Me

to form a smile. "I'm Benjamin Bradford, Director of Locomotive Services."

Ahh, I see now I know you because Dad was about to fire your lazy ass. He said your department was losing money left and right. She thought back to the reports that she'd read. That was the department that the company was losing deals in. *Hmm...*

"Okay so we're all here, as you know I've taken a look at the reports and spreadsheets. It appears to me that we've lost some major deals in the past eight months. Anyone care to elaborate?" No one spoke up. "Alright, let me start by saying first of all we lost a good deal to overhaul three of Amtrak's locomotives. Second we lost a major deal to produce two new locomotives to CSX plus they also needed six new box cars. So that would be deal number three, shall I continue Mr. Bradford?" The man fumbled, looking questioningly at Frasier Higginbotham. "Uh Mr. Bradford, I'm over here." She craned her head around to see his eyes.

"It was...production...it's their fault. Production is so slow, they can't..." he was shaking. "They can't get anything completed on time. They blame logistics for not getting the parts to the right places and on time. They...production... they caused us to lose these deals, not my department."

Ian could tell there was definitely more to the story, something was seriously amiss with the entire situation.

"Okay, if you say that's what it was, then I believe you. But, Mr. Bradford, what did you do to try and overcome these obstacles and save the deal?" He didn't speak. "My father, grandfather, and great grandfather prided themselves on being able to not only make a deal, but close a sale and stand behind their word and finish the project under schedule to please the customer. I don't see where you even tried to close the deal. It looks to me like you let, what is it..." She looked down at the report. "Four, you let four deals slip away without any effort to save them."

"I worked on them, I..." he looked over at Frasier again. This was beginning to really piss her off. "Production couldn't do it, they couldn't get things straight with logistics and by the time we had a date for them they had already filed contracts with someone else. What was I suppose to do? I did everything. The plant...caused it."

Ian shook her head. *Does he think that I won't go and investigate this? How stupid do these two think I am? I know Frasier is in on this, he has to be. My father would be on his way to the plant right now if he were here. You think I won't go out there don't you? Ugh men!*

"This meeting is adjourned until I return, I will be leaving this afternoon for Grand Junction. I will personally find out what happened with these deals Mr. Bradford. Until then, you are not to do any deals without speaking directly to me, is that understood?"

"Yes ma'am. Miss Wiley, I didn't cause this, you have to understand..."

"I'll find out who *did* cause this, and probably others as well. Good day gentlemen." She reached into her pocket and pulled her cell phone out. She'd already transferred copies of the department reports for the entire year onto her laptop, this included production and logistics as well.

"Giles, I'm ready whenever you can be here."

"I'm out front ma'am."

Just Me

"Good man, I'm on the way out." The double door opened and Ian walked out into the snow covered ground.

"G'day, Miss Wiley."

"You have no idea....no idea." She slid into the car and unbuttoned her suit jacket. Her eyes slammed shut. *Oh dad, I wish you were here. This is big, real big. I don't know if I can take these idiots out of here without you.*

"That bad, young Wiley?"

"Well...how do you feel about a road trip?"

"Excuse me?"

"I need to be in Grand Junction in the morning right after the plant opens."

"*That* bad huh?"

"Yeah."

"I can drive you, Miss Wiley, your father use to tak…"

She cut him off and he stopped in mid sentence too. "I already called a private airline. My flight leaves at eight a.m."

"How long will you be gone?"

"I don't know. I booked a pretty nice room at the Hilton. They have a twenty four hour concierge and a car service. I should be fine, I'd say I'll be back by Friday, but who knows at this point."

"I'll get your luggage ready." He said as he pulled the car up to the front door and got out to open the door for his passenger. Ian went into the house and Giles parked the car in the garage.

Chapter 8

Ian straightened her charcoal gray suit jacket as she walked into the Wiley Steel Corporation production plant in Grand Junction, Colorado. From the outside it looked like a giant warehouse, equally as large as four or five football fields. The gray, steel constructed building stood out from the trees in the forest line. A massive bronze statue of Ian's great grandfather was in the foyer leading to the reception desk. The front of the building was made of various offices and conference rooms, leaving the rest of the enormous superstructure for design, fabrication, and production. She assumed the gated parking lot behind the building was probably a football field size of its own, although she really didn't have clue how many people the company employed.

"Excuse me, may I help you?" The receptionist had long rust colored brown hair that was twisted into a bun and skin that never saw the rays of the sun, making her appear in her late thirties, but Ian figured she was probably middle-aged.

Ian set her briefcase down and stuck her hand over the tall counter top. "I'm Ian Wiley." The woman's golden brown colored eyes went as round as saucers as she smiled and returned the gesture.

"Mr. Masters didn't tell me he was expecting you. It's very nice to see you again, Miss Wiley." She tried to

Just Me

remember the last time that she'd seen the young heir. She was probably a teenager then.

Ian smiled and looked at the name plate on the counter. "Thank you, Mrs. Cragen. Can you please point me towards Richard Masters' office?"

The woman stood and walked around the counter. The blond was surprised to see the receptionist stood eye level with her. Ian wasn't extremely tall, but above average height for a woman.

"Go down this hallway here, take a right and continue to the end, you'll run into his secretary."

"Thank you." Ian picked up her briefcase and strode down the hall. Her black silk shirt felt cool against her skin under her heavy jacket.

~ ~ ~

"It's good to see you again, Miss Wiley." The taller man appeared every bit of forty, trim and happy, but his solid gray hair gave his age away. Still, he was handsome for an older man.

"I'm sure you know I'm here on business." She smiled. "It's been a few years since I was last here. How about a tour of the plant first?" She set her briefcase down and he locked the door to his office on the way out.

They started down the main hallway. She recognized most of the framed photos covering the walls. They were similar to the ones in the corporate office hallways. All of them, photos of her great grandfather, her grandfather, and a few of her father over the years, as well as many projects they had accomplished. Rich stopped outside of the office door closest to his. The plate on the door read, Cassidy Harland, Director of Logistics.

He knocked and opened it, but the room was empty. Just then a shorter woman with sandy blond hair came by with coffee. She stopped at the secretary desk across from the offices. "Kathleen, where's Miss Harland?" She took a sip of her coffee trying to remember where she knew the blond from. She definitely looked important. Mr. Masters was giving her the 'answer me now' look.

"She's out in the plant somewhere, I think."

"Okay." He went to walk away, but decided he had better introduce the Company's owner since she was inches from introducing herself. "Kathleen, this is Ian Wiley." The woman came seriously close to spitting her mouthful of coffee all over the woman she was being introduced to. Ian smiled and shook her hand.

Ian followed the tall man down the next hallway through a door that led to the working part of the building. They went through the design and fabrication rooms. She was pleased with meeting everyone, they, on the other hand, were scared shitless. She knew her father had visited the plant, usually every other month or so. She guessed they weren't use to seeing her and that's what the big deal was, although she *had* visited the plant with her father, as recently as two years ago. Maybe some of these people were new.

Rich took her around the production floor. Many of the machines were going and she was required to wear a hardhat if she went any further. She opted against it. There was no need to watch a machine cut steel. Instead, he took her over to the production floor manager's office. Darren Johnson looked about Rich's age with white hair and a thick white mustache. He took his hardhat off and reached out to shake the woman's hand when Ian was introduced to him. She leaned to return the shake when a spunky brunette in a black pants suit walked into the room. Ian stared at the woman who dropped the file she was carrying when she saw the blond standing in the room looking back at her.

"There you are. I've been looking all over this place for you." Rich snorted and bent to pick up the papers.

"I..." *It's her! Oh my god! She's here. Why is she here?* She could hear Rich talking to her and now standing contently waiting for her reply. *Find your voice Cassidy. Say something!* "I've been down here working with Darren on a new deal. It needs to be out of here next week."

Ian met cool gray eyes with her steel blue ones. The woman standing across from her had her jet black hair pulled up off of her neck in a clip. Her light pink blouse stood out under the black jacket. Ian could swear the woman's skin had blushed to that color all over.

"Oh. Anyway, Cassidy Harland, this is..." Ian cut him off and stuck her hand out to the other woman that stood eye level to her. Ian, was wearing flat, lace up dress shoes and imagined the brunette was probably in shoes with at least two inch heels to make her that tall.

"Ian Wiley." She smiled as she felt a trembling hand touch her own briefly.

"It's nice to meet you, Miss Wiley." *Damn, damn, damn it to hell and back! I almost got it on with my god damn boss! Oh my god, I was going to have a one night stand with her! Holy shit!* She took a deep breath, taking in the sight in front of her. *She's gorgeous.*

"Well, we should get back to the office. I'm sure you've seen enough of the plant." Rich smiled quickly. His face went thin when he remembered she was *here on business.*

"Yes, you're right Rich." She turned to follow him out of the office and whispered as she walked past the still stunned woman. "You got your name."

Ian took a deep breath and continued down the hallway. *My god! How the hell was I supposed to know she worked for me? Great Wiley, this is just what you need. She's beautiful.* The woman that had been labeled by Ian as *the one that got away*, now had a name, a name that was on a paycheck every other week with her computer generated signature on it.

~ ~ ~

"I need to know what happened with the deals on these accounts." Ian tossed a file full of reports on the desk.

"What are these?" Rich sat at his desk reading the reports. "I don't know anything about a deal with Amtrak and our account with CSX doesn't have any locomotives or box cars listed on it for the past year."

"So you're telling me that these deals never came across your desk for production?" Ian tried to contain her frustration.

"No, Miss Wiley, I've never seen these."

He turned to his computer and pulled up Amtrak and showed the past two years history on the account. Then, he typed in CSX and showed her the past two years account history for them too.

"If these came down to my department they'd be listed here."

"This doesn't make sense. These deals didn't go through because production was backed up and logistics was too slow."

He took offense to her words. "There is no way, me and Cass would've known if we had a deal that was behind. These deals you're referring to never made it to production. I swear to you, I've never seen them."

"Do you have a conference room we can meet in with the Logistics Director?" She realized his office was plenty big enough, but she was uncomfortable not sitting at the head of the table.

"Yeah." He called down to production and asked Cassidy to meet him in the conference room in ten minutes. She crossed her fingers hoping the infamous Ian Wiley was long gone.

She was slightly disappointed to see Ian standing in the corner talking on her cell phone. Cassidy took a seat across from Rich and watched Ian walk up to the head of the table and sat down when she ended her call.

"Did you bring her up to speed?" She looked at Rich, he shook his head no. *Great.* "I have reports for four major deals that were supposedly cancelled or rejected due to slow-moving production and delayed logistics. These deals have cost the company millions of dollars in the past eight months."

Cassidy looked at Rich with questioning eyes.

"I don't know anything about it Cassidy. I've checked the accounts on my end and I don't have any orders that match these deals." He looked like he was sitting in a vice that was slowly squeezing him.

She tucked a loose piece of dark hair behind her ear and hesitantly looked at Ian. "I don't know anything about this. My department is running very smoothly. In fact, in the three years that I've been here and year and half that I've been director, we've never been behind with a shipment." She was so nervous her teeth were chattering.

Rich seconded her statement. His fists were clinched together and his knuckles were white. "We've never been behind in production. This doesn't make sense, Miss Wiley."

Ian stretched her neck, trying to appear normal. She was fuming inside, past the point of pissed, heading down the path of rage. "This doesn't make sense to me either. I've been through the locomotive books a hundred times in the corporate office. I'm going to need both of you to pull your files for the past…" She mentally tried to remember how long Fraser Higginbotham had worked for the company. She knew Benjamin Bradford had worked for her father for probably ten years. "five years." If something was going on, her father would've found out, no this, this is a recent problem. "I'm going to head back to my hotel and go through some of the other files that I brought with me. I'll meet with both of you tomorrow morning. Please keep this in this room. The other directors are already aware of this and the fact that I'm here. I met with them yesterday."

She stood and ran her hand through her short hair, her blue eyes were almost black. Cassidy tried desperately to make eye contact with her before she left the room, but Ian was gone as quickly as she had appeared.

~ ~ ~

"Come on Cass, its ladies night at *Playerz*, at least have one drink with me and Wendi." She tossed the clip on the dresser and let her shoulder length black hair flow

Just Me

freely.

"Yeah, we haven't seen you since Aspen!" Wendi chimed in.

"I'm really busy with work guys." *I have to see her again tomorrow, ugh! I don't know why I'm so drawn to her. It's not like anything will happen now, or ever. She's your boss!*

"That's not an excuse and you know it." Both women said simultaneously.

Cassidy knew they were right. She'd done everything she could at the office, even stayed two hours late to help Rich get all of the files together for the meeting. "Fine, I need to shower. I'll be there in an hour." She sighed.

The bar was already packed at eight thirty. *Do straight people only go to one bar? Or is this the only night they go out?* She sat at the small high top round table. The waiter came by and winked, meaning he'd return shortly.

"So, what's got you so busy at work girlie?" Wendi was contemplating grabbing the waiter's ass when he came back over, but she decided to wait a little longer.

"What can I get you?" The shirtless Italian looking man was probably barely twenty one. His dark brown eyes seemed to be looking right through Cassidy's tight, baby blue colored, scoop neck sweater. Her black jeans and zip up leather ankle boots completed the outfit. Her black leather jacket was hanging on the back of her chair.

"What are you guys drinking?" She looked at both of them with Martini's. *Eww, never mind.* "Ugh, bring me Soco on the rocks."

"Lime?"

"No." He disappeared into the crowd.

"Oh my god, did you see how tight his little black jeans are? Mmm!" Wendi was definitely in heat and on the prowl, as usual.

"Yes sir!" Trina agreed and high-fived the redhead. Cassidy rolled her eyes.

"Don't straight-hate!" They all laughed.

"So really, how's work? You seem like you're pissed off." Trina's voice took on a more serious tone. When Cassidy's drink arrived she sipped it at first, then, gulped half of it down. She felt the bourbon go straight from her empty stomach to her aching head.

"We have some major issues going on." She shrugged.

"Okay?"

"My department is involved, well technically it is anyway."

"Oh no, is it bad?" Wendi emptied her Manhattan glass and nodded to the waiter for another.

"I'm not sure, it could be nothing. The owner of the company was at the plant today."

"Oh that always sucks. I hate it when my boss is snooping around. Is he a jerk?" Cassidy downed the rest of her glass and ordered another when the waiter appeared with Wendi's drink. Trina decided to go ahead and order another Cosmopolitan while he was there.

"No. Not from what I saw today. She's–"

"A woman!" Wendi almost choked. "I thought–"

"Mr. Wiley died a few months ago. Don't you remember that?" Cassidy shot her a look.

"Yeah, I just–"

"She's his only child and heir to a fortune." Happy to see her glass reappear Cassidy chugged half of it again.

"At least she's not a bitch. It sucks that she's snooping around your department though."

"Ha! That's not even the half of it." *Why does it have to be* her, *of all god damn people?*

"Okay? What else is going on? Did she say something to you? Is she an old bag? What?" Trina could see the unsettled look on her friends' face, even in the dim light her eyes seemed dark.

"Do you remember the bar in the ski lodge, in Aspen?"

"Yeah." Both women looked puzzled.

"The blond with piercing blue eyes?"

"Oh yeah, the one you were smitten with. I swear I thought you were going to have one hot steamy night of sex with that woman. She looked at you like she wanted to devour you from top to bottom, then start all over again. She made me think about becoming a lesbian. She was really attractive. What about her?" How could Wendi forget? She and Trina gave Cassidy hell for a week, they thought she'd be the one to hook up with someone, instead they both did.

"She's the infamous Ian Wiley…my boss." Cassidy tossed back the contents of her glass and raised it up to the waiter. He turned to get her another.

"Oh my god, Cass!" Trina spoke first.

"Holy shit!" Wendi was right behind her. She swallowed the rest of her drink and ordered another too.

"Yeah, you're telling me." She sighed and drew out the breath she'd been holding.

"What did she say to you?"

"Nothing. Well it was strictly business. I told you she's here because something's up. She has us pulling all kinds of files and records. I don't know. We're meeting with her in the morning."

"Are you going to talk to her? I mean about you know, Aspen and everything?"

"No. There's no way I will cross that boundary with her. She looked as shocked to see me as I was to see her. I'm sure that's a side of her that I, as an employee, wasn't supposed to see."

"How come you didn't know it was her in the bar?" Trina asked.

"I'd never seen her, only heard her name a hundred times. I met her father. She looks a lot like him, but I never put it together in that bar, like a millionaire would be sitting at a tiny ski lodge bar picking up a strange woman."

"Wow, this is really weird, I wouldn't know what to do." Wendi felt nervous.

"I'd quit my job." Trina retorted.

"What! No, I'm not quitting my job. So, I may know a little secret about the company's owner, who happens to be my boss, I'll just keep it a secret and go on like it never happened."

"How are you going to do that? You guys shared a pretty heavy moment. I've never seen a woman unhinge you like she did."

"Oh well. I'm just thankful I didn't sleep with her, my god."

"No shit! That would be a huge mess."

"I'll drink to that, amen sister!"

~ ~ ~

Cassidy shifted slightly in her chair, fighting off a

Just Me

hangover with a headache from hell. They'd been sitting there for three hours. She knew there was nothing to hide. The records in her department were squeaky clean. Still, the powerful blond sitting in front of her made her skin crawl with nervousness and her blood boil with lust. She fought the fire between legs with rattling nerves.

"Damn it." Ian sat back forcefully in the chair. "None of this adds up." *I'm going to have to dig deeper, I think I may have only scratched the surface. There's nothing left to do, except call for an audit of the entire company. Oh Dad, I wish you were here to handle this. I don't know if I can do it. And if that woman looks at me one more time with that scared to death look in her eyes I'm going to smack her. How was I to know she worked for the company? Thousands of god damn employees and I had to try to fuck one of them. More than that, she's so damn attractive. I would've probably tried to see her twice.* A grin crossed her face, not going unnoticed to both Rich and Cassidy.

"What do you think happened?" Rich asked as he thanked god the fuck up wasn't in his department, or in the plant at all for that matter.

"I'm not sure. Maybe these deals were just turned down or rejected by the director. He's blaming you guys, but the records indicate that he's lying to me. Either way, I'll figure it out." She stood up and shuffled all of the reports together and slid them into her briefcase. "By the way, the plant looks good, Rich." She forced a smile and walked out of the room.

"Well, that went over like a terd on a waterfall." He loosened his tie and sat back in the chair.

"Yeah, you're telling me. I don't want to be the one to piss her off. I'm just glad it doesn't have anything to do with me." Cassidy cringed, thinking about how mad Ian looked when she left the room. *She didn't even say bye, hell she didn't even look at me for that matter. I guess I was just another girl in a bar to her. Damn it, damn it to hell. Why me?*

"Miss Harland?" Their joint secretary had messages for Cassidy and Rich. She called to the first one that she saw. "You have a message." Cassidy grabbed the piece of paper. She had no problem reading Kathleen's loopy handwriting.

Change your mind yet? I'm sorry, I didn't know. I'll be at Antonio's if you're hungry around 7 p.m. She knew who it was from, but couldn't figure out why. "Thanks. Did they leave a name or number?"

"No, she called for you. When I said you were in a meeting she said please give her this message. I wrote down everything she said and then she hung up."

"No problem." Cassidy went into her office and shut the door. *One p.m. now, six hours to decide.*

~ ~ ~

Cassidy had worked until six and rushed to her apartment to shower and change. She new Antonio's was a fairly nice place so she opted for pair of nice black jeans and a plum colored V-neck sweater. She zipped up her black leather ankle boots and snatched her black leather jacket from the rack on her way out. She left her hair down and the small breeze blew it around slightly on her shoulders. The light snow that fell earlier was already gone.

"Seven exactly, how'd I know you'd be so punctual?" Ian spoke, her blue eyes twinkled in the low lighting of the restaurant. She was in a white turtle neck and regular blue jeans, her brown leather jacket hung on her chair. Cassidy stripped out of her jacket and hung it on the chair before she sat down.

"You've seen my records. You know I don't cut corners Miss Wi..." Ian reached across the table and brushed her hand over Cassidy's. Cassidy thought her hand was on fire from the heat as their skin touched. She felt her heart skip a beat.

"Since the secret is out, you now have the name that mattered to you so much. It *is* nice to meet formally though, Miss Harland. But, please call me Ian."

"Are you sure? I mean you're..."

"Cassidy, you can't expect me to sit here and treat you like an employee. I'm above that, I thought you would be too."

"I am. I just don't know what to say, I'm still in shock."

"So am I. A little embarrassed too, I might add. You met me under...well, intense circumstances."

"Don't worry, your secret's safe with me." Cassidy said sarcastically as she slid her hand out from under Ian's.

"And what secret might that be?" Ian questioned as the waiter came by. She ordered an expensive bottle of wine to go with her main course of veal parmesan. Cassidy quickly ordered shrimp primavera. As soon as the waiter walked away Cassidy answered her.

"Your motives...the bar..." Cassidy wasn't sure if she should even say anything.

"It's not like I'm asking you to sleep with me. Cassidy. In fact, I've never asked you to sleep with me." Ian replied as she swallowed some of her wine.

"Oh please…you were cruising that bar, twice I might add!" Cassidy tried not to make a scene. Her voice was barely above a whisper, but the nervous frustration was obvious.

"Touché." Ian smiled with a raised eyebrow. "So what are you going to do, out me now? The big bad Wiley is a woman seeking woman for casual sex."

She drank some more of her wine and stared at the woman across from her. Cassidy's eyes were bugging out of her head, she was scared to death and Ian knew it.

"I…I would never…" Cassidy's hand shook as she brought the wine glass to her mouth. *Drink, swallow, drink, swallow. God get me out of here! What the hell was I thinking? She's going to tear me to pieces!*

"It's okay Cassidy, I'm only giving you a hard time. That person…that was a side of me I hope you never see again." Ian seemed very serious. When Cassidy looked up she met bright blue eyes that seemed to hold her. She wasn't sure what to say back to this woman.

"I…don't…I barely know you…I mean…"

"Let's start over. I'm Ian Leland Wiley, I don't frequent bars for women, anymore, and I'm really sorry, if I had known you worked for Wiley Steel I never would've subjected you to that side of me, ever."

"Okay, so what now?"

"What do you mean?"

"Where do we go from here, you're my…my boss…Ian." It tore Ian's heart in two when Cassidy spoke her name. *Why am I so captivated by you?* Cassidy thought.

"Well, yes, you're right. I'm glad we've cleared things up between us. I should definitely change the subject to business, but I don't want to talk business with

Just Me

you. That's not why I invited you and that's not how we met."

"Okay, what do we talk about then?" *I can't believe I am sitting here having this conversation with you. You're my boss and I think you're the most gorgeous woman I have ever met. But, you're definitely complicated, that's for sure.*

"How long have you worked for Wiley Steel? How did you get into logistics? Where did you go to college? What's your degree in? Tell me about you, Cassidy." Ian poured herself another glass of wine, willing it to douse the fire between her legs.

By the end of their dinner Ian knew everything about Cassidy and Cassidy knew nothing about Ian. Ian paid the bill and offered to walk Cassidy to her car. When Cassidy pushed the button to unlock her SUV Ian grabbed her hand. Cassidy turned around to face her, inches from her wet lips. There were standing face to face, Cassidy could see Ian's eyes twinkle in the moonlight. She felt dizzy as the blood in her head went south. *My god she's going to kiss me!*

"I had a nice evening Miss Harland. I'm glad we were able to get past everything and start over." Ian was trying not to fumble her words. *Don't kiss her, for god's sake she's an employee don't kiss her!*

"Thank you for inviting me, I enjoyed it." Cassidy swallowed hard enough for Ian to hear it.

"Goodbye." Ian smiled, let go of her hand and turned towards the hotel that sat across the road from the restaurant.

Chapter 9

The private jet landed shakily on the recently plowed and salted runway, then turned left to taxi towards the private hanger. Ian could see the black luxury car with tinted windows idling next to the open bay door. The salt and pepper haired man stood next to the car, formally dressed as usual in his black cut away style tuxedo with a black vest and a black ascot. He was watching the plane as it rolled to a stop close by. The blond grabbed her briefcase that was sitting next to her and retrieved her luggage from the over-head compartment. She proceeded down the staircase and Giles met her at the bottom to carry her suitcase.

"Good Morning, Miss Wiley." His lips formed a smile. The Englishman still carried his accent, although he'd lived in the States for almost thirty years. "How was your trip?"

Ian looked up at him as she slid into the car. He could see the frustration in her deep blue eyes, when she didn't answer he shut the door and walked around to the driver side. She sat quietly in the back, staring at the trees and melting snow banks along the short ride back up the mountain.

"Giles, stop at the cemetery please." He was a little concerned, Ian hadn't gone anywhere near the cemetery since the funeral. She even made him avoid that road at all cost when he drove her anywhere.

"Would you like me to stop at a flower shop first, Miss Wiley?" He didn't want to speak, but he knew she needed guidance, especially now.

"Yes, please." He turned down a side road and stopped outside of a small family owned florist. "Take my Visa, Giles. Get a combination of yellow orchids and pink carnations." He returned to the car fifteen minutes later and handed the bouquet to her when she opened the door.

Minutes later the black car cleared the Iron Gate and proceeded to the left. A large marble statue stood by itself, lightly covered by a thin layer of snow. When the car stopped, Ian got out on her own and shut the door. Giles got out and stood next to the car. He watched her walk slowly through the snow covered path and stop in front of the famous Bernini 'Apollo and Daphne' statue. Ian bent down and wiped the snow from the inscription. *Leland and Lorraine Wiley, two loving souls that lived together, passed together, now exist beyond our imagination together.*

Ian felt the tears run down her face as she read it. She continued to lean forward, squatting with her hand on the statue. She laid the flowers against the marble.

"I wish you were here dad, I don't know if I can do this alone. God, I have been so mad at you for leaving me like this. I'm not ready, dad." She used her free hand to wipe the tears. "I miss you both so much. I've needed you more than ever lately, mom. You were always there to offer the advice that dad shied away from. I'm so sorry I never told both of you when I had the chance. I was a coward. I'm sure you know now, if you're really watching me like Giles says you are. Oh boy, if that's true I really am sorry for the things you've witnessed since you've been gone. I told you I'm not strong enough to do this." A gust of cold wind sent chills up her spine. "I promise from here on I'll do my best for you both. You deserve that and so much more, mom and dad. I love you both dearly and miss you more everyday."

She wiped the tears from her eyes again before she leaned forward and pressed her lips to the cold marble. She stood up, turned around and walked back down the path towards the car. Giles was waiting with a small package of tissue. She took them from him and threw her arms around his neck. He held her tightly, clearly knowing he was all the young woman had left in her life. She quietly whispered…"Thank you Giles." He almost thought he imagined it as she let go of him and slid into the car, wiping her eyes again, this time using the soft tissues.

~ ~ ~

Friday night Ian found herself sitting at the familiar *Snow Drift* ski lodge bar. The bartender had brought her usual to her as she sat on the corner of the square bar. She finished the glass and ordered another while she contemplated going after the tall blond sitting across from her. When the malignant bartender returned with her second glass she quickly slung it back and set the glass down on the bar with a loud thud. *Not tonight Wiley, it's time to move on.* Her mind drifted to the 'one that got away'. She shook the memory from her head, pulled her keys from her pocket, and left the bar…alone.

~ ~ ~

Just Me

Monday morning the blond rushed down the stairs, tossed her dark blue suit jacket neatly on the chair by the foyer, and walked into the kitchen. Giles waited for her to sit, taking in the crème colored blouse she was wearing and the dark blue pants. He smiled, straightened his ascot and walked over to her.

"May I get you anything, Miss Wiley?" He waited, silently counting as she picked up the crossword puzzle of the newspaper, that and the funnies section being the only parts she'd read. The young woman reminded Giles of her father more and more everyday.

"Mimosa and a piece of white toast." He shook his head and walked out of the kitchen with her breakfast, a large glass of chocolate milk and pumpkin pancakes. She ignored the man when he set the food down, then began to eat contently. She sat the paper aside and called him into the dining room.

"I have an important decision to make today Giles." He nodded. "I know dad never talked about the business with you. He relied on that twit of an assistant for everything."

"I take it you don't take kindly to Mr. Higginbotham?" He stood like any other English butler, his hands behind his back and his attention directly on her until she cleared her plate.

"No, he's a snake in the grass, I know he's up to something. I just can't prove it."

"I see." He took her dirty dishes to the kitchen and loaded them in the dishwasher. She was putting her jacket on when he came out of the kitchen.

"Shall we leave now, Miss Wiley?" He went down the hall and pulled the keys from the wall in the study. "I'll need to take you in the Land Rover today. It seems they forgot to pave our road and driveway this morning."

"It's okay. Giles, I'll drive myself today. I'm going to need to run some errands this afternoon anyway."

"Only if you're sure, Miss Wiley. It's very out of sorts for you to drive yourself to the office." She took a deep breath and sighed. She knew he was right, Giles always drove her father to the office, then came home to see to the house until her mother was ready to go out. Her father had only bought the Land Rover because he sometimes felt like driving himself if he wasn't going to work.

"You're right, let's go."

~ ~ ~

Ian sat behind her gigantic mahogany desk staring at her laptop screen. She'd been engrossed for three hours now, searching website after website for a professional and very discreet account auditing firm. Auditing the books was by far her last resort and at this point, that's all she had left. She closed the window and brought up Wiley Steel production logs any time Frasier decided to rear his ugly head. Something about that man made her skin crawl. *You may have fooled my father. What am I saying? I'm sure he was on to you, you stupid ignoramus. I just can't seem to find the file he had on you, either way, I know you have something to do with this.* That was all she needed. Ian picked up her cell phone and dialed a number from the website on her computer.

"Good afternoon, thank you for calling Acco

Just Me

Consulting Firm, how may I direct your call?" Ian was staring at the website at the Bio's of the upper management for the company. She was surprised to see that the offices were located in the Grand Junction area. She was expecting Denver or Colorado Springs.

"Yes ma'am, may I speak with Larry Maxwell, please?" The woman on the other end sounded a little confused.

"May I ask who's calling ma'am?"

"Ian Wiley." She let out the nervous breath that she'd been holding. *God I hate this.* A minute later a deep voice came on the line.

"Good afternoon, this is Larry Maxwell."

"Mr. Maxwell, this is Ian Wiley, of Wiley Steel Corporation."

"It's a pleasure to speak with you, Miss Wiley. What can I do for you?" She tapped her pen on the edge of the file folder laying on the desk by the computer.

"Before I get started, I need you to understand that this conversation has to be very discreet. No one may know that I contacted you."

"Yes ma'am, all of our business deals are completely confidential."

"I believe my company is in need of an account audit."

"Okay, please specify the reason for the audit. What makes you think your accounts need to be audited?"

"Please understand Mr. Maxwell, this is my very last recourse. I do not want to do this."

"I understand. Who does?" He smiled through the phone trying to console her.

"I believe I may have a corrupt employee."

"Okay, go on." He was taking notes.

"We have a few account deals that mysteriously never made it to production. I know this probably sounds a little off, but I know there is no reason for the deals to be rejected. I've pulled all of the accounts and reports and I can't seem to find out what happened. I'm going to start making calls tomorrow to the account holding companies and other steel corporations to find out if we were undersold, and if so, who got the bid on the deals."

"It sounds like you know what direction to go in Miss Wiley. Why would you need to audit your accounts?"

"Because I need to know how long this has been going on and who's behind it. I also need to see if they've taken anything other than a few million dollar deals, if you know what I mean."

"Yes ma'am, I think I can definitely help you determine whether or not your records and accounts add up."

"Thank you, I'll need this done as soon as possible. Are you available to start tomorrow?"

"I won't be there personally, but I will send you one of my best account managers. Give me your fax number and I'll send over the paperwork for you to sign, in the meantime, I'll check her schedule real quick." Ian gave him the number. Light sounds of Rod Stewart played when he put her back on hold. *I hope I'm doing the right thing. I don't know what else to do, if I let this continue and I'm right, then whoever is doing this will wipe us out, slowly but surely.* She signed the paper and sent it back to him. He charged the five thousand dollar fee to her personal Visa card while she waited. The music stopped.

"Okay Miss Wiley, I have everything taken care of, Katrina Sylvan will be there…what is the location that I should send her to?"

"I'm sorry, the corporate offices are located in Aspen. It's a two and a half hour trip from the production plant in Grand Junction."

"That's not a problem. She should be there around ten a.m."

"Mr. Maxwell, please give her my cell number and have her stay in the hotel. She will need to contact me when she's ready to meet and I'll have my driver come get her. I cannot let the directors or my assistant in the offices know why she's here."

"Yes ma'am, I'll let her know."

"Thank you again." She hung up.

Chapter 10

The black car pulled up in front of the Aspen Grand Hotel and Ian saw a woman standing by the doors in a black skirt suit and a black overcoat. Her sandy colored hair was shoulder length. *I know I've seen her before.* The woman slid into the car next to Ian when Giles opened the door. Her brown eyes grew large and her eyebrows disappeared into her hair line. She looked scared to death. The blond was nervous and thought for sure she'd seen this woman sometime somewhere. She extended her hand.

"Hi, I'm Ian Wiley." The other woman returned the gesture unsteadily.

It's her, oh my god! Holy Shit! "Uh…I'm Katrina Sylvan, it's nice to meet you, Miss Wiley." Ian smiled softly and nodded.

"I hope you've been briefed on my situation." Giles started the car and continued to drive around town as Ian had instructed him to do.

"Larry…uh…Mr. Maxwell gave me the details. It may help me out if you explain exactly what you are looking for though."

"Basically, I have a few major deals that didn't go through and I'm trying to find out why and if there have been any others. I purchased a laptop for you to use, I've downloaded all of our account information to it. I have a

Just Me

stack of thirty disks that are also in that case." She pointed at the black leather laptop case on the floor. "Those disks contain all of the deals that were drawn up at the corporate office, all of the deals that went into production, and all of the logistics regarding those deals for the past five years." At the word logistics the sandy haired woman sitting next to Ian cringed. She took a deep breath and exhaled slowly.

"This is going to be a lot of work."

"I know, trust me, I've been over all of this a hundred times and I still can't come to a conclusion, but I do have a hypothesis. That's why you're here, to either prove me right, or I hope, prove me wrong. Anyway, while you're doing all of this I'll be making some very serious phone calls. One way or another I will find out what's going on." *I really do hope that we were just underbid, but deep down my gut is telling me otherwise.* "I've arranged everything so that there's no need for you to go to the corporate offices, everything is on that computer. If it's not, tell me what it is and I'll get it for you. None of my staff knows about this audit, and it will remain that way. You have my personal cell number, please call me if you need anything." The car pulled back up at the hotel and the sandy haired woman stepped out.

"Again, thank you Miss Sylvan, I hope you are able to help me out."

"I'll do my best, Miss Wiley." Giles shut the door and went back around to the front. He'd heard the entire conversation, but like hundreds of others that he'd witnessed from her father, he would keep this a secret and not speak to her about it.

~ ~ ~

Trina went back to her hotel room with the case and contemplated calling her boss and backing out of the assignment. She'd known it was a well respected corporation that needed a very private account audit. He never told her the company name or the name of the person she would be meeting. Her hands shook as she fumbled with the key card and opened the door. She set the case down by the small desk and went into the bathroom area. She quickly splashed cold water on her face. *Please don't let Cassidy be involved in this.* She dried her face and went back over to the desk and removed the laptop and plugged the battery cord into the wall. She desperately wanted to call Cassidy and tell her everything, but she knew she signed a protection oath, just like a lawyer or a therapist. She was unable to disclose any information about her assignments to anyone, especially an employee of the company she was working for.

Trina set the small desk up with the laptop and file disks. She added a pen and a small note pad to the arrangement and went to work reading through the files one at a time and comparing them to the records.

~ ~ ~

Ian went into the office as usual. She sat behind the large desk and pulled up the accounts in question. With a small sigh she stretched her neck and wiggled out of her light gray suit jacket. She hung the jacket on the back of her chair and straightened the long sleeves on the black silk blouse that she was wearing. A loud knock on the door grabbed her attention quickly. *God your jumpy,*

Just Me

Wiley, calm down! She closed the window on the computer screen.

"Come in." As soon as the door opened she smelled his musky cologne before she saw his brown hair. He was chewing on the corner of his thick mustache as always. His black suit was wrinkled, the obnoxious red and yellow stripped tie stuck out against his white shirt. "What can I do for you, Frasier?"

"I need some paperwork signed for the locomotive department. I'm trying to get to the bottom of these missing deals and I need to check some of the bank records to make sure we don't show deposits or worse, withdrawals, during the dates of these accounts." He walked over to the desk and slid the bank paperwork over to her. She picked the four pages up and read through them.

"That won't be necessary, Mr. Higginbotham, I've already taken care of that. I already know that we didn't have any bank transactions on those dates." *If someone stole the money or sold the account off it didn't go through our bank at all. Whoever is behind this isn't that stupid, but I do find it curious that you're determined to help me, I thought you hated me you rat bastard.* "I'll hold onto these though, in case I do wind up needing this information. Thanks."

She slid the papers into her desk drawer and watched as the color drained from his face. He nodded and asked how far she had gotten to finding out about the deals. She told him she was no further than a few weeks ago when she first found out about it. He assured that he'd do his best to help find out the problem. As soon as he left the room she brought the account screen back up and dialed the number to the Amtrak Corporation.

Half a dozen phone calls later she finally got a hold of the buyer for Amtrak. All he could tell her was the file was set up to be contracted out to Wiley Steel, a bid was made and then retracted by Wiley Steel, therefore the deal went to another company. He was unauthorized to give her the name of the company that received the contract. She slammed the phone down in aggravation, then picked it up again and dialed the number that they had on file with CSX. Unfortunately, the buyer for that company that handled the locomotive contracts was on vacation and no one in the office could help her.

Ian sat back in her chair. She couldn't get one picture out of her mind. It wasn't haunting, more uplifting than anything, every couple of days when she least expected it she'd see the beautiful brunette smiling at her. *Cassidy, Cassidy Harland. Completely off limits to me, but I can't help thinking about her. I thank god everyday that she's* the one that got away. She blinked the picture away and dialed a number that was scribbled on a piece of paper in her briefcase.

"Hello?" Trina ran over to the phone.

"Hi Miss Sylvan, this is Ian Wiley."

"Oh hello Miss Wiley, what can I do for you?" Talking to the woman made her nervous, so nervous in fact she thought she needed a drink every time she had anything to do with the woman. *God Cass would kill me if she knew I was here doing this, talking to her and meeting with her. Hell I'm auditing her records too. What the hell have I gotten myself into?*

"I'm just calling to see how things are going with the files, is everything working okay?" *You could tell me where I know you from, god I hope I didn't go to bed with*

Just Me

you and don't remember...oh god, maybe that's why you're so freaked out around me. Great Wiley!

"Yes ma'am, everything is going fine, I've only been through a few of the files though. This is going to take a few more days. There's a lot of information to match up."

"Yes, like I said, I've been staring at this hodgepodge for a few weeks now. I guess I'm looking in a haystack for a miracle, not a needle."

"Well I assure you Miss Wiley, if there's one to be found, I will find it." She tried to cover her discomfort.

"Okay then, I'll call you in a few days to check up, please feel free to call me if you need anything else." Ian hung up the phone and decided to call it a day.

~ ~ ~

As soon as Trina hung up the hotel phone her cell rang. *God does it ever end?* She ran across the room and picked it up.

"Hello?" She answered without checking the caller ID.

"Hey, it's ladies night where the hell are you?" The spunky voice was loud, as usual.

"Hey Wendi, I'm working out of town. I got here yesterday." She sounded tired.

"Where's here? Where the hell are you? I thought you didn't have to travel much anymore?" Wendi sounded a little pissed that she was deserted on their bar night, but she understood 'the job'.

"I'm in Aspen. I really don't travel much, I only handle the major accounts and this one is private and very major so my boss sent me to take care of it here instead of my office. I only get in this deep a few times a year. Most of my auditing I can do from my office."

"What company is it this time?"

Shit. "I can't tell you that, you know it's confidential." She sighed.

"Aspen, hmm…I'm sure I can think of a few big companies in that area, but only one major comes to mind. One that may be having a small internal problem if I do recall." She took a breath. "When are you going to tell Cass that you're auditing her?"

"God damn it Wendi keep your mouth shut. I could not only lose my job, but get sued if it got out. Please, for me, please don't say anything."

"I'm not going to say anything, Trina. She deserves to know. She's your best friend damn it."

"I know, trust me, I know. It's tearing me apart and that Wiley woman scares the shit out of me."

"Oh my god! You are not working with…what's her name…uh…"

"Ian…Ian Wiley."

"Yeah that's her, you're working with her personally?!"

"Have to, it's *her* company." *This is just great Katrina, you let the neighborhood cat find out you had a mouse. The entire world is going to know by sun up. You should just tell her, at least do it before motor mouth!*

"Wow, this is big huh?"

"Yeah she seems to think it is, but I haven't seen anything yet. I'll be here a few more days though."

"At least tell me, does it involve Cass? I mean personally?" *Please say no, please say no.*

"No…"

"Thank god!"

Just Me

"Well, I'm auditing the entire company, that means her records and accounts are included."

"She's so straight laced, she'd never do anything wrong."

"I know, like I said, I haven't seen anything so far."

"I promise not to say anything to her, but so help me if you don't and she finds out about this, she will never forgive you."

"I know."

~ ~ ~

"Good morning, young Wiley. Can I get you anything?" He smiled at the young woman. He had seen her sneaking out to the bar still at least twice a week, but she wasn't staying out all night and she wasn't coming back drunk. Most importantly, she wasn't drinking herself to death at night in her room. *Baby steps.* He told himself.

"I'll have a Mimosa and a piece of cinnamon toast." She yawned as she sat patiently. Giles, dressed habitually in his 'English Butler' outfit, returned to the table with a large glass of chocolate milk and a plate of blueberry waffles. Ian held in her ear to ear grin and began devouring her wonderful breakfast.

Giles stood in the kitchen and watched her eat. *One thing I can say, that kid can eat. She was always such a good child. Leland, you and Lorraine would be so proud of her.*

~ ~ ~

Ian was sitting at her desk staring at the computer screen as usual, a hundred different scenarios running though her blond head. Her cell phone rang in the clip on her belt.

"Ian Wiley."

"Hi Miss Wiley, I'm sorry to bother you so early…"

"Nonsense Miss Sylvan, I'm in the office everyday at eight, what can I do for you?"

"I'm missing a production file from a little over a year ago. I've found everything around it, but this one looks like it was missed when you made the copies. Also, can you check on the status of two possible deals that went on during that time?"

"Sure, tell me exactly what you need and I'll drive over there myself. I can't trust the buffoons I have working for me right now."

An already shaky voice turned to trembling at that point. Trina tried desperately to covey all of the information that she still needed. Ian could still hear the tremors in her voice. *Why is she so scared of me? So we slept together, I'm not into rough sex so I know that's not it, maybe she was expecting more? All I know is I need to straighten this out between me and her, I like being intimidating, but I'm afraid she might pee her pants or something around me, she looks* that *scared!*

~ ~ ~

Giles drove the car and Ian sat in the back punching the keys on her laptop. Two and a half hours later they arrived in front of the Wiley Steel Corporation. She smiled when she saw the statue of her great grandfather.

Ian straightened her black pants and jacket before she walked in. She waved at the receptionist who looked like she was going to faint, then proceeded down the hall. The joint secretary appeared dumbfounded. Apparently, it was a little odd for Ian to show up unannounced. As soon as she knocked on the door the familiar voice called out to her. As the door opened Ian stepped inside, she saw Cassidy standing in front of the large brown desk, Richard Masters sat behind the desk. He almost fell out of his chair as he rapidly stood up.

"Miss Wiley…good morning…what can I do for you?" He practically ran Cassidy over to get to Ian with his hand extended. Ian shook back and smiled behind him towards Cassidy.

"I'm actually glad to catch you both. It seems as if I didn't get all of the information when I was here last." She squared her shoulders and closed the door. He waved her to the chair behind his desk, she obliged and sat down. Rich and Cassidy sat across from her. "I missed a production file from a year and a half ago and I need some clarification on two particular smaller deals that were supposed to go through a year ago."

She pulled the papers out of her briefcase listing the exact information that she needed. Cassidy fidgeted in her chair wishing she'd kept her suit jacket on She felt very unprofessional sitting with them since they were fully dressed. She sat in her black suit pants and pale green blouse. When Ian reached out to hand the paperwork to her she saw the light blue sleeve of Ian's shirt stick out past her jacket sleeve. She couldn't help noticing the platinum cufflinks on the shirt. In the back of her mind she figured those cufflinks probably cost as much as the limit on one of her credit cards. She chastised herself for losing track of the conversation.

"So, if you two could get this together for me as quickly as possible that would be great. I need to drive back for a meeting this afternoon." She stood up and motioned for Rich to take his desk back.

"Miss Harland, I'd like to tag along with you for a little bit if you don't mind. I don't get to talk to you as much as I do the other directors." She watched Cassidy's gray eyes turn the lightest shade of blue. She was certain she could feel the heat radiating from the other woman.

Great, she wants to follow me around, ugh! As if I haven't had a hard enough time trying to get past having a casual dinner with you. You're my god damn boss for crying out loud! And I'm completely lost when I look into those gorgeous sapphire blue eyes. "Sure Miss Wiley, my office is right next door here."

Ian smiled and followed Cassidy out of the room. When they stepped into her office Cassidy went to offer her desk chair just as Rich had done earlier, but Ian refused, stating Cassidy would need it since she was supposed to work on the missing deals and records.

"I'm sorry Cassidy, I don't mean to make you nervous. This isn't exactly easy for me either, just so you know." Ian sat in the chair by the door and watched in awe as Cassidy ran a nervous hand through her hair.

"I'm trying not to be. I mean it's hard, you're you and I'm...well I'm your employee." *This is beyond weird...what the hell am I suppose to do?* "I sincerely hope you find out what's going with these deals. Personally I'm not happy about being partially blamed for it." *There, I said it, I can talk business with her whether she likes it or not. We're sitting in my office for god's sake!*

"I never doubted your work, Cassidy, I know you aren't involved."

"Is it really more than a bad bid?" She questioned, hoping she was wrong. The company had always been so family driven. She never thought anyone at Wiley Steel could be corrupt.

"I'm not at liberty to say anything about it at this time. When I have all of the facts everyone will know about it. Right now, all I can say is, so far, I haven't seen any problems with your department. You shouldn't worry so much." Her smile flattened. "Unless you have something you want to tell me?" Cassidy's gray eyes looked like she was being scolded like a child.

"No...of course not...I'd never..." Ian stood up and smiled again. Her blue eyes sparkled.

"It's okay, I'm only giving you a hard time, Cassidy. Like I said, I know you're not involved." She walked over behind the desk next to her. "So, show me what it is that you do. I mean, I know what you do, but I'd like to hear it in your prospective."

"Uh…" *I don't think I could do anything with you standing that close to me. My god I'm liable to spontaneously combust from the heat between my legs and the pounding in my chest.* "Well, as soon as a deal goes through Rich and I receive emails regarding the time and date deadlines, and the specifics of the project. He meets with the Production Manager to come up with the best plan of action. In the meantime, I'm already checking routes, freight costs, fuel surcharges, and so on. Then, Rich and I meet to compare notes and give the department director a more realistic and legitimate date time for completion. Basically, as you know, my job is to make sure the parts or machinery make it to the correct location on time, preferably early, and by using the lowest cost to get it there." The corners of her mouth turned up into a semi-smile. Ian nodded in agreement.

"Thank you. Now, I'd like to know more about you, but only if you will accompany me to lunch." Ian cocked her head to the side and waited for the answer. Cassidy restlessly tapped her pen against he keyboard. *Aww, she's so damn nervous around me, it's too cute. What the hell am I saying? What am I doing? She's an employee Wiley, don't do this…*

"Yes Miss Wiley, I would be delighted to have lunch with you." She used her best 'you're the boss and I'm the employee so I had better go' voice.

"Great, I'll call for my car. Will you be ready in ten minutes?" Ian contemplated asking Rich to lunch as well. How would this look?

"Yes ma'am." When Cassidy walked out to the waiting car she saw Rich talking to Ian. The man standing by the open rear door looked like a servant from an English Channel movie. She snickered under her breath.

"Ah, there you are. Giles, this is Cassidy Harland, she's the Logistics Director. Miss Harland, this is Giles Fontaine, my Butler." The Englishman smiled thinly and spoke with a pristine accent.

Ian slid into the back seat next to Cassidy and Rich rode up front with Giles.

"I know you two are very busy today, especially since I will need to be heading back soon with that new information that I asked for, but I wanted to thank you both for not only doing this for me, but doing it very discreetly. I appreciate honest, diligent employees."

Just Me

"Thank you Miss Wiley. I'm sure Miss Harland and I are in agreement when I say that I enjoy working for Wiley Steel. The family environment sets a very eminent gesture to the rest of the corporate world."

"Yes, I agree with you Rich," Cassidy butted in. She could feel the heat pouring from the woman next to her, even though they weren't touching, she could swear they were.

"So Cassidy, how long have you been with Wiley Steel? Forgive my ignorance, I know I can find out anything about any of you if I go to our Human Resources Manager in my office, but I like to personally know the five main people that help keep this corporation going, that being my five directors." She looked over at Cassidy and smiled openly, unaware of Giles watching in the rearview mirror.

"Well, I've been with the company a little over three years, I've been the Director of Logistics for close to two years now."

"Where did you go to college?"

"University of Colorado. You?"

"I went to Colorado State." She smiled sheepishly. "Rich, I believe you went to U.C. didn't you?"

"Yes ma'am, but I graduated many, many moons ago." He laughed.

~ ~ ~

After an hour long lunch at one of the finest restaurants in Grand Junction, they all returned to the plant. Ian spent most of the lunch talking business with the two of them, going over various deal scenarios. In the back of her mind she was taking notes, trying to figure just how those majors deals never made it to production. If they had, there was no obvious way that these two wouldn't follow through and complete them.

Ian let Rich and Cassidy go back to work, explaining that she needed to run an errand and would return in a few hours for the documents, just in time to get on the road before the afternoon traffic. At that rate, she'd be back in Aspen in time to meet with the auditor. As the car drove off Giles sensed the secluded blond needed to talk. He noticed her talking on her cell phone before he could speak to her.

"Hello Miss Sylvan, how is the research going?" She could hear the timidity in the other woman's voice. *That's it; I need to talk to her about this. I feel terrible, I never thought I'd run into one of those women again. Karma, that bitch has it out for me! Either way, I can't let her go on like this, I feel smaller and smaller around her. It's bad enough that I didn't recognize or even remember her for that matter.*

"I'm down to the point where I'm waiting for the rest of the records that I asked you about." Trina tried to sound professional. In the back of her mind she prayed Cassidy didn't hate her when this was finished.

"I'm in Grand Junction now…" She heard a gasp on the other end of the line. "Are you okay?"

"Uh…yeah…yes ma'am, I just didn't expect you to go to the plant." *Oh my god!*

"I told you I'd personally get the information, at this point I don't trust anyone. I really hope all of this turns out to be just sour bidding on our part." *But my gut tells me otherwise.* "Anyway, I was hoping that you'd join me for dinner when I return. I can give you this information and we can discuss your findings so far."

Trina's mind raced. *Dinner! What the hell? Oh man…this is so wrong, I really need to tell Cass, she's going to be so mad at me.* "Uh…sure, what time will you be back?"

"Probably around five, but just in case, how about I pick you up at six?"

"Sure, I'll bring my notes with me."

"Sounds good." She hung up the phone and tossed her head against the headrest in the back seat. A deep sigh escaped her throat.

"May I ask, what's got you so troubled young Wiley?"

Oh Giles…" *Where do I start? How about the fact that I'm completely infatuated with one of my employees, or the fact that I had careless, meaningless sex with the woman that I have scrutinizing the records for my entire company and don't even remember her.* "I'm just stressed. I'm sure a lot more than dad ever was." Her voice faded to a whisper, she hoped he didn't hear the end of that sentence, but knowing Giles, he heard it.

"You've been running around like a chicken with your head cut off lately. Might I make a suggestion?"

"Please, feel free." She starred out the window.

"Slow down."

"I can't, at least not right now." *I know I'm close, I can feel it.*

~ ~ ~

Trina stood out front of the hotel watching for the black 'rich and famous' looking car. She'd spoken to Wendi again and decided that she needed to talk to Cass.

Waiting this long was hard enough, she couldn't imagine not telling her and then letting her possibly find out on her own. *Maybe, maybe nothing will come of this. Maybe it was really just poor judgment and not some secret embezzlement scam.* The car pulled up, she politely waited for the tuxedoed man to get out and open the door for her.

"He's such a gentleman." She said as he closed the door.

"That he is, you should see him at home. He keeps me in line." She smiled.

Ian ordered a nice bottle of Pinot Grigio to go with their Italian dinner. She tasted the first glass and nodded for the waiter to pour full glasses for both of them.

"Thank you for asking me to dinner. This place is really nice." Trina took in the Italian sculptures and paintings, the place looked like a museum of Little Italy.

"You're very welcome, I don't come here as often as I'd like. The chef is magnificent." She took a deep breath. *It's now or never Wiley.* "So...uh...I have to admit I had ulterior motives for bringing you here tonight." The sandy haired woman felt a lump rise in her throat.

Oh no! Oh dear god don't let her be interested me! Trina wanted to down the entire bottle of wine. She starred at the table cloth. *Don't look at her. Don't look at her.* She looked up at sincere blue eyes staring back at her. *She looks sad.*

"Katrina, I wanted to..."

"I'm straight!" She blurted out. "I'm sorry. I mean I'm not interested in you like that." The confusion on Ian's face made her think she jumped the gun.

Just Me

"No, I mean I'm not...well I thought..." *Shit!* Ian tried to find her voice. "You look familiar, I thought maybe...look, not to get personal, but I went through a rough time not long ago, I thought maybe I'd slept with you and didn't remember you. I felt déjà vu when I met you a few days ago." *Great Wiley, you look like an idiot sitting here, and you just outed yourself.* The woman across from her wasn't sure what to say or do. "If that's what had happened, I wanted to apologize to you and ask you to be please be secretive, I'm not out to anyone."

"Miss Wiley..." *Damn it...do I tell her about Cass? Son of a bitch, she thinks she slept with me.* "Let me assure you, we never slept together. That I can be sure of, I am very in tune with men." She smiled shyly. "I do need to be honest with you though." She downed the entire glass of wine that was sitting in front of her. Ian took that as an opportunity to finish her own glass. The waiter appeared to pour them two fresh glasses. "Although you've never met me, we have seen each other. So you're not going crazy." She smiled and Ian laughed.

"Well then, where do I know you from?" She asked as she sipped her wine. She moved the glass to make room for the waiter to set down their entrees.

Oh man, well, it was fun having a career while it lasted. I'll never get another job in this line of work again. "I was here on a weekend ski trip with some friends about two months ago."

"Okay?"

"You saw me at the *Snow Drift* ski lodge bar. Do keep in mind, I had no idea who you were, actually, none of us did. It wasn't until I met you the other day, that I realized I had seen you there."

"Did I talk to you? I don't remember when I saw you. I'm very good with faces, that's why I remembered seeing you. I just wasn't good at anything else during that time of my life. I'm very sorry if I was rude to you or anything."

"Oh no, no, you didn't speak to me, you did however, talk to one of my friends. Truth be told, you did not sleep with her." Ian's fork slipped from her hand and bounced off of the floor.

"I...uh...so you're...uh friends with Cassidy Harland?" She didn't have to see the other woman nod, she knew she was had. *Great, you've seen my alter ego. Could this fucking state possible get any smaller? Talk about degrees of separation. Not only does the damn girl work for me, but I hired her best friend to examine my company's records, including the accounts of her friend.*

"Please don't be mad, I tried my best to keep the confidentiality that you strongly desire." Nervousness went to an entirely different level, she was now scared. Her green eyes felt moist. She ran her hand through her sandy colored hair and wiped the small tear from the corner of her face. *My job is going down the toilet as I sit here and force myself to eat this two hundred dollar dinner.*

"I'm not mad at you. Wait, you didn't...oh no Katrina, please tell me that you haven't said anything to Cassidy."

"No, I...Miss Wiley, she's my best friend."

"Yes."

"I know she's not the person that you're searching for, I've been through everything that involves her. I've known her for ten years, she'd never…"

"I know she's not the problem, but she is

involved, she is one of my Directors. I can't have anyone find out about the audit."

"She will hate me when she finds out." Another innocent tear fell. Ian wanted to reach out to the woman. Hurting Cassidy was the last thing that she would ever want to do.

"Let me tell her."

"Oh no! She'll be so mad at me."

"Well, she's going to be seriously pissed at one or even both of us. Let her be pissed at me. Hell, they'll all be pissed at me when they find out, but this is the only way."

She squeezed her eyes closed. Part of her wanted to act like a giddy teenager and ask if Cassidy had ever talked about her, or even told her who she was. "All right, you can tell her, but not until your work for me is completed. Once I have your report, I can go on my own to try and figure out the rest of this puzzle. I'm not telling anyone until I know for sure what caused my company to lose the deals. When you've submitted your report she'll be cleared of any preferential treatment during the investigation. Miss Sylvan, as far as I'm concerned, we never had this conversation." She finished her second and last glass of wine.

"Yes ma'am, I agree with you." Trina also finished her last glass. *Don't say anything, it's not your business. Cass can handle herself.* She swallowed the thought of telling Ian how bewildered Cassidy was over her.

Graysen Morgen
Chapter 11

Another month passed, the audit was over and Ian sat in her fathers' study reading the fifteen page report. The only findings were a few small deals that never went through over the past two years, leading up to the four major deals that Ian originally ran into. All in all, seven million dollars worth of deals scattered over a two year period were turned down before they ever made it to production. This left her completely puzzled. Somewhere, somehow, someone was benefiting from these deals. Why else would Wiley Steel give up a deal? Production and logistics weren't even aware of the deals, therefore they weren't to blame. *Someone stopped these deals. Who? I know you have something to do with this 'rat bastard'. I know it and I'll prove it.*

~ ~ ~

Christmas was less than a week away, which meant Cassidy's birthday was also a week away. Her parents had decided to go on a European Tour for the Holidays, so they sent her birthday and Christmas gifts a week early and gave their love through the phone line. She guessed this meant it was time to grow up and get her own life. They just tried to put it mildly. She knew they had planned and saved for this trip for almost three years

Just Me

and she was happy for them.

"Hey, 'soon to be' birthday girl." Wendi smiled and toasted Cassidy. Trina held her glass high too. "So, what are we doing for your birthday?"

"What?"

"Well, your parents ditched you, so you get to celebrate the big three 'oh with us." Trina and Wendi held their heads together and smiled from ear to ear. They had already decided what to do. Both of them knew the anxiety their dark-haired friend was going through with her boss being the one person to take her breath away with only a simply smile.

"I don't know. I mean I have a few extra days off since Wiley Steel is closed the day before and after Christmas, but I don't know what I want to do." She sipped her drink and sat on the couch. They were all standing in the kitchen of her apartment.

"We have it all figured out. Have your bags packed, we're leaving after work tomorrow." Wendi announced.

"Okay? And where are we going?" She didn't like it when those two got together to conspire against her.

"Aspen–"

"Oh hell no, we are not! Huh ugh, no way!" She shook her head from side to side.

"Yes we are. We booked three rooms at the *Snow Drift*. We're going snowboarding and snowmobile riding for three days, along with celebrating your birthday and Christmas, of course."

"Do you guys remember what happened last time we were there? I do not want to go through that again. Besides, what if she's there?"

"So what, you've told both of us how she's been

very nice to you at work. What's the big deal?"

"That's just it, *work*. She's my god damn boss, I have to have a work relationship with her."

"Okay?" Trina looked at Wendi. Her breath caught in her throat. "Oh."

"Yeah, big oh, I can't get her out of my head. She's driving me nuts!"

"Well if she's there then we'll run interference. Won't we Trina?" She nudged the dazing woman next to her.

"What…uh…oh yeah, yeah we'll take care of her for you." She was thinking about her involvement with Ian and wondering how it would go when Cassidy finally found out about it.

The next evening Cassidy, Wendi, and Trina were all sitting at a table in the bar at the ski lodge listening to Christmas Carols on the jukebox. Cassidy had a glass of Soco in front of her; the other two had various Martini's. It wasn't until Ian walked up to their table, that any of them realized she had walked in. Cassidy immediately noticed the difference in the precocious blond when her business suit 'costume' was on the hanger in her closet. Ian was dressed in blue jeans, a white long sleeve tee shirt, and a black leather jacket. *This is the real you, the you that makes the blood rush from my head to my crotch faster than I can speak.*

"Hi Miss Wiley, Merry Christmas." Cassidy tried to be as professionally polite as possible.

"Cassidy, how are you?" She examined the matching glass in her hand. The brunette smiled shyly when she saw Ian compare their drinks.

"I'm good."

"Tomorrow's her thirtieth birthday, she's

celebrating." Wendi butted in. Cassidy kicked her under the table and Trina spit her drink back into the glass. Ian laughed out loud.

"Well, I should leave you ladies to it then." She reached over and laid her hand on top of Cassidy's. "Merry Christmas, to all of you, and Happy Birthday, Cassidy." Her blue eyes twinkled and she walked back over to the bar.

"If I didn't know any better, I'd say she's into you Cass." Wendi spoke the truth as always.

"I can't believe you told her about my birthday and how old I am, damn it Wendi!"

"Oh calm down, she doesn't care how old you are, although, she is younger than you." Trina added.

"How do you know?" Cassidy shot her a look.

"Uh…I…she looks young…"

"I think she's twenty six."

"Okay, that's not bad, Cass."

"She's my god damn boss!" That came out louder than she intended it to and just as the songs were changing so the bar was particularly quiet. She dared not look up towards the bar. Of course Ian was sitting there and heard the entire statement. She looked in their direction and Trina shrugged her shoulders. "I'm tired, let's go to bed." *Before I embarrass myself even more.*

~ ~ ~

A soft knock on the wooden door woke Cassidy out of a restless sleep. *Morning already? Yeah Happy Birthday, Merry Christmas, woo fucking hoo!* The sarcasm was scary. "Who is it?" She called out as she looked through the peep hole. The picture on the other side was a distorted forest. "What the hell?" She pulled the door open; thankful she was wearing a pajama top along with pajama bottoms. The person at the door had a giant bouquet of yellow roses mixed with baby's breathe, a card, and a small package wrapped in red and green foil paper. She took the items into her room, thanked him with a tip before she closed the door. The flowers had no card so she opened the enveloped card.

Cassidy,
I hope you like the flowers. They reminded me of you. Happy Birthday! The gift also reminded me of you. Merry Christmas! P.S. I would like to invite you and your friends to my home for Christmas Dinner. My Butler makes entirely too much food and I would enjoy it if the three of you would join me. He'll be in front of the ski lodge at five p.m. If you don't want to go, I will understand completely. I do ask that you let him know so he's not waiting around. By the way, I know I'm your boss, although the entire bar didn't know who you were talking about. Again, Happy Birthday and Merry Christmas!
Signed. *I.L. Wiley.*

"Holy shit."
She sat on the edge of the bed and tore the paper open to uncover a thin black velvet box. *Oh no.* She opened the box to find three front row tickets to the Harry Connick Jr. concert for the following week.
"Wow!"
She couldn't remember telling Ian that she was a huge Jazz fan. Trina had mentioned it to Ian when they were in the restaurant, she was trying to come up with a

way to soften the blow when she told her about the work that she was doing for Ian.

"What's with all the noise?" Wendi and Trina were beating on the door. Cassidy opened it with shimmering eyes and a wide smile. "What's gotten into you?" They both took in the flowers on the little table, torn up wrapping paper on the bed, then the thin expensive looking box in her hand.

"What the hell?" Wendi stared at her.

"It's her, all her. It's like she knows me."

"Her?" Trina looked around for someone else in the small room. "Who?"

"Ian Wiley." The other two women gasped at the same time.

"She did this?"

"Yeah, the flowers, the card,..."

"What's in the box, Cass?" Trina's heart was pounding.

"Three front row tickets to Harry Connick Jr. next week!" She was squeaking like a small child.

Holy shit! "Wow, that's really nice of her." *I never said Who, I just said she likes jazz, blah, blah, blah. I never even went into any details about it. How the hell did she know? Lucky guess.*

"That's not all, she's invited all of us to have Christmas dinner with her at her home. The butler will be here at five to pick us up."

"Whoa!"

"I know, we don't have to go. The gesture was certainly nice though."

"We are *so* going!" Wendi was all about seeing the inside of that mansion.

"I don't know guys. She's my boss, and she's

already gone kind of far, don't ya think?" She gave them a questioning look.

"Girl, you better have your ass ready to go at five or I'm going without you."

"Me too." Trina added and shrugged.

"What the hell do I wear?" Wendi and Trina looked at each other.

"Shopping!" They said simultaneously. Cassidy laughed and shook her head.

~ ~ ~

It was noon and Ian was pacing the floor in the formal living room where the Christmas tree was located. *Well by now she's received the gift and the flowers. Please let her come to dinner, I know this is not exactly the best thing to do, but I can't help it. Keep it friendly, professional as usual.*

"Young Wiley, you're wearing a hole in the rug."

He knew she was worn out and running on adrenaline only. Their trip to the cemetery first thing this morning took a deep toll on the young woman. She put the odd combination of flowers between the angels and leaned against the marble statue. Ian cried until there were no more tears, kissed the inscription, and wandered back down the path to the car. She turned back and smiled one last time. The flowers were pretty unsightly, but they were a mixture of her mother and father's favorite flowers.

After returning to the house Ian showered, and exchanged gifts with Giles. He'd bought her a beautiful gold pendant of a guardian angel. It had two small colored gemstones on each side of the angel. She realized one was her mother's birthstone and the other one was her father's. She cried and he wrapped his arms around her. She gave him a two thousand dollar gift certificate to the tuxedo store that he shopped at, a raise, and another rare coin for his collection. He always wondered how she was able to get her hands on items that seemed to be out of reach, such as the tickets that he overheard her purchasing for a completely sold out concert next week and the rare coins she always gave him for his birthday and Christmas. *She's so much like both of her parents. A perfect mold of two genuine people.*

"Sit down already." He scolded.

~ ~ ~

"I can't believe we are doing this. She's my boss for crying out loud!"

"Oh calm down, get your thong out of a wad. Cass!" Wendi growled.

"She doesn't seem so bad. I don't know why you're so scared of her." Trina suggested.

"I'm not scared of her!" *I'm scared of the way I feel about her.*

"Look, here comes the car. Woo hoo, 'Lifestyles of the Rich and Famous' baby!" Wendi hooted and smacked Trina's arm.

Giles pulled the car around and stepped out to greet them. He held the door while all three women slid into the back seat.

~ ~ ~

Ian continued to pace the floor in the formal

living room in front of the large bay window. She ran a restless hand through her short blond hair. *What the hell am I doing?* She let out a deep breath followed by a long sigh. Her heart stopped beating completely when the black car pulled through the Iron Gate, drove up the circle drive and stopped across from the front door of the house. Giles stepped out and straightened his tux, before he walked around the back of the car to the right rear passenger door. Ian's heart wasn't beating and she knew she wasn't breathing. *If she's not in that car I'll die right here on this floor.*

Giles pulled the door open. The spunky redhead slid out of the car and moved away from the door and Katrina was next to vacate the black car. Ian felt herself getting light headed and dizzy from the lack of oxygen and blood flow as she watched intently. Wendi and Trina looked in awe at the massive house in front of them, neither woman noticed Ian standing in the window staring out at them. Giles had a teasing thought about closing the door and letting Ian, who he saw in the window, completely lose her mind thinking the third woman had not joined them for dinner. Instead he reached and grabbed her hand as she stepped out onto the snow covered ground, taking in her surroundings with amazement.

As soon as she saw Cassidy, Ian let out the breath she'd been holding, her heart beat rapidly, allowing blood to flow into uncharted territory. *She's beautiful.* The three women were dressed in wool slacks and various blouses. They all had black overcoats on. Giles walked ahead of them and opened the right side of the double front doors. He waved them in and took their coats, hanging them in the large closet off to the right. Cassidy held her breath as she looked around the large foyer.

The floors were dark teak wood that contrasted beautifully against the crème colored walls, which were hung with a variety of paintings. Marble statues sat on either side of the long winding staircase in front of them. Twinkling lights seemed to be glowing in a room off the left, Trina cocked her head to see further into the room, that's when she saw Ian walking towards them from the center of that room.

Ian's blue eyes sparkled and her smile went on for days. She was dressed in gray slacks and a maroon colored V-neck sweater that hugged her upper body tightly. Her sun-tanned arms stuck out of the three-quarter length sleeves. Trina recognized the silver Rolex with diamonds in the face that she wore on her left hand surprisingly since she was left handed. Cassidy had her back to that glowing room until she heard a familiar voice. She spun around so quickly she almost knocked Wendi over.

"Hello everyone. Merry Christmas and welcome to the Wiley Estate." She spoke softer. "My home."

My god she's gorgeous. It took everything Cassidy had to pull her attention away from the deep blue eyes staring directly into her soul. She stepped forward and offered her hand. "Thank you so much for inviting us, Miss Wiley—"

"Please, you're guests in my house, call me Ian." She winked and smiled innocently. *I'm treading on thin ice above freezing cold water. I hope I know what I'm doing. Who the hell am I kidding?*

"Thank you." She took a deep breath. "Ian."

Cassidy turned towards the women standing behind her bewildered. "These are my two best friends,

Wendimena Blanchert," she pointed to the redhead that cringed when she heard her full name announced, "and Katrina Sylvan."

The sandy haired woman stepped forward and shook Ian's hand. "Please call me Trina." The redhead was right next to her extending her hand as well. She shot an *I hate you* glance across her shoulder towards Cassidy.

"It's very nice to meet you and please call me Wendi." Ian could sense the desperation in the woman's voice.

"It's my pleasure to meet you. You have a lovely name." She smiled.

"You should hear my middle name. Sometimes I wonder what drugs my parents were doing." Wendi laughed and Cassidy's eyebrows flew up. She wanted to knock her best friend out for embarrassing her. Ian laughed with her.

"Really? Well now I have to know what it is and the story behind your name."

Ian waved towards the living room and the three women walked into the large room, complete with a fireplace in one corner, a grand piano in the other corner, two large sofas across from each other on top of an elegant oriental rug with a Chippendale wood table in the middle. The twinkling lights were coming from the eight foot Douglas Fir Christmas tree that sat next to the piano. Wendi and Trina sat on one sofa and left Cassidy to sit next to her boss. Somehow she thought her friends were up to no good. Ian sat last and grabbed Cassidy's hand that was lying on the soft cushion next to her. She let it's warmth go right through her, it trembled lightly. The touch happened so fast no one noticed except Cassidy.

"Happy Birthday!" The blond smiled charmingly

Just Me

and let go of the hand.

"Thank you." *Shit you dummy, you never mentioned the gift or the flowers. What a moron. She probably thinks you're shallow.* "And thank you for the beautiful flowers, I love roses, I wouldn't know where to begin with the gift, I love jazz and Harry Connick Jr. is my favorite. Thank you so much."

Yes! Jackpot! "You're welcome."

She tried not to stare, but she couldn't stop thinking about running her hands through Cassidy's shoulder length black hair and kissing her tenderly at the base of her neck. *Holy shit! Where did that come from? Giles help!* Just then the Butler appeared in the doorway.

"Pardon my interruption, would any of you ladies like a beverage?" He stood poised with his arms by his side and his hands clasped behind his back.

"I think a nice bottle of wine would be good, Giles." She glanced at everyone, the women nodded in agreement.

"Yes ma'am, may I recommend a fine rose, to go with dinner?"

"Sure, I haven't been down to the cellar lately. Bring up whichever one will go best with the feast that you've been preparing all day." She smiled and he grinned and nodded before leaving the room.

"Forgive me for saying so, but you two are quite comical." Trina met sincere blue eyes. Ian took a deep breath.

"Yes. Giles and I, well we've been through a great deal. He was with my family before I was born." She drifted into memories of her childhood with her parents and Giles. "So, weren't we discussing that unusual name of yours, Wendi?"

"I was hoping you forgot." Wendi smiled. "My father named me after his mother and my grandmother, therefore, Wendimena Agatha Blanchert at your service." She did a mock bow.

Both of her best friends were staring at her, they knew about her name, but never expected her to tell a total stranger. And she wasn't even drinking yet.

"I still think you have a wonderful name. There is absolutely nothing wrong with having a strong family name. I'm named after my father and grandfather." She poked herself in the chest. "Ian Leland Wiley, in the flesh."

Wendi smiled and leaned across the table to extend her hand, they shook hands and laughed. Both completely understanding the childhood and torment the other faced with having a 'different' name.

"Well, I don't know about you Cassidy, but Katrina Marie Sylvan didn't give me any problems in school, I guess I'm just normal." She teased.

"Actually, my name has a story behind it."

"Do tell." Wendi was waiting for this, she'd never heard of any name story in Cass's family.

"Uh…okay, my parents wanted a boy and a girl, Cassidy and Calamity, from Butch Cassidy and Calamity Jane." Wendi laughed while Trina and Ian choked back and smiled. "Two years before I was born, my mother was pregnant and gave birth four months prematurely to a baby girl that they named Calamity. She died within the hour due to complications, her lungs weren't completely formed. Anyway, two years later I was carried to term and born with no complications and since they had named the first child Calamity, that left Cassidy for me. So, that's how I became Cassidy Elaine Harland."

Just Me

"That's a very special story Cassidy, thank you for telling it." Ian looked at her with admiration. *It took guts to tell that story.*

"You're welcome."

"Wow, I'm surprised you never told us, Cass." Trina spoke first. Wendi was wiping the tears from her eyes.

"I guess I haven't thought about it in years."

Giles came into the room with three glasses of blush colored wine. He gave Ian his best, *do not spill this on the rug*, look, she smiled and he left the room once again.

"What's he cooking? It smells delicious." Wendi gathered courage to speak, shocked at the tears that fell from hearing the heartfelt story. *You big sap.*

"Uh…turkey and ham with probably fifteen side dishes."

"Holy shi…uh…wow that's a large amount of food." Wendi saw the razor sharp look Cassidy gave her. Ian laughed.

"Try living here, I'd weigh four-hundred pounds if I didn't work out regularly. That man has cooked for an Army my entire life." *An army of one now.* She missed her parents. This was one of the hardest days since they'd been gone. Somehow spending it with strangers seemed to make her happy.

~ ~ ~

No one was aware of the two feet of snow that fell while they ate. Giles had outdone himself with a mouthwatering turkey and a honey glazed ham, complete with stuffing, green bean casserole, sweet potato casserole, garlic butter acorn squash, mashed potatoes and giblet gravy, broccoli cheese casserole, and four different types of bread. Not to mention a blueberry pie, raspberry cheesecake, and chocolate silk mousse pie. Before she ever sat down, Ian went to the old man and asked him to join her at the table, telling him that he was now the only family that she had and therefore needed to share this holiday dinner with her. He choked back tears and joined the group.

Three hours later the women sat back in the living room. Wendi and Trina enjoyed coffee mixed with Irish Crème. Cassidy joined Ian with a nice brandy cordial. Giles worked feverishly packing up the leftovers and cleaning the kitchen. It was close to ten p.m. when Giles walked back into the living room. The fireplace was burning and the multi-colored lights were twinkling on the tree. The women were engrossed in conversation over the latest movie stars in the headlines. Ian wasn't much of a movie buff, but Wendi and Trina could tell her anything she needed to know about the movies. Cassidy seemed to be in her own world listening contently to the soft jazz that played on the stereo.

"Pardon me, Miss Wiley–"

"Yes Giles? She stood and walked over to him. "What is it?"

"The snow is falling harder, there's at least two feet on the roads going down the mountain."

"Wow, I didn't remember hearing anything about a heavy snowfall tonight. I can take them back in the SUV."

Cassidy could tell they were deep in conversation as they walked over to the window. Ian shook her head as she looked out. The front yard was covered in a blanket of white.

"Is everything okay?" Cassidy called out. Ian turned towards her.

"We have about three feet of snow on the ground and the roads are covered."

"Oh my god." *We're stuck here.*

"It's not that bad, I can take you back in the SUV." All of the women were up now looking out at the snow covering everything. Giles butted in.

"Perhaps they should stay here tonight, Miss Wiley."

"What, oh no that's not necessary. Thank you though." Cassidy tried not to look nervous.

"It's dangerous out there Cass, he has a point." Trina agreed.

Blue eyes met gray ones, they held one another softly. "It's settled then…" Ian spoke before tearing her eyes away. "I have plenty of room. You can all stay here tonight. Giles will take you back as soon as the road clears in the morning." She stepped around the brunette and sat back down on the couch to finish her brandy.

An hour later, Trina and Wendi were dosing on the couch.

"I'll have Giles show all of you to your rooms."

The women followed the salt and pepper haired man up the stairs. They saw what appeared to be two master suites at opposite ends of the hallway with two small rooms in the middle on the left side and two small rooms in the middle on the right side.

"Here you go ladies. Miss Blanchert you may stay in here and Miss Sylvan you may stay in that room there." He pointed to the room next to it. "These rooms share a bathroom between them. "Miss Harland you may stay in the room over here." He took her across the hall.

"Is that your room next door?" She hoped she didn't have to share a bathroom with the butler. She was already in a panic for having to stay the night. She didn't want to invade their space even further. The corner of his mouth turned up slightly.

"No ma'am, you see the rooms at both ends?"

"Yes."

He pointed to one end. "That's Miss Wiley's room and the other one was…it was her parent's." she nodded. "My room is downstairs."

He made sure everyone was settled in and wished each of them good night. Cassidy was too agitated to sleep. She was freaked out about being in her bosses' house, with whom she was infatuated, and now sleeping down the hall from her was going to drive her insane. She changed into the tee shirt and pajama bottoms that Ian had lent her to sleep in. She was nice enough to lend all of them some sort of outfit to sleep in. It was up to them whether or not they slept in it.

~ ~ ~

"Come in here Giles." Ian called out as she heard the man come back down the stairs. "Sit down, take a load off." He smiled and sat across from her. "Is everyone squared away?"

"Yes ma'am. I could sense the nervousness in Miss Harland."

Ian chewed on her bottom lip, surprised that she wasn't drunk, actually, none of them were. Most likely because they spaced their drinking out over a matter of hours with an enormous meal in the middle to soak it all up.

"I'm sure you're right, she's probably scared to death. I'm her boss and trust me, I've heard her say that more times than I care to count." She laid her head back against the cushion.

"May I speak freely?"

She opened her eyes and stared at the man across from her. She considered slapping him for even asking, after everything they had been through. He knew he was her only family and she treated him as such.

"I'm not a hard ass like my father, Giles. Besides, if you didn't 'speak freely' on a regular basis around here, who would keep me in line?" She grinned. Her mother and father had always treated Giles as if he were family. Out of respect for them, he never once spoke out of context.

"I guess you're right. I'm sorry, young Wiley."

"What's on your mind old man?" She closed her eyes.

"Miss Harland seems to be rather intimidated by you. She acts very reserved around you." He stared at the fireplace.

Ian opened her eyes and waved around at the room. "And you wouldn't be a little intimidated by all of this? Besides the fact that she works for me, I'm sure me opening up my home to her has been a little too much for her to take in."

"I'm sure you're right. Can I get you anything before I go to bed?"

She opened her eyes and looked at him as he stood up.

"No, I'm fine, thank you though." He turned to walk away. "And Giles…Merry Christmas." She smiled and he returned the gesture.

Ian ran both hands through her hair and stared at what was left of the fire burning to her left. She closed her eyes, willing her mind to focus on something besides the brunette asleep upstairs down the hall from her own bed. Her eyes flew open when she heard foot steps.

"Hey, I'm sorry I didn't mean to wake you. I couldn't sleep so I wanted to come down here and look at the tree again." Cassidy looked adorable in Ian's white CSU tee shirt and black cotton pajama pants.

"Come sit down. You didn't wake me by the way."

Cassidy brushed her hair back with a swift motion from her left hand and sat on the couch facing Ian. That was a safe distance she thought as the embers from the fire glowed just enough to cast a shadowy haze of light in the room. The twinkle lights danced on the walls. "I'm going to go change, will you be here when I come back?"

"Sure."

Ian ran upstairs quietly and changed into dark blue satin pajama bottoms that matched her eyes. She tossed her pants into the hamper, along with her sweater and bra. She put on a thin baby blue tee shirt that hugged her nicely and went back downstairs.

"That was quick." Cassidy tried to breath, but found her lungs compressed tightly as she took in the sight before her. *She's so incredibly sexy, even in pajamas!*

"I even brushed my teeth." She smiled and shrugged. "Do you want something to drink or anything to eat?"

"No, I'm fine, thank you. Did Giles go to bed?"

"Yeah about a half hour ago."

"Oh."

"So you like the tree huh?"

"Yeah, it reminds me of being home." She stirred unconsciously.

"If you don't mind my asking, why aren't you with your parents for the holidays?"

This caused even more stirring from the smaller woman.

"They…uh…they went on a European tour…and ..well.."

"Abandoned you huh?" Ian knew the feeling, she had felt as if her own parents had abandoned her, but for the rest of her life. She got up and walked over to the other couch and sat down next to Cassidy, their thighs almost touching. Cassidy was trembling. "Are you cold?"

"Uh…no."

Ian looked into light gray eyes that seemed to reach into her heart. "You know you don't have to be so shy around me, I'd never do anything to hurt you."

"You're…but…you're my boss."

God damn it, not again. I'm just trying to be your friend right this minute, not have my way with you! "I know that, thank you for reminding me *again*. You sounded sad, I'm trying to be a friend." She drew out a long breath and sighed.

"I know I'm sorry."

"Don't be, we obviously know we're attracted to each other, there are ways around it." *There, I said it.* Ian's mind was racing and her heart was doing back flips.

Change the subject, change the subject, change the subject. Don't have this talk with her, not now, not like this. "Uh…so…uh…uh Giles, he seems to be a very nice man."

What the hell? "Uh…yeah, yes he is. Giles is the only family I have. He's a very big part of my life."

"That's good, I'm glad you have him. I wouldn't…I mean…I'm sor…"

Ian sensed exactly what Cassidy was trying to say as she fumbled her words. Ian reached out and placed her fingers under Cassidy's chin and gently turned her so they were facing each other.

"Cassidy, I don't talk about my parents, well to anyone besides Giles. Yes, he has been a big help to me since their death. I miss them so much, I don't know where I'd be if Giles wasn't here with me. I was going through the worst part of my entire life when you met me. I'd given up on the world and to be honest, thought about not living anymore. I spent most of my days and all of my nights so drunk that I couldn't see straight. It helped me forget for those few hours, until the pain of reality would come back, then I'd start all over. I was slowly killing myself. Giles found the courage to go against anything and everything that he knew as a *servant* basically, and tossed me around a little bit until I woke up. He made me see life for what it was worth, he taught me how to miss my parents and respect their death as a part of my life." A few tears fell from her blond lashes and rolled down her cheek. "I owe him so much." She took her hand away from Cassidy's face but continued to gaze into her eyes. Cassidy could feel the pain radiating from the woman next to her.

"I…I'm so sorry…I…"

Ian cut her off.

"No. I'm sorry, very sorry that you met that side of me, a side that I hope never surfaces again."

Cassidy broke the eye contact and looked down at

the table in front of them. "Are you sorry I…found out about you?"

"About what? The fact that I was a drunk? Or sleeping with women? Or both?" She took a deep breath. *I never meant for the conversation to go this far, now what?* "Cassidy, Giles was the only person that knew about what happened to me when my parents died. He never judged me, just did the best he could to take care of me. I never told my parents I was gay, and frankly, I never told Giles for that matter, but over the course of the last six months I'm sure he noticed."

She bent forward and put her head in her hands. "I'm the soul heir to a multi-million dollar family fortune, I can't be outed. That would ruin the reputation of the company and the media would tear me apart because I can't produce the next Wiley heir!" Ian let out the deep breath that she was holding when she felt a warm hand rub gently across her back. "Not only do you know about me, but now your friends too. Maybe it was a mistake to bring you all up here."

"I don't think it was, just like I don't think meeting you the way I did would change anything. In fact, it makes me not only see, but feel how human you really are." She felt Ian shift under her hand. "Ian…if I had met you at work, with your title and everything that went with it, well I can tell you for sure I would not be sitting here with you right now. You scare the hell out of me in your power suit!" *There I said it.*

Ian sat up and gazed into her eyes once again. Cassidy didn't want to blink; afraid she'd lose the feeling of those beautiful blue eyes staring deeply into her.

"Cassidy, I never meant to scare you, I'm not the person you met in that bar and I'm not the power suit either."

"Then who are you? All I know is your name is Ian Wiley and you own a major corporation. Plus you happen to like alcohol and women."

"That's just it, since my parents death I haven't known who I am. I just exist, trying to do what is right. I get up everyday and go run that company just like my father and grandfather did."

"What do you want to do instead?" Cassidy could see the wet tears on the blonde's face in the glowing light of the fire burning close by.

"I…want…" She sniffled. "I want to call home and talk to my dad, have him tell me the latest news on Wiley Steel, and speak to my mom about everything else in my life. I want to sit down and tell my parents that I'm gay and I'm sorry." She wiped her face with the back of her hand. "I will never be able to do any of that. I have to accept it and move on, I guess that's what I've been doing."

"You're an incredible young woman and with everything you are going through, you seem to put yourself aside to do what you were meant to do, no matter what."

"It took me a while to learn how to do that. I was very selfish after they died, that's how I was when you met me."

"Maybe, but you're a very strong person, Ian."

"I don't want to be this overbearing power suit that scares you, Cassidy."

"I know you have to be at work, but here, now, you're not scaring me at all. Just be yourself. Wiley Steel is on hold until Monday morning." *I can't believe I just said that. Where is this confidence coming from? She's so confused, hell I'm confused, I'm falling for her, oh my god* . Cassidy stiffened all of a sudden and pulled her arm back to her own body. Ian noticed the sudden change.

"What's wrong?"

"Nothing, I …uh…I…"

Ian turned her body slightly towards the smaller woman. "I see the scared deer in the headlights looking at me again. Please, talk to me Cassidy–"

I can't. "It's nothing. I just realized how everything has changed between us. It'll be very hard to see you in the office and forget I know so much about you. That's all."

"Yes, that's an obstacle, but it's not like we're sleeping together or in love for that matter." *That would be impossible. If anyone found out, no, Wiley, don't tell her.* "We've just become friends. There is nothing wrong with that. But, you're right, in the office I can't let on that I personally know you. It's not like you see me often anyway. Although…"

She wasn't ready to tell her, but now was as good a time as any. "You will see me again, probably a few more times within the next few months. That leads me to something that I need to tell you." She reached over and grabbed Cassidy's slightly smaller hand, the warmth stung her skin. "Please promise that you will not be mad and if you have to be mad, take it out on me."

"What?" Cassidy stiffened. "Why would I be mad at you? What are you talking about?"

"You know there is a serious issue going on with the corporation, no one knows exactly accept for myself. I've involved no one."

"Right?"

"All of the records and accounts that I had all of

the departments pull for me didn't make sense, so I hired an account auditing firm," She watched the color fade from Cassidy's face. "You understand that you cannot say anything to anyone about this."

"Yes."

"The auditor only found a few minor irregularities that I'm working on now."

"Wow, I…I don't know what to say…I'm sorry Ian, I can't even begin to imagine what that must be like for you or that anyone would steal from the company."

"Well, I wouldn't go that far, I don't think it's that bad, so far anyway. But, that's not all."

"There's more?" *Oh no, my department, it's my department isn't it?*

"The auditor…it's Katrina Sylvan." Ian released her grip on the smaller hand when Cassidy pulled away and stood up.

"What! How could you?!" Her voice seemed to travel through the entire house.

"Ssshhh, you're going to wake the house. Sit down." Ian tried to calm the woman. "Listen to me, I didn't know who she was and she wasn't told it was my company until she arrived here. I knew I recognized her, but I thought I had maybe slept with her and didn't remember. She informed me about how we really met. Anyway, she was highly recommended and did a very good job."

"Let me get this right…you hired my best friend to audit my records? How could you do something like that?" Cassidy was shaking. *Oh my god I'm yelling at my boss in her home in the middle of night. I am so fired!* Her voice was still higher than Ian wanted it to be, so she stood up and grabbed the smaller woman, forcing her sit

Just Me

back down on the couch.

Ian's voice took on a higher tone this time. "Listen to me please, Cassidy. She audited the entire company and I didn't know who she was, I called the best company that I could find and asked them to send me their best. She arrived the next day. I only found out that she knew you a few days before she was finished." Both women turned towards the doorway when they heard footsteps. Wendi and Trina were standing there staring at the two women on the couch yelling at each other.

"Uh…is everything okay?" Wendi asked quietly.

"How could you, Trina?!" Cassidy turned away from her.

"I told her, I had to. I'm sorry." Ian stood up and walked over to the window, afraid to look back at the chaos that she'd just caused. *And to think, I stopped myself from kissing her at least ten times. What the hell am I doing?*

Trina and Wendi walked over to the couch and sat across from their angry best friend.

"I'm sorry, it was a private meeting. I had no idea who she was or even the company's name. It was very confidential, besides Cass, you know I have a confidentiality agreement clause with my contracts. I couldn't tell you, I would lose my god damn job." Trina ran her hand through her sandy colored hair and shook with frustration.

"She felt terrible, Cass." The redhead added softly.

"You knew! What the hell!" Cassidy was yelling at both of them.

Ian had had enough and marched back over to the couch. She stopped a foot from the couch. "For crying out loud, it's one o'clock in the morning! So we had a business deal that involved you and we couldn't tell you about it. Grow up Cassidy!"

No one noticed Giles come into the room in his dark green pajama bottoms and matching button down top. His hair was disheveled and he was wearing glasses.

"Is everything okay Miss Wiley?" He asked patiently. Ian shot ice cold blue daggers at Cassidy as she turned towards the doorway.

"Yes." She caught up to him and placed her hand gently on his forearm. "It seems that Cassidy didn't agree with my most recent business decision and she's voicing her opinion. I'm very sorry we woke you."

"It's no trouble. I just wanted to make sure you were okay. May I get you anything?"

She laughed. "No Giles, we're fine. Please," She nodded towards the hallway. "go back to bed, get some sleep, I'll handle this."

"Goodnight then." He turned and left the room. Ian ran her hands through her short hair and sauntered back over to the couches.

"I think everyone should call it a night before too much is said that no one really means."

Ian turned her back to them and began to walk out of the room. Cassidy stood up and moved in Ian's direction. She felt horrible for what happened. They had become so close in a matter of a few hours and now everyone was fighting. She couldn't imagine how Ian was feeling at that moment.

"I'm very sorry Miss Wiley…uh…Ian…"

"You don't trust me. You're back to acting reserved." Ian turned around to face Cassidy after she spoke.

Just Me

"After everything that we talked about tonight how could you say that to me?" She felt a tear escape her eyes as she tried to choke it back. Ian leaned forward and wiped it away, completely unaware of the two friends sitting a few feet away watching every move.

"You know better than anyone that there are parts to me. I'm not one whole person, I have several 'costumes' if you will. There are things that I cannot share with you, not because I don't want to, but because you're an employee and…well...I'm your boss."

She looked past the shorter woman standing in front of her. "Goodnight ladies, I'm sorry for all of the confusion. I hope we can all get past this and enjoy a nice day tomorrow. It's supposed to be beautiful. I'd like to show the estate to all of you before you go back. It's not often that I have guests up here." She worked out a smile, then turned and left the room. *Goodbye what little happiness I was starting to feel, welcome back depression and hostility.*

~ ~ ~

Ian came downstairs to find her house was completely empty. *There's no way everyone's still asleep.*

"Giles!"

She walked around the first floor of the house, no sign of the salt and pepper haired man. *Hmm.* She went back upstairs, quietly knocked on the door of the room she knew Cassidy had been given. When she didn't hear anything she opened the door and peered in. No one was in the room and the bed was freshly made.

"What the hell?" She went back downstairs, the

Grandfather clock in the living room chimed. *nine a.m. and no one is here.* All of a sudden the color drained from her face and she sat on the sofa. The only rational thought that came to mind was the women woke up and wanted to leave so Giles took them back. *I didn't get to say goodbye, we ended on such a bad note, everything went horribly wrong.* She was too busy sulking in her own self pity to hear the door open.

"Good morning." Ian turned around to see Cassidy standing in the doorway, her two best friends and Giles all behind her in the foyer. "I'm sorry we didn't wake you, Giles said you'd still be asleep when we returned. We needed to go shower and change into clean clothes."

She hoped her shyness didn't show on the surface. Ian ran a hand through her hair and stood up, walked past Cassidy and glared at Giles. She did however stop and tell her it was okay, they weren't her captures.

The three women followed her to the dining room table and Ian sat in her customary seat at the head of the table. Cassidy sat to her left, Wendi and Trina sat to her right. Giles walked into the dining room from the kitchen.

"May I get you anything Miss Wiley?" He silently counted…and habitually she answered him.

"Four Mimosa's and four pieces of cinnamon toast." Ian said solemnly. All three women looked from her to Giles and started to object. He smiled and raised his hand for them to not speak. Cassidy looked at Trina and shrugged. Wendi's eyes went as round as saucers, but no one spoke.

"So, I only have two snowmobiles, we'll have to ride in pairs today. Is that okay?" Everyone nodded as no one wanted to speak. They were still in shock from the breakfast order.

Alcohol and a god damn piece of dry toast, there is no way I'll last all day on that. Is she nuts?! Cassidy thought to herself. *Maybe she's a Looney Tune. What the hell was I thinking?* Giles appeared carrying a small tray with four tall glasses of chocolate milk. Seconds later he sat four plates of banana nut pancakes down, one in front of each of the women. Ian nodded to him then took a long swallow of the milk. Cassidy, Trina, and Wendi weren't sure what the hell had just happened. They all looked at each other dumbfounded while Ian began eating her flapjacks. Cassidy shrugged and started eating and the others followed.

~ ~ ~

Ian opened the first bay of the garage to get the snowmobiles out and the three women followed her inside. Wendi happened to notice the little black sports car sitting on the other side of the Bentley, next to a large black SUV.

"Who's car is that?" She asked with a smile. Ian looked over her shoulder at her prize possession, black Lotus. Then she turned back around like it was nothing.

"That's Giles'." She said with a thin grin, but continued to act as if it were only a simple automobile with no meaning to her.

"No way!" Wendi was thinking the older man was sounding sexier by the minute. She stepped around Ian and walked over to the car that was backed in. The license plate read: YLESGRL. One rust colored eyebrow rose up and a sly smile crossed her face as she walked back over to them. Both of the snowmobiles were now sitting in the thick white snow to the left of the garage.

"Who's Wiley's girl?" Wendi questioned.

Ian shrugged her shoulders. "The car."

"And who's Wiley?"

"Me." Ian said with confidence.

"Ah ha! I knew it was your car! It's sweet, I bet it hauls ass!" She was grinning ear to ear like a little kid. "Why don't you drive it?"

Ian knew she was had. *My wild side has reared its ugly head!* "I do drive it, just not on these salted slick roads. I don't care to wrap it around a tree. When Giles doesn't drive me, then I drive my dad's Land Rover. As soon as the snow stops for good I'll be driving my Lotus again." She said as she climbed onto her snowmobile. Wendi climbed onto the other one that Ian's mother and father had always shared, Trina jumped on the back with her. Cassidy rolled her eyes at her friends and climbed onto the back of Ian's machine. She tried not to sit close enough to touch her though.

"Hey Wendi." Ian yelled.

"Yeah."

"When it warms up, maybe I'll take you for a ride."

Wendi disagreed. "Nah, I'll take you for a ride." She started up the snowmobile and took off, leaving a small rooster tail. Trina was thanking god that she'd been holding on. Ian glanced over her shoulder.

"I don't bite…unless you want me to." She winked.

Is she flirting with me?

"You better hold on to me or I'll leave you on your butt in the snow." Cassidy gave in a slid up behind the taller woman and wrapped her arms around her waist.

Both women could feel the heat burning between them, even though they were wearing layers of clothing and ski jackets. The vibration of the machine mixed with the feeling of the smaller woman wrapped around her was enough to make Ian's center melt. She took a deep cold breath and gunned the throttle. They caught up to the other pair that was now cruising slowly next to them.

Ian would stop occasionally to show them areas of the property and explain what part of the mountain they were on. She took them up around the right side to a man-made trail between the trees. Cassidy closed her eyes and held on tighter, the trees were coming dangerously close. She knew Trina was probably scared to death with wild and reckless Wendi driving. Ian came to a stop a few yards away from a cliff that looked out over a ravine. Cassidy got off the snowmobile and walked up closer to peek over the edge.

"It's beautiful up here." She turned to face deep blue puddles staring into her heart. Ian was standing right behind her.

"Thank you. I use to come up here with my dad. This was our…secret spot. I haven't been up here…since…their death." She almost whispered the last words.

Cassidy sensed the sadness, reached back and grabbed Ian's hand. With the thick gloves on they couldn't interlock their fingers, so she just held her hand.

Wendi was a few feet away taking in the scenery, completely unaware of the women next to her. Trina, however, noticed and smiled. Deep down she was hoping the two of them would see the love between them. She could it see from the very beginning.

"If we go back down over there," Ian pointed to

her left. "We'll come up on the hill where I snowboard. I have to chase the local's out of there all the time. It's the only part of our property line that isn't behind the gate."

"I remember seeing you out there the last time we were here." Cassidy added.

"Yeah, I saw you too." Ian smiled.

They got back on the snowmobiles and continued to ride around for hours. Ian showed them all of the beautiful spots that only magazine's tell about. Giles had lunch ready when they arrived back at the house.

"This is wonderful Giles. You're an amazing cook." Trina complimented between bites of turkey melt sandwich and homemade chicken noodle soup.

"Thank you, ma'am." He nodded with the corner of his mouth turned up.

"We have entirely too many leftovers. I would be happy if you would join me for dinner again tonight." Ian held her breath. Cassidy was trying to think of an excuse, hoping her friends would help her out. Deep down she did want to come back, she enjoyed being around Ian. In fact, every part of her enjoyed it.

"That sounds like a gre–" Wendi was trying to talk when Trina kicked her under the table.

"We need to go take care of a few things this evening don't we Wendi, but Cass, you should come back for dinner."

"What do you mean you have things to take care of?" Cassidy shot her an *I hate you* look. Wendi was rubbing her hand on her, now bruised, shin.

"We are meeting up with Charlie and Derek for dinner." Trina said. Wendi looked at her quizzically and Trina raised her eye brows trying to do her best *shut up* impression.

Just Me

"Uh...okay..." Cassidy was confused. Ian just sat there watching the conversation.

"You know...the guys we met last time we were up here."

"Oh yeah, you still talk to them?"

"Yeah. We were going to invite you to go with us tonight."

"When are you guys going back to Grand Junction?" Ian asked.

"We are supposed to go back tomorrow, but since Christmas fell on a Thursday this year, we are all off today obviously, so we can actually stay until Sunday." Trina explained. Cassidy knew something was up. She just couldn't put her finger on it. Wendi wasn't talking and Trina was digging herself one huge pile of bullshit.

"I see. So I guess you're free for dinner then Cassidy?" Ian looked over at her.

"It seems that way, yes."

"Please join me. I'm going to be eating turkey and ham forever." All of the women laughed.

"In that case, yes, I'll join you."

"Excellent."

~ ~ ~

Cassidy was standing out front of the hotel waiting for the black car when a familiar black SUV pulled up next to the curb. Ian hoped out and walked around to the passenger side. She opened the door and waved at the brunette to get in. Once Cassidy was situated, Ian shut the door and got back in the driver seat.

"Where's Giles?"

Ian noticed Cassidy had changed clothes, and

more than likely showered. She was now wearing casual black pants, a crème colored scoop neck sweater and the black leather jacket that Ian had seen her in before. Her black hair hung loosely on her shoulders. Ian had also showered and changed into khaki's and a dark blue V-neck sweater that matched her eyes. Her brown leather jacket was laying on the backseat.

"I don't know. I guess he's probably using the microwave right about now." She smiled at the look on the other woman's face. "I'm kidding, I told him I wanted to come get you. He's been in the kitchen for at least an hour and is probably whipping up something new with all of his leftover ingredients. That man could make a culinary masterpiece out of bread and water." She smiled and Cassidy laughed. "Besides, I'm trying to show you *me*, not your boss, and not the drunk woman chaser."

"So who was I with today?"

"*Me*. Just me."

"Good, I like that one."

"Me too."

When they went inside Giles was busy in the kitchen. He had brought a bottle of wine up from the cellar and left it chilling for them.

"Would either of you care for a glass of wine?" He stood poised as always, politely waiting for an answer. Ian looked over at Cassidy who nodded.

"Sure, two glasses please, Giles." Ian sat on the couch in living room, Cassidy sat across from her. "You seem nervous again."

"I am."

"Don't be, I promise I wont talk about Wiley Steel at all tonight. What happens at work stays at work. Deal?"

Just Me

"Does that mean what happens here stays here?" Cassidy raised an eyebrow with curiosity.

Ian wasn't sure where this was going. "Uh…sure…well obviously I can't go into the office Monday and tell everyone I spent Christmas weekend with you, now can I?"

"No of course not."

"Okay then, what happens with our friendship stays with us. I know I shouldn't see you like this, but truth be told Cassidy, if you didn't work for me I would want to date you. I find you very intriguing, I really enjoy being around you. As I said last night, I have to live my life in the closet. I could never risk anyone finding out. My being friends with you like this is probably just as bad."

"I thought we weren't talking about Wiley Steel?" *Did she just tell me she liked me? Get your ears checked Cassidy.*

"Touché." Ian grinned and took a sip of her wine. *What have I started? I can't get you out of my head Cassidy. God I shouldn't be doing this, I know I shouldn't see her anymore.*

"Then we have a deal." Cassidy reached forward and Ian's hand met hers halfway across the table between them. The spark could've been blamed on static electricity, but both women felt it and held on tightly as if it were something completely different. They sat across from each other staring and searching for some sort of sign from the other. The sound of Giles' voice startled both of them.

"Dinner is ready. Miss Wiley." He turned and went back to the kitchen.

Cassidy sat on the left side of the head of the

table, which was where Ian sat. Soft candles were glowing in the center of the large table. Giles returned with two large bowls of homemade turkey pot pie.

"This looks delicious, Giles." Cassidy stated as she stuck her fork into the bowl.

"Thank you, ma'am." He walked away to give them some privacy. They ate and talked about the different areas of the mountain that they saw earlier. After Giles served them dessert he added a few logs to start a fresh fire in the living room and then went back to his own room. If Ian didn't know any better, she'd swear he was up to something.

~ ~ ~

Ian sat on the couch next to Cassidy, their thighs touching slightly. The snow fell lightly on the ground outside as they sat in the glowing light of the fireplace talking. Cassidy tried not to bring up her parents, but that seemed to be the only thing on her mind, except for the smoldering heat radiating off of the gorgeous body next to her. It always hurt Ian to think of her parents, but somehow listening to this woman talk next to her made her miss them without hurting so badly. Cassidy changed the subject when she asked Ian what it was like growing up in what she would call *royalty*, on the most beautiful mountain that she'd ever seen.

"Well, I...from the time I can remember, I guess I was about four or five, I spent the summers fishing in the streams with my father when he wasn't working, which wasn't often due to his schedule. My mother would spend her days working on various art deals. She owned one of the local galleries for years, that's where the art influence comes from."

"I can see it. This house is a work of art all on its own, but the masterpieces that fill the walls and the statues that adorn them are absolutely amazing. I feel like I'm in an art museum when I'm here." Cassidy smiled.

Ian continued to talk about her childhood. This was the first time she spoken of it in many years.

"Yes, sometimes I do too. My mother would take me to different shows, teaching me about different pieces and how to read to them. She taught me so much about feelings and how to understand them. To me she was a piece of art all by herself. She reminded me of an angel. She was very graceful and pure. My father was strong-willed and powerful, but he was sentimental and loving at home. As I got older he took me with him to the office and the plant. He would show me everything that he was doing and explain why he was doing it. When my grandfather passed away my dad took the reins of the company. I must've been around ten. That's when he began spending more and more time crusading in the corporate world. I knew one day all of it would be mine, even at that young age. Giles did the best he could to fill in when they weren't there. My mother finally sold her gallery and began to take a more formal role as *the* Mrs. Wiley. Both of my parents pushed me to succeed in everything that I did, when I graduated with a full academic scholarship they cried. I remember the day I told them, it seems like yesterday."

She looked over at the brunette sitting next to her. Cassidy had laid her head on Ian's shoulder and fallen asleep. Ian wrapped her arm around her and settled into the corner of the couch to get more comfortable. She watched the rise and fall of Cassidy's chest until she dosed off.

Cassidy opened her eyes to a semi-dark room. She was on the couch, so warm. The couch was so soft and warm against her. She turned her head. *Ian! Oh my god I fell asleep with her, on her! Shit!* Her heart raced. Their bodies were tangled together. Ian had her arms wrapped around the smaller woman. One of Cassidy's arms was between them. The other one was draped over Ian's stomach and extended up between her breasts. Cassidy's hand lay flat against Ian's chest just above her breasts, almost over her heart. Cassidy was scared to death. *What the hell do I say or do if and when she wakes up? I'm stuck here, like this. It's not that bad. She's so comfortable. She looks like an angel sleeping. She's your god damn boss!* The last thought in her head stung, this caused her to stir gently. That's all it took to wake the sleeping beauty underneath her.

Ian's eyes flickered open, slowly taking in her surroundings. That's when she noticed the smaller woman lying in her arms, their faces inches apart. Cassidy stared deeply into sparkling blue eyes. Ian studied Cassidy's face, her gray eyes ran deeper than she could ever have imagined. Before any words could be spoken, both women simultaneously closed the gap between them. Their lips met softly at first, neither woman pulling away or rushing for more. The kiss was gentle and innocent, when Ian's lips parted Cassidy's tongue explored deeper, tasting as much of the other woman as she possibly could. Ian allowed the entrance with a soft moan, her tongue followed suit, each mouth and tongue massaging the other passionately.

Ian's hold on Cassidy became tighter and she pulled the smaller woman tightly against her, completely

Just Me

aware of the flames between her legs. Cassidy slid her hand further up, brushing along Ian's jaw and her neck until she could feel the whispers of short hair on her fingertips. She ran her hand through Ian's short hair. Both women were sure they'd be bruised, but neither one stopped the intoxicating kiss. They drank form each others mouth with a fiery passion, their tongues never parting. Their hands wandered, feeling as much as they could of each other. Cassidy pulled away just enough to catch her breath and playfully bit Ian's bottom lip as she broke their contact, that's when she looked into dark blue eyes swimming with desire. *Oh my god!*

All Ian could do was stare at this magnificent woman lying in her arms. The kiss had completely taken her breath away. Her mind couldn't control the pounding in her heart, the burning in the pit of her stomach, or the powerful throbbing between her legs. *What have I done?!*

Cassidy removed herself from Ian's embrace. She slid over to the other end of the couch. Her body was trembling from the loss of contact. Ian sat up and stared into the darkness. She was sure the sunrise wouldn't be far away. Her body was freezing everywhere that their bodies had been infused. The fireplace was almost out, except for one orange ember glowing in the ashes.

"I–"

"I'm–"

Both of them tried to speak first, neither one knowing what to say. They sat in silence for another few minutes. Finally Ian started.

"I'm sorry…I never meant for that to happen." She continued to stare at the darkness outside. The woman next to her stared at her palms, which were folded into her lap.

"I'm sorry too. It's not your fault."

"Do you regret it?" Ian spoke softly.

"No." Cassidy answered back with a whisper. *And that scares the hell out of me.* "You should probably take me back to the lodge."

"Yes. You're right." *Making love to you would tear me apart, I can't give you the lifestyle that you deserve, no matter how bad I want you. It could never come out of the bedroom.*

Just Me
Chapter 12

Two weeks later Ian finally received the return phone call that she'd been waiting for. The buyer for CSX explained how he inquired with Benjamin Bradford of Wiley Steel about building two new locomotives and six container style box cars. He went on to say that Wiley Steel bid extremely high, almost a hundred thousand dollars above his total budget, but he knew the Wiley name and wanted to go with them. Three days later he received a call from Frasier Higginbotham saying that they could not complete the order. The production lines were extremely backed up and they would be months away from the agreed deadline. CSX was forced to pull out and go on with another company. All Ian needed to hear was the name of the other company, J.R. Hinkley Metals. She knew something was up. Hinkley was nowhere near capable of handling the kind of deals that Wiley executed daily. She hated snooping around her own company, but it had to be done, she finally found the answers she was looking for. All of the deals that were pulled or turned away over the past couple of years went to J.R. Hinkley Metals.

"It's time to put the banana in front of the monkey." She smiled.

~ ~ ~

Ian seemed to pour herself completely into Wiley Steel for the next few weeks. Giles wasn't exactly sure, but he could tell something had happened. He was half expecting the young woman to retreat back to her wild and reckless side. She was quiet and secluded, spending hours in her fathers study while she was at the house. In fact, she spent more time at the house in the study than she did in the corporate office. Giles knew she was working on something, her ears were steaming from thought, but the sadness remained on the surface.

The sudden death of her parents had thrown the young blond for a loop. Slowly she figured out how to unwind it, but Giles was sure something had tightened the knot once again. If it wasn't for his constant checking on her, he was sure she wouldn't be eating and alcohol would once again be her comfort. Luckily, he knew the signs from the last time. He vowed to never let her go that far ever again. Anytime he tried to get her to talk she seemed to withdraw, only speaking about the business or her parents a little and reminiscing her childhood with him. It seemed as if she was stepping over a void every time he asked about her three friends that visited over the holidays, she would simply shrug and say she didn't have time to talk.

~ ~ ~

Cassidy continued to go to work as usual. Her heart leapt into her throat every time she heard a knock on her door. She'd told her friends about her events of that night.

Just Me

"Oh my god Cass." Trina was shocked. Wendi was more intrigued at the fact that she ran away instead of following through.

"What made you stop? I mean she's gorgeous, if I were gay I'd be after her!"

"It's not that simply Wendi. She's my boss for crying out loud! Sleeping with her would be a huge mistake." Cassidy downed the entire glass of Soco in one sip and waved for the bartender to bring her another.

"Who pulled away first?" Trina watched her best friend's face. She could see the straining lines from not eating or sleeping. *She's really taking this pretty hard.*

"I...I don't know, I guess I did. Hell I was on top of her!"

"Woo hoo!" Wendi hollered, only loud enough for them to hear it.

"Damn it Wendi." Cassidy smiled and shook her head.

"Was it good? Is she as good a kisser as she comes off to be?" Wendi wasn't letting up. Trina was glad someone was asking. *She wanted all of the details too.*

Cassidy took a deep breath and closed her eyes. *It was the most extraordinary thing that I have ever felt. My body was on fire, burning for her touch.* "Yeah, she's a great kisser."

"Well then, what's the problem?"

"She doesn't want me like that. I mean, we could never...she's my boss, it just doesn't work like that Wendi."

"Have you guys talked about it?" Trina sipped her drink when the bartender returned.

"No, there's nothing to talk about." There never

will be. End of story.

Cassidy leaned her head back against her desk chair and smiled, recalling the headache she woke up with the next day. She had prayed to the toilet gods for hours. She swore she'd never drink again. Eventually her friends dropped the subject of Ian Wiley as the weeks went on. Before long, two months had passed. March wasn't far off and spring was around the corner. That alone was enough to give her hope. Hope for what, she wasn't sure.

~ ~ ~

Ian sat behind the large mahogany desk in the giant office. A soft leather couch sat along one side of the room. The rest of the walls were covered with photos, diplomas, certificates, and other important or sentimental documentation. She'd just made the second dreaded phone call. She hung up knowing she had all of bases covered since she'd started the ball rolling the day before when she made the initial call from the study at the estate. She cradled the receiver on the phone and dialed a familiar extension on the intercom. After that she called the number back and left the speaker phone going. The tiny light on the corner of the phone was only noticeable on her side of the desk.

"Yes." The male voice answered.

"Benjamin, this is Ian Wiley. Can you meet me in my office right now?" Her tone was strong, suggesting he would meet her no matter what he was doing.

"Uh…yeah…yes ma'am, I'm on the way."

A few minutes later she heard the knock on the

door.

"Come in." She sat with her hands folded on the desk. The screen saver was running on her computer. She wasn't surprised to see Frasier Higginbotham come through the door. *Rat bastard!* "What can I do for you, Frasier?"

"Miss Wiley, Benjamin Bradford said you called a meeting."

She wanted to smack the smirk off of his face and stomp on it. Instead she kept her cool. "I did." She said flatly. "Between him and myself."

"Oh, well then, would you mind if I sat in? We have some new deals to go over–" She cut him off.

"Not right now Frasier, I need to speak to Mr. Bradford alone. I'll brief you when I'm finished." All he could do was nod and back away. The man waiting in the hall next to him walked inside of the room.

"Shut the door and have a seat Benjamin." He did as he was told. She knew the *rat bastard* wouldn't be able to listen in. There was no way he could ease drop, someone would see him lingering in the hallway.

"What can I do for you ma'am?" His skin was pale white, she knew she scared the shit out him and she hadn't even spoken yet. She crossed her arms over her chest and leaned back in her chair.

"Well, you can start by telling me the truth." She stared sapphire blue daggers directly into his eyes.

"Uh…what…what do you mean? I don't understand–" He fumbled over his words as if English was a foreign language to him.

"I'm not going to beat around the bush, Mr. Bradford. You know what happened to those deals with Amtrak, CSX, and a few smaller companies. I want the truth and I want it right now."

"We…I told you, production and logis–"

Her voice went up one octave. "Benjamin you know as well as I do that I've already been to the plant and seen the records. Those deals never made it to production, therefore logistics never saw them either. Now, let's try this again. What happened to them?"

"I…I don't know, I told you." She could see him shaking in the chair across from her.

"You told me a little white lie, as a matter of fact, you've told me a few of them. Listen to me Mr. Bradford. It is in your best interest to start from the beginning and tell me the truth."

"There's nothing to tell." His voice was trembling. "We couldn't meet their deadlines and…and well that's it."

She slammed her fist on the desk, hard enough to rumble everything sitting on it. "I promised myself that I wouldn't get mad, Benjamin, but you're seriously pushing my patience here. Let's try this, I already know what happened and who the deals went to. You need to tell me how this happened. Now I'm only going to ask you one more time, after that, well, I guess we will see what happens then wont we?" She dared him to lie again. Her eyes bore holes into him.

"I…we…" He took a shallow breath. "The deals, we overbid…then forced them to pull out. We said we couldn't complete the orders." His forehead was covered with beads of sweat.

"And you did all of this on purpose?"

"Yes, but I …we…"

"Who is we? Who helped you with this?"

"Frasier Higginbotham, it was all his idea." He

hung his head.

She could feel the blood boiling in her body. It took everything inside of her to hold back. She desperately wanted to ram this asshole's head through the concrete wall and spit in his face on the other side. "Why did you two do this?"

"Hinkley…Frasier made a deal with Hinkley."

"What deal?" Now she had three people to beat the shit out of.

"We would purposely mock up our bids and production so that the companies would have to go to Hinkley. They were cutting Frasier and me a small part of the profit."

"Okay how long has this been going on?"

"I don't know a year or two."

"How many deals Benjamin?" Her voice was even higher now, and her tone lower.

He swallowed loud enough for her to hear it. "Uh…I don't know…"

"How much money then?"

"I…I really don't know…I've gotten a little over a million so far." He looked away form her. All of a sudden a deep voice was heard through the room.

"Miss Wiley I believe we have enough here. The authorities are waiting outside of your door for him."

"Thank you Max."

"Who's…who's that?" He began fumbling around looking for the person that had been speaking. Ian turned the volume off on the speaker phone, stood up and started to make her way around her desk.

"That was Maxwell Guthrey, of Guthrey and Meyers, Attorney's at Law." She smiled. He was never prepared for what happened next. Her fist met his face with extreme force, his head rocked back as if her hand had gone through him. Blood squirted from his nose and trickled from his mouth where a tooth had been. Her hand hurt and she figured she fractured it, but she didn't care. As soon as he tried to come at her she swung the door open. Four Aspen Police officers rushed in and grabbed him. One of the men turned to her.

"What happened to his face?" He smiled.

"I don't know, he fell out of his chair." She grinned; her right hand was behind her back. She was surprised to see the power in her right hand considering she was actually left handed. *You're lucky I didn't shoot the son of a bitch.*

"That bitch broke my nose." He was trying to stop the blood, that's when he realized his tooth was also gone. She smiled and waved as they handcuffed him and escorted him from the building. Ian went back to the desk and turned the volume back on.

"Max?"

"Yeah, what happened?"

"He's gone."

"What about Higginbotham?"

"They're waiting for me to talk to him. He has no idea. I'm about to call him in here."

"Okay, make sure they're out of sight."

She called Frasier into her office and began the same speech that she'd given Benjamin Bradford. Frasier also didn't bite at first. Her hand throbbed, she knew it needed ice and this only made her angrier. She was passed the point of pissed off.

"I don't know what you're talking about. We've already been over this."

"I audited the records, Frasier. I know what you

Just Me

did, besides your little buddy just ratted you out."

"What?" He looked confused.

Her voice went up. "I said Benjamin just told me what you and he did. He told me all about Hinkley."

"You dyke bitch!" He jumped out of the chair. "You don't deserve this company, if your father knew you were a dyke he would've given it to me. I should be running this place not you!" He was screaming at her. She stood to meet him face to face, with the large desk between them. The brown haired man stood a few inches taller than her.

"You rat bastard, my father was about to fire your stupid ass before he died." She said flatly with a loud tone.

"This place deserves to go into the ground. You'll run it there anyway. I was only making some money and setting myself up to take over when you did, you lousy bitch!" He leaned forward to hit her and she moved around the desk, knowing damn good and well her attorney was recording and witnessing all of this.

"You missed. See that's the problem with you Frasier, you do everything half-assed. That's why I caught you."

He tried to hit her again. She grabbed his collar and shoved him against the door. He was surprised at the strength coming from such a small person. When he came off of the wall she caught him square in the mouth with her left hand and all of her body weight behind it. His whole body rocked back. The cops heard him hit the wall and were already halfway into the room when she hit him. None of them saw the blow though. Now her left hand hurt just as bad as her right. Frasier lunged at her, but the cops grabbed him before he could get her. He was screaming at her all the way out to the patrol car waiting out front.

"My god Miss Wiley, are you okay?" The deep voice called out. She ran over to the desk and grabbed up the receiver.

"Yeah." She let out a deep breath. "I'm fine."

"That was close. At least we did get confessions from both of them. I'll have this in front of the grand jury by Monday. We have enough documentation to take Hinkley down too."

"Good, that's what I was hoping for. Keep me updated. I'm sure this will drag on for a year."

"Not if I can help it, but you know how the corporate world can be." He tried to console her, he'd been her father's lawyer since he took over the business when she was ten.

Ian hung up the phone. She took a deep breath and looked down at the purple bruises forming on her hands. *God damn it!* She sighed and called Carey Stewart and William Goody into her office. Once they arrived she called the plant and asked Richard Masters to call Cassidy Harland into his office, shut the door and leave the speaker phone on.

"Okay now that I have everyone's attention I'll get to the point. Obviously Mr. Goody and Mr. Carey, you guys can tell by the mess that there was a small scuffle in here." Both men looked around and nodded. "Mr. Benjamin Bradford, Director of Locomotive Services, and Mr. Frasier Higginbotham, Executive Assistant, are no longer with the company." She heard gasps from all around, everyone was questioning her. "I caught both of them in a scandal with J.R. Hinkley."

"What! Oh my god!" Richard Masters couldn't

hide his surprise. "That son of a bitch!" He was disgusted.

"It's okay Rich. I know, trust me. That's why some of the pictures are laying on the floor in broken frames. Things got a little physical with both guys." She looked down at her purple hands that throbbed as if they were in vises.

"I'm sorry, Miss Wiley." Rich apologized for losing his temper. Cassidy sat in silence, wishing she was in that room instead of two and a half hours away on the phone.

"Anyway, I know none of you were involved. Just so that all of you know, this will be a long courtroom battle and we're now down one director. I can run without an assistant, that's not a big deal, but we will need to step it up and try to straighten out this mess with Locomotive Services.

"I can definitely help out, Miss Wiley."

"Thanks. William."

"Me too." Carey Stewart added.

"Alright, it sounds like this isn't going to affect us on the home front." She smiled. "Just so all of you know the entire records for Wiley Steel have been audited and everything else is clean. I want to thank each of you for being trustworthy employees. William, you and Carey will be a big help to me here. Rich, you and Cassidy…" Her heart skipped a beat. "You two are always on top of your game, thank you both."

"Let us know if we can help in anyway, Miss Wiley." Cassidy spoke with respect for the company like everyone else, but the blond could hear the concern in her voice. She felt her pulse race when she heard the brunette speak.

"Thank you Cassidy, I appreciate it. Okay everyone, that's all I have so far. Thank you all. I know this is a pretty big mess, but I believe in this company, just as my father and grandfather did. I'll do anything and everything in my power to keep this corporation at the top." *No matter what.*

Just Me
Chapter 13

The middle of February brought more snow than Ian ever cared to see. Her precious *YLESGRL* sat in the warm garage begging to be driven fast and loose. *Damn the weather,* she thought as she sat in the study staring out the window. She'd spent the past week on the phone, talking to her lawyers as well as the State Attorney's office. She wished with every ounce of her being that her father was still alive to handle this. Part of her knew she was strong, but the other parts were scared to death. Then, she had the ever-present thoughts of the moment she shared with Cassidy on the couch. With tomorrow being Valentine's Days she decided to do something that her heart and mind were fighting over. She dialed information to get the phone number that she needed.

"Hi, I'd like to order your nicest bouquet, please." Ian leaned back in the chair and ran her hand through her messy short hair.

"Yes ma'am, would that be roses or–"

"Yes please, how about an array of yellow and pink with baby's breath."

"Yes ma'am, we can definitely do that. One dozen then?"

"No. Let's go with two and make it perfect, the cost doesn't matter."

"Yes ma'am. Who and where is this being

delivered to?"

Ian thought for a second, she didn't know Cassidy's home address, she could of course call the office to find out, but then that would be conspicuous. "It's going to Cassidy Harland. Are you familiar with the Wiley Steel Corporation?"

"Yes ma'am."

"Good, she's one of the executives there. Please deliver it to her office."

"No problem. I'm assuming you want this delivered tomorrow morning?"

"Yes, please."

"Okay. And, what would you like the card to say?" Ian almost dropped the phone. She had completely forgotten about that part. *What would she say? What could she say?* Everyone would already be asking about the flowers and who they were from. She knew Cassidy was professional and would never dare tell them they were from Ian, but still, what the hell would she say on the card?

"Uh…" Then it hit her. "Please put this on the card: *No regrets, only friendship to build on. Sorry I can't be, Just Me.*"

"Okay, I got it." The woman repeated it back, and Ian paid for it with a credit card that she had in Giles' name so that she didn't get hassled when she made purchases over the phone. This had been a secret between them since she was old enough to get credit cards.

Bad idea Wiley. What have I done now? I can't seem to control myself when it comes to this woman. Ugh!

~ ~ ~

Just Me

The young man parked the large white van at the curb and stepped out. As soon as he walked into the massive building he heard the receptionist speak from behind the tall desk on the left.

"Hi, I have a delivery for Cassidy Harland."

She could barely see the man behind the giant vase of flowers that he was holding. "Thank you, if you would just set them on the counter over there, I can sign for them." She reached up and scribbled on his clipboard. As soon as he was outside she called the extension for Cassidy and Richard's shared secretary. Ten minutes later the bubbly young woman appeared at the desk. She looked shocked when she saw the arrangement. Nevertheless, she grabbed the large vase and took it back to the brunette's office. Cassidy was over in the production room so the secretary left the beautiful mass of flowers sitting in the middle of Cassidy's desk and waited for what seemed like hours.

"What the hell! Kathleen?" Cassidy called out louder than she meant to when she went into her office.

"Oh, Miss Harland, those were delivered a little while ago." She hesitated, trying to hide the curious smile.

"Who are they from?" Cassidy turned towards her. Kathleen only shrugged her shoulders. Cassidy moved closer to the desk and sniffed the sweet aroma. "They're gorgeous!"

She grabbed the tiny card and removed it from the envelope. Her facial expressions were enough to drive the secretary over the edge. Cassidy smiled and tears filled her eyes. She put the card back in the envelope and slipped it into her inside coat pocket. She moved the vase to a nearby table since they took up most of her desk.Cassidy turned towards Kathleen, who seemed to be waiting anxiously to find out who sent the bundle of roses. "They're from a secret admirer." Kathleen's face went pale. 'I'm kidding, they're from a friend." It was the truth, she and Ian were friends, only friends and they would stay that way. *Do I call and thank her? Do I mention it at all? Do I...oh hell, I don't know what the hell to do when it comes to her.* The secretary left her boss alone in her thoughts.

Four hours later, Cassidy was perched on her couch staring at the elegant looking arrangement sitting on the dining room table in her apartment. The knock on the door shook her back to reality. She swept her dark hair back off of her shoulder.

"Hey Cass, we knew you'd be sitting here alone on Valentine's Day." Wendi pushed her way inside, followed by Trina.

"You two are something else." Cassidy shook her head.

"What the hell is this?! Trina look!" Wendi was eyeing the flowers and physically searching them for the card.

"You won't find it. I hid it an hour ago." Cassidy smirked and went back to her warm seat on the couch.

"Well? Who are they from?" Trina sniffed the delicate scent.

Cassidy simply shrugged. "My boss."

"Who?" Wendi turned to Trina as they both spoke at the same time.

"Ian?"

"Yep."

"Holy shit! What did the card say?"

Just Me

"Not much and everything." She ran her hands through her long black hair.

"What? No riddles tonight, Cass. I'm not into playing games with you. Let me see the card." Wendi barked in protest. Cassidy walked into her bedroom and came back out with the envelope. Her best friends read it together and handed it back to her.

"That's heavy. Talk about riddles." Trina shook her head.

"What does she mean by that?" Wendi asked.

"What happened between you two that night, Cassidy?" Trina asked.

"I already told both of you, nothing happened. We talked for a while and fell asleep on the couch. Look guys, she's my boss and nothing will ever happen between us. Even if we wanted it to, it just wouldn't work out. We're friends." *That's all.*

"Are you in love with her?" Trina asked. Wendi almost slapped her. Cassidy looked at both of them, ignoring the question.

"Let's go out. Who wants to sit alone on Valentine's Day?"

"I hear ya!" Wendi smiled and clapped her hands together and shot a piercing gaze at Trina when Cassidy left the room to change her clothes. "What the hell did you do that for?" She whispered harshly.

"Because she needs to admit it, hell they both do. You and I both saw it. You can't deny the heat between them." She whispered back.

"So they were lusting after each other. Do you really want her to get hurt?" Wendi growled quietly.

"No. I don't think Ian would hurt her. She looks at her like she's the only woman in the world."

"She's also her god damn boss, Trina."

"I know that."

"Good, stay out of it." On that note Cassidy walked back into the room wearing jeans and a baby blue sweater. She grabbed her leather jacket on the way out the door.

Once the three women arrived at the bar Trina decided to speak again.

"Have you called to thank her?"

Wendi looked like she was about to go off on Trina.

"No."

"Why not?"

"It's complicated, Trina. What the hell would I say?" *No you have no idea how difficult this is for me. I can't explain what's going on because I don't even know myself.*

"Thank you would be a start." The sandy haired woman shrugged and sipped her drink as soon as the waiter set it down. Cassidy downed the glass of Soco in one sip.

"Have you given any thought to applying for one of the open positions?" Wendi changed the subject.

"No, I mean the Locomotive Director position probably pays higher than mine, but I don't know if I would want to live in Aspen and I'd have to work in the corporate office."

"What about the other one?"

"What other one? Oh you mean her assistant?"

"Yeah."

"No I wouldn't want to do that. You're practically her bitch twenty-four-seven. No thank you." She laughed.

"I can see where I wouldn't want to do that

either." Trina finally joined the conversation.

"How's the legal battle going?"

"I don't know. Honestly, we haven't heard much about it."

"I haven't either, I gave her attorney's the copies of my reports last week. That's the last I heard about it. I'm sure I'll have to testify or at least give a deposition eventually."

"I'm sure we all will. I still can't believe this mess."

"Believe it or not Cass, I see this sort of thing a lot in the corporate world. People get greedy." Trina finished her Martini and ordered a round of chocolate covered strawberries for the table. "Let's celebrate." She smiled.

"The fact that we're all single, on Valentine's Day?" Wendi laughed.

"No, the fact that we always have each other no matter what." Trina put her glass up, they toasted in unison.

Chapter 14

A month passed, Cassidy found herself sitting in a quiet room in the back of the office section of the Wiley Steel production plant. She was alone, awaiting the arrival of Mr. Guthrey, to take her testimony about the business scam that Higginbotham and Bradford had been involved in. Richard Masters, Director of Production, had given his statements earlier that day. To keep everything legitimate, she was told to take the day off and be there at four p.m. to meet with him.

When the door opened, a tall man with jet black hair that matched Cassidy's, walked into the room carrying a briefcase. His dark brown eyes seemed friendlier than his appearance; the charcoal colored Armani suit was crisp and reeked of power. Cassidy didn't see the blond enter behind him until she shut the door and sat in the seat next to him. He extended his hand with a smile.

"Miss Harland, we spoke on the phone, I'm Maxwell Guthrey and I'm sure you know Ian Wiley."

"Yes sir, it's nice to meet you…" She looked at the blond. "And it's nice to see you again, Miss Wiley." Her tone was flat, but polite.

"Okay, let's get started then." He went through each of the questions in his list and she answered them to the best of her knowledge as the small device in the center of the table recorded every word. Ian never spoke. She sat in silence acting only as a witness. Cassidy found herself glancing towards Ian every so often. She was always looking back. Her amazing blue eyes were cloudy, as if they were deep in thought.

After three hours the meeting was over. Cassidy shook hands with Mr. Guthrey once again, this time she also offered her hand to the blond. Ian returned the gesture softly. Both women felt the heat that passed between them as there hands touched briefly, then the bitter cold that was left when their hands released. Mr. Guthrey and Ian stayed in the room to talk in private after Cassidy walked out.

"I think we have everything we need from Wiley Steel. The next step is going through all of the records that we subpoenaed from J.R. Hinkley Metals. I'm sure that'll have us buried in paperwork for another month. After that, well," He took a deep breath and quickly let it out. "We go to trial."

"Sounds like the war is slowing starting. I can't tell you how much I hate this Max."

"I know, but your daddy would be very proud of you."

"Thanks." She smiled lightly. *What would he think of me being gay? The great Wiley heir leading the throne with a woman on her arm?*

Ian decided to stop at Cassidy's office on her way out of the building. Sure enough the brunette was sitting at her desk.

"Come in." Cassidy smiled tenderly.

"You were supposed to take today off." Ian spoke dryly.

"Yes, I know. It's Friday. I should be happy to

have a three day weekend. Actually, I only came in here for a piece of paper." She slid the small piece of paper across the desk. Ian glanced at it.

"What's this?"

"My address." Cassidy's entire body was trembling. *What the hell am I doing? Thanking her for the flowers, that's it I'm being nice to her.* "If you're staying in town tonight, I'd like to cook you dinner..." She hesitated, praying her secretary could not hear their conversation. "As a thank you for the flowers and all of the dinners and so on that I shared with you in your home." *There I said it, it's out. The ball is out of my court, for once.* Ian shifted in her chair.

"What time should I be there?"

"Eight, if that's okay."

"Yeah, it's already past seven, I need to get to the hotel and change first." She looked down at her business suit, wishing she was already in jeans.

"Sure, I'm not far from the Hilton. I'm assuming that's where you're staying."

Ian smiled. "Yes it is."

~ ~ ~

Cassidy paced the floor, dinner was in the oven keeping warm and the bottle of chardonnay was chilling in the wine cooler on the table. She was hoping her friends didn't decide to stop by unannounced as usual. Both of them knew about her deposition today and would more than likely inquire about it. The knock on the door brought her out of the daze she had floated into.

"Hey."

"Hi, thanks for inviting me, I wasn't sure if I

should bring anything." Ian said shyly.

"No, you've done enough, it's my turn." Cassidy's voice sounded almost seductive, she chastised herself for being so forward. Sex was not on her mind. Okay sex was on her mind, but not just sex and definitely not with her boss. For some odd reason the woman standing in front of her clad in jeans, a polo, and a leather jacket was the complete opposite of the power suit boss that she was speaking of not having sex with. *She's still your god damn boss, no matter what she wears!* Her nerves began taking over her body.

"You have a nice place." Ian looked around at the modernly decorated tiny apartment. The couch was the color of smooth chocolate. It contrasted perfectly against the crème colored walls and carpet. Two small wooden tables sat on each end of the sofa, a matching coffee table sat in front of it. The entertainment center on the opposite side of the room was also wood. It housed a moderate sized TV and a few other electronics. A small breakfast bar with two stools separated the living room and kitchen. The dining area was off to the side of the kitchen, and a small hallway was off to the right. Ian suspected that led to the master bedroom and probably a much smaller spare room.

"Thanks. It's nothing like your home though." Cassidy moved close to the other woman. "Please, let me take your coat. Dinner is in the oven, I've prepared a Caesar Salad to start." She took Ian's coat and draped it across one of the bar stools. The blond followed her in the dining area.

"Something smells good."

"That would be Lasagna." Cassidy poured two glasses of wine and walked back into the kitchen and returned with two bowls of salad placing them on the small dining table and then she sat down across from Ian.

"I wanted to say thank you for the flowers. They were beautiful."

"You're welcome."

"Trina and Wendi went nuts over them." She laughed.

Ian thought of the crazy pair of friends and laughed as well.

"The office was a little more difficult. Kathleen, my secretary wouldn't leave me alone about them. Rich was even a little curious."

"No one's ever sent you flowers before?"

"No, well not to work." She thought of the time Ian sent her flowers to the ski lodge for her birthday.

"Do they know about your personal life?" Ian questioned as she ate her salad.

"No. No one knows anything about me except Trina and Wendi. My parents have never asked. I'm sure they know." Cassidy's cell phone rang at that precise moment. *Speak of the devil pair!* "Please excuse me, if I don't answer they will just show up here."

Ian laughed and nodded her head. Cassidy went into the living room. She answered sharper than she had intended.

"What?"

"Whoa! What crawled up your ass?" Trina yelled.

"Sorry, I'm a little busy. Can I...can I call you back?"

"Busy? You? Since when? Who's there? Where are you?"

"I'm at home and I have company. I'll call you when I'm alone."

Just Me

"Who is it?"

"None of your business." She growled low, trying not to be overheard was hard enough in the small apartment.

"Uh huh…who is she? And since when do you have a date that Wendi and I don't know about?"

"Look, do me a favor and let Wendi know that I'm occupied at this moment so she doesn't decide to show up. I'll call you later and tell you about the meeting, if that's why you're calling."

"It is, but now I'm more intrigued to find out who's at your house right now."

She whispered. "It's her, okay."

"What? Who?"

"Her." She said through clinched teeth.

"Her? Huh?"

"God damn it Trina, you know who." She heard a gasp on the other end of the line.

"Oh my god, Ian's there? Why is she at your apartment?"

"I invited her to dinner to thank her for the flowers and you are rudely interrupting me at the moment."

"Shit, okay I'm sorry. I'll call Wendi. Hey I want the details when she leaves."

"Fine! I gotta go." She slammed her phone closed and walked back into the dining area.

"I'm so sorry. It was Trina with a hundred questions."

"Did you tell her I was here?"

"Yes, I'm sorry. If I hadn't she might have shown up here." She laughed. "They both would have."

"It's okay."

Cassidy cleared the table and returned with two heaping plates of homemade lasagna. She poured two more glasses of wine and sat down. Ian was the first to bite into the main course.

"Wow, this is excellent!"

"Thank you, I don't cook much, but when I do it's usually something Italian. For some reason I love Italian food."

"Me too. Giles makes a huge array of different foods, but I've always liked Italian the best." She smiled and continued to enjoy her meal as she ate. Ian tried to overlook the desire building in her body. Ever since the passionate kiss that they shared on the couch, her libido had been screaming at her. Seeing Cassidy today was all it took, her heart raced and her body yearned for the dark-haired woman across from her. *A friendly dinner, that's all this is. Behave Wiley!*

"I don't know how you live with him. He spoiled me and I was only there a day or two." She smiled.

"I guess I'm use to him." She took a sip of her wine. "Honestly, I don't know what I'd do without him." She grinned.

"So how long are you in town for?"

"I drove in early this morning. With today being Friday, I guess I don't really have to be back until Monday. I have a few things I need to do in the office. Not having an assistance is crucifying. I'm reading through at least fifty resumes everyday. I'm also hiring for a new position. Did Rich tell you about it?"

"No. What is it?"

"I'm sorry, I hate talking business when I'm not in the office and I really don't like to talk about it around you."

Just Me

"We don't have to talk about work."

"Good." She could see the questions on the brunette's face. "It's a new director position. This one will be totally new, I'm trying to broaden the market and reach out to the steel construction industry. A lot of buildings are built out of the same steel that we use everyday. I know it won't be a major dollar difference, but it gives us expansion and that's always positive."

"That sounds interesting. I can't wait to see how it does." Cassidy seemed excited and that alone made Ian happy.

"Me too. But now I'm looking for an assistant, a Locomotive Services Director, and a Construction Director. I'm pulling my hair out." Both women laughed. The smile on Cassidy's face could melt the polar icecaps. At least, that's how Ian viewed it, warm and endearing, but seductively hot when she wanted it to be.

"I have tiramisu for dessert." Cassidy challenged with a smile as she stood up to clear the table.

"I can't believe you made all of this." Ian admitted she couldn't cook near as well. She was very thankful for Giles in many ways.

"Well, I have to confess, I purchased the dessert, but I did make the salad and lasagna."

"Ah ha! You almost let me believe you were perfect." Ian laughed. Cassidy gave her a crooked grin with a raised eyebrow.

"Want some coffee to go with this?" Cassidy set the plate of cake in front of Ian; blue eyes searched her face as she answered.

"Sure, do you happen to have any Irish Crème?"

"Of course, I was about to ask if you liked your coffee dirty."

"I rarely drink coffee, but when I do I love it dirty." The end of that sentence rolled seductively off of her tongue. Ian was shocked at what she'd just done. *Damn it.* Cassidy heard every word, but decided not to touch it with a ten foot pole.

They finished their cake and moved to the couch. Both of them were nursing their coffee mugs, anything to keep from staring too long at the other.

"It's getting late, I should probably go." Ian stood up. Cassidy mimicked her, following closely as the blond made her way over to the door. Ian turned to face the smaller woman who was practically standing against her.

"Thank you for dinner, I had a wonderful time." She bent her head slightly to kiss Cassidy's cheek, but Cassidy had other plans. She turned her head to meet the softest lips that she'd ever tasted. Everything from the last kiss that they'd shared came rushing back full force. Ian was against the door with her arms wrapped tightly around the smaller woman, pulling her against her thigh. Ian could feel the heat of Cassidy's crotch seeping through her jeans. They continued to explore each other's mouths. Ian pulled away slightly to playfully bite Cassidy's bottom lip, a moan escaped the smaller woman as she stuck her tongue out and traced Ian's lips, producing a moan from the taller woman.

"We should stop this…I don't…Ian I want you, I've wanted you since the first night I saw you. This is crazy."

They continued to press their lips together, kissing with raw emotion, their tongues tangled together in a heated battle to be inside the others mouth. When Cassidy came to her senses she tried to pull away but strong arms held her tightly, refusing to let them part.

Just Me

"Where's your bedroom?" Ian whispered huskily as she placed small kisses on her neck and nibbled on her ear. Cassidy was too lost in the heated flood between her legs to realize that she was leading her boss to her bedroom.

Both women kicked off their shoes and tossed their socks in the corner. The room was dark, except for the small shadow that the parking lot lights cast across the wall. Cassidy pulled Ian's shirt and bra up over her head and added it to the pile of socks and shoes. Ian followed her moves until they were standing naked next to the bed. Ian moved first, she ran her hands down Cassidy's chest caressing her firm round breasts, teasing the sensitive nipples with soft pinches. Sliding her hands further to Cassidy's flat stomach and around to the small of her back.

Her mind was lost in the feel of the incredibly soft skin under her hands. Cassidy tangled her fingers in Ian's short hair, pulling her down into an electrifying kiss. Rough and wet, she bit Ian's lip and glided her tongue past the sensitive spot that she had just claimed with her teeth. It took two small steps for them to hit the bed. Cassidy laid down first pulling Ian on top of her. Neither woman could deny the pain between their legs. The wanting and needing to be touched was overtaken by the powerful desire to feel every inch of the other person.

Ian ran her tongue slowly across Cassidy's chest, stopping to tease each nipple with her teeth before drawing it between her lips to cover it with wet heat. She continued south, placing tiny heated kisses on Cassidy's stomach all the way to her hairline, then each thigh before moving painfully slow back up to capture her lips. Ian's thigh slipped across Cassidy's center. She could feel the warm liquid cover her leg and the faint shudder of the smaller woman under her.

Cassidy rolled Ian over and straddled her. Their tiny hairs tangled together as they thrust into each other. She brought Ian's hands up to caress her breasts as she looked down into the beautiful blue puddles sparkling at her. She softly rocked back and forth as Ian flicked her thumbs over stiff nipples. She was too engrossed to feel the wet spot on the sheet under her. Ian lowered her hands to reach behind Cassidy and squeezed her ass pulling her forward and sliding lower on the bed in one fluid motion. Cassidy caught on quickly and settled herself on Ian's mouth. When Ian's tongue opened her she felt her body tremble. The heat from Ian's mouth on her was almost enough to make her lose control. Ian continued to slowly lick back and forth in teasing strokes, stopping to suck the mound of muscles that swelled with every touch. Cassidy was close. She knew it would be over all too soon. She rolled off of Ian and pulled Ian on top of her.

"I want you inside me…I want to see your face."

She tasted herself on Ian's lips, then on her tongue as she slid her tongue deep inside Ian's mouth. Ian reached down and easily slid two fingers inside of Cassidy. The burning heat and muscles surrounding her fingers tightly contracted as she worked her fingers in deeper, then all the way out. Cassidy moaned and gasped until she was once again filled with Ian's fingers. Cassidy held Ian tightly in her arms, kissing her and thrusting her hips forward to match every stroke. She reached down between herself and Ian to place her fingers in Ian's blond wet curls. Ian's breath caught in her throat as her legs opened, her body begging desperately to be touched. She inched her way up enough for the smaller woman to reach inside of her without altering her own rhythm inside of Cassidy. She felt Cassidy's fingers circle her clit, then enter her in one fluid motion. Their hips rocked together, forcing deeper and faster penetration. Both women were panting and thrusting together desperate for release. Again they kissed as if this were the last time intensely tasting every part of each others mouth until Cassidy pulled Ian's tongue into her mouth sucking in and out slowly. Ian began to tighten around Cassidy's fingers that were plunging deeper inside of her. The kiss broke while they frantically rode each other. Cassidy's sharp cries were first, followed closely by Ian's as they held each other tightly and came together, not once but twice before they finally stilled their fingers.

Neither woman moved, they stayed inside of each other tangled together. Ian scanned gray eyes for some sort of comfort. Cassidy stared openly into the deep blue eyes looking down at her as they slid out of each other. Ian wrapped her arms around Cassidy and delicately kissed her lips.

~ ~ ~

When Ian awoke at three a.m. tangled with Cassidy, reality slapped her across the face. She quickly dressed and snuck back to her hotel. She showered and packed. By five a.m. she was checked out and back on the road. *What have I done?* She turned the radio in the Land Rover as loud as it would go, trying to drown out the thoughts in her head. She would be back in Aspen in two and a half hours, back to sanity.

Cassidy realized she was alone when she woke. Why would she think she wasn't? All of a sudden visions of the past few hours flashed through her mind. *Oh my god. What the hell have I done?* She sat up wondering where Ian was. She scampered over to the light switch and illuminated the room. Her clothes were all that was left. Her mind raced with thoughts that she couldn't control. A hot shower would wash away the memory or so she thought.

Chapter 15

"You did what?!" Trina's voice was vicious.

"You heard me. Don't make me repeat it." Cassidy spoke with what sounded like her last breath, quiet and composed.

"Cass, I...wow...I don't know what to say."

She sighed. "Me either. I feel so empty, like I fell into this dark hole that I can't climb out of Trina. It's fucking scaring me."

"I'm sorry honey, I know you're hurting. Have you talked to her? Has she called you?"

"No."

It had been three weeks since she had dinner and sex with Ian in her apartment. The only contact they had was through the lawyers. Ian was completely wrapped up in the lawsuit from hell, heading into the trial of the century. Cassidy spent her days working vigorously now that Ian had hired a director for the new construction department, and the locomotive department was finally being run correctly although two other directors were simultaneously running it together until Ian filled that position.

Ian still hadn't found an assistant so she was working sixty hours a week in her corporate office. Giles could tell something was wrong. He knew the obscured blond all too well. Ian had been acting strangely since she arrived home from her last trip to the plant. He wouldn't push, that wasn't his place, but if she wanted to talk he would be there. He would watch closely to keep her out of trouble and to keep her from falling back into her old ways.

~ ~ ~

"Hell no I'm not settling Max, a million dollars isn't worth my time on this god damn telephone!" Her voice rose higher. "Tell them, I'm a Wiley through and through, and they can kiss my ass!" She slammed the phone down. "Deal? If Hinkley thinks I'm going to fold like a cheap plate they're stupider that I thought. God damn idiots! Ugh!" She sat back in her chair and rubbed her temples, trying to sooth the nonstop pounding between her ears. *Not now.*

A month had gone by since Ian spent the night making love to the beautiful brunette. Everyday she fought off the memory of that night and the pain that it caused. Trying to forget everything that happened was by far the worst thing to do. Cassidy would more than likely be devastated. Deep down Ian knew in her heart how she felt, but she couldn't ignore the right-winged world on the surface. Her love for another woman would ruin her and everything that her family stood for. Not to mention her lack of producing the next heir to the corporation. Would sharing a life with the most intriguing woman that she'd ever met really be that bad? No, their life together would probably be perfect, until they left the house to go work every morning under scrutiny by the corporate world. Then there's the small fact that Cassidy is Ian's employee. That alone would be enough to bring down the house. Instead, Ian decided the best way to handle the situation would be to forget it ever happened. Her mind might let go of the images in her memory, but her heart would beat only one name.

~ ~ ~

Ian finally hired an assistant, the first week of April. Her lawsuit was moving along at a snails pace. Hinkley was obviously digging for dirt on her to countersue. This only meant more delays and appeals. The blond worked vigorously training her new subordinate.

Clark Watkins was roughly two inches taller than Ian, with light brown hair and big brown eyes. He was semi-muscular and tan. Ian could see why the straight women went after him. He was sort of cute, if you were into boyish good looks, and of course, a penis, both of which she wasn't. Clark spent his first week learning the business.

He worked with William Goody, Director of Railway Transit. First, he learned all about railroad tracks and how they're made, as well as how they sold the parts. Then, he was passed off to Carey Stewart, Director of Metro Transit, here he learned about metro and subway system tracks, how they work and how the parts are sold. Ian finished his first weeks training by explaining the Locomotive Department and the new Construction department herself.

"I know this is a lot of information to digest in one week Clark, but coming from a background in the steel industry you should pick up on the lingo pretty quickly."

"Yes ma'am, I understand most of what I've been told since it's relative to my last company. I have also learned a great deal of information about the railroad industry."

The brown haired man appeared less nervous around his superior as the week went by. Friday afternoon, he sat across from her in her office admiring and respecting her as he had on Monday morning. He now understood why it had taken him over a month to get the position. To him, this was like working as the President's Chief of Staff. He smiled inwardly at that thought.

"Enjoy your weekend off, but make sure you read all of those parts manuals that William and Carey gave you, along with the ones that we went over yesterday."

"Not a problem, ma'am. Being single leaves me with plenty of time on my hands." He grinned.

Ian knew he had worked for various companies in the steel industry during the past ten years, but his latest position was managing the headquarters of a major automotive factory. This gave him the credentials that she was looking for, even though he was barely thirty. He had enough experience to push him to the top of her candidate list. He finally won her over in his third interview.

"Monday morning my personal driver will take us to Grand Junction. It's about two and a half hours away. We'll spend the day with the Plant Director and the Logistics Director." She paused when Cassidy's face appeared in her thoughts. "After that we'll tour the plant."

"That sounds interesting, I've never seen how the parts are actually made, I spent most of my time in the office on the phone."

She laughed at his honesty.

"Well, this will be your only time to see it, unfortunately, you'll be in your office on the phone for the rest of your career at Wiley Steel." He laughed with her.

"At least I do give you a chance to see how my company works, maybe that's why we stand out. We work as a family. Anyway, I'm going to leave you there in a hotel for a few days. I expect you to work closely with the directors at the plant, these two can make or break a deal. Get to know them."

"I'm looking forward to it, ma'am." He straightened his red tie behind his black suit jacket.

"Good, I think you will be a great asset to me, as well as the rest of my team. One thing that I want you to remember and always keep in the back of your mind Clark, you are the liaison. All of these directors will go through you to get to me. I expect you to be capable of handling every issue by the beginning of next month." As soon as he left the room she ran both hands through her hair and sighed. Going back to Grand Junction was not something that she was looking forward to. She was looking forward to meeting and having multiple conversations with Cassidy even less. *You are professional. It's time to* be *professional.*

Ian was glad to be back at the estate. After dinner she retreated to the study to go over paperwork as usual. The blond hadn't stepped foot in the formal living room since the last night that she'd spent with Cassidy in there, the night they shared the kiss that changed her life. Instead, she seemed to find the bottom of the glass of Southern Comfort more and more. Not quite as often as when her parents passed away, but close enough to begin to scare Giles.

"Young Wiley, you seem as if something's bothering you." The Englishman stood in the doorway. Ian looked up to find caring eyes staring back at her.

"It's nothing Giles. I'm just a little stressed." She tried to raise the corner of her mouth, but a smile was the farthest thing from her mind.

"Forgive me for being so disorderly, Miss. I see sadness in you once again, and you're talking to the bottle…I…" Ian caught the tear that fell from her eye as she cut him off.

"Giles, I expect you to be straightforward with me. Hell you saved my life. I know you're the one person that can see right through me." She pushed away from the desk and walked over to the tiny sofa against the back wall. "Come sit down with me." He sat on the worn leather couch. "I'm glad you worry about me, you know you're the only family I have now."

"I hate to see you like this young Wiley. The past few months you've seemed so happy, especially when Miss Harland is around." At the sound of her name another tear slid down her face. This time Giles saw it.

"If you only knew the half of it." She finished the glass of bourbon that she was nursing. "I'm gay Giles…I never…." Another tear escaped. "Mom and dad, I…" As the tears began to fall faster the salt and pepper haired man wrapped his arm around her shoulders and pulled her close to him.

"I know, I guess I've known for a long time. It was never my place to say anything. Your mother and father loved you unconditionally. I'm sure that would never have changed. You're an amazing person Ian

Leland Wiley. Don't let anything stand in your way. You haven't yet, why start now?"

"This is big Giles, I can't even produce the next god damn heir. How am I supposed to run this company as a lesbian? We're already going through the wringer with this lawsuit, coming out will only add fuel to Hinkley's fire."

"Yes well sometimes we take the good with the bad." She smiled as a lone tear fell.

"My dad use to say that to me."

"I know."

"The worst part of it all is I'm in love with Cassidy." *Oh my god, I've never said that about anyone, to anyone. What's happening to me? Oh Mom and Dad I wish you were here. I miss you both so much.*

"Why is that so bad? She's a very nice woman and I must say she's very beautiful." He blushed slightly. *You poor kid, you've already been through so much. I hate seeing your pain continue.*

"That she is Giles, but she's also an employee of Wiley Steel."

"Ah, I see now where all of the fuss is."

"I can't just start up a relationship with one of my subordinates. Could you imagine? My god I'd be a fool."

"Please forgive me, but I do believe you've already passed that point, young Wiley."

She sat in silence for the better part of five minutes. Desperately trying to hold her breath, finally she let out a long sigh and sank her head into her hands. "I slept with her."

"I figured as much."

"Yes well I ruined any chance I had with her when I left without warning in the middle of the night.

The simple truth is I haven't bothered to contact her since then."

"Hmm…it seems you have gotten yourself into a bit of a dilemma."

"Huh, that's putting it mildly." She huffed. "I told you I hired a new assistant this week didn't I?"

"Yes ma'am."

"He and I have meetings scheduled at the plant all day Monday. A very large part of the day we'll be with her. By the way, you're driving us. I'm coming back and he's staying over for a few days. I'll send a car for him when I think he's ready to come back."

"Does she know about these meetings?"

"Yeah, I'm assuming she does. I spoke to the Production Director today and set everything up."

"My advice if I may?"

"Of course, have I ever said anything to you about speaking out of context with me, Giles? I told you, you're my family now, I expect you to keep me in line." This time she did smile.

"Be honest with her. Tell her how you feel."

"I can't do that, not now, not when I'm there for meetings. I don't even know how to say anything to her at all. Much less, pour my heart out. I need to decide what to do about her and all of the consequences that come along with her."

"You once told me you're a Wiley. Wiley's don't quit and they don't back down. If you really love her, then you will love her no matter what the consequences are."

"Thanks Giles."

~ ~ ~

Just Me

Monday morning Ian came down the stairs dressed in a black business suit with an olive green blouse underneath, the silver Rolex shined against the tan skin of her left wrist.

"Morning, Miss Wiley. Can I get you anything?" The butler stood at attention in his usual ascot style tuxedo.

"Mimosa and a piece of toast." She sat at the head of the table in her ordinary seat.

"Yes ma'am."

He returned with a large glass of chocolate milk and a stack of blueberry pancakes. Without another word spoken, he went back to the kitchen cleaning.

An hour later they picked up Clark Watkins. He seemed slightly on edge as he slid into the back next to his blond superior.

"Good morning." He spoke nervously and she ate it up. If her assistant seemed scared of her then so would the rest of the world. This alone made her smile.

"Looking forward to seeing the operation behind the brains?" She grinned.

"Most definitely, I've heard a lot about the plant from the directors."

"It'll hold up to the talk I'm sure."

~ ~ ~

Two and a half hours later the black Bentley pulled through the round driveway around the bronze statue of Ian's great grandfather and stopped parallel to the main double doors. Giles gracefully opened the door and Ian strutted into the building with Clark hot on her heels.

"Good Morning, Miss Wiley." The receptionist stood at attention.

"Hello, Mrs. Cragen." Ian smiled kindly. "This is my new Executive Assistant Clark Watkins. He has replaced Fraiser Higginbotham."

"Yes ma'am. Nice to meet you." She smiled.

Ian proceeded down the hallway. She stopped periodically at different photos when Clark questioned her about one of them. He'd spent the better part of a day looking at the photos and reading the captions in the corporate office. She stopped in front of a large desk where a sandy haired secretary sat. She was staring and smiling ear to ear.

Ian searched her brain for the woman's name. *Kathleen.* "Kathleen, this is Clark Watkins, my Executive Assistant."

"It's nice to meet you." Clark said.

"You too sir, Miss Wiley, Mr. Masters is expecting you."

"Thank you." Ian walked passed the door to Cassidy's office. Her heart skipped a beat, jumped into her throat and caused her to cough to catch her breath as she walked into Richard's office.

"Good Morning, Miss Wiley." He noticed her obvious choking. "Everything okay?"

"Oh yeah, yeah, went down the wrong pipe." She cleared her throat embarrassingly. "Richard, this is my new assistant Clark Watkins. Clark this is Richard Masters, Production Director." Rich stood an inch taller than Clark. They shook hands and returned awkward grins at each other.

"It's nice to meet you, I've heard a lot about you."

Rich spoke with a deep voice.

"Where's Cas…uh…Miss Harland?" Ian cut in.

"She is aware of the meetings. She's probably out on the floor somewhere, I can never keep up with that woman. I swear she stays in shape from running around this place all day long."

A playful smile graced Ian's lips as she remembered every inch of Cassidy's trim body and silky smooth skin. *Snap out of it. My god you look like a love struck teenager!*

"Let's go ahead and take the tour of the production floor, maybe we'll run into her over there."

They began walking through the maze of hallways until they reached a heavy metal door. On the other side of the door Rich took them through a second, smaller maze of offices. Clark was introduced to the design crew before shuffling along to the production floor manager's office.

"Hey Darren, this is Clark Watkins. He's Miss Wiley's new assistant." The white haired man stood up from the chair behind his desk.

"It's nice to meet you, and it's good to see you again Miss Wiley, as always it's a pleasure." He smiled. She remembered seeing him a few times before when she came to the plant with her father. Rich and Darren had been with the company probably close to twenty years each.

"Have you seen Cassidy?" Rich asked.

"Yeah, actually she was just down here going over a deal that we need to ship out tomorrow. She had to switch carriers at the last minute and wanted to make sure that we'd be able to ship at eight a.m. instead of ten a.m. like originally planned."

"Oh, is everything taken care of?"

"Of course." He smiled.

"Good, well if you have a few free minutes do you mind taking us on a tour around the equipment? I'm sure Mr. Watkins would like to see it."

"No problem, look in that room over there and grab hardhats and safety glasses for everyone."

~ ~ ~

An hour later, Ian and Clark were back in Richard's office with him. "Let's move into the conference room so we can all sit down and go over the numbers for the first quarter since I'm here."

"Sure, let me go check Cassidy's office, if she's not there I'll call her cell."

A few minutes later the door opened to the small room, Ian was sitting at the head of the table with Clark on her right. Rich walked in and sat next to Clark, leaving the seat across from Clark and on Ian's left open.

"Nice of you to join us, Miss Harland." Ian said with a hint of sarcasm.

"I'm sorry, I've had some problems with one of our carriers this morning. It seems their drivers decided to go on strike this week." Ian could see the pain in Cassidy's gray eyes starring daggers at her. "It's nice to see you again Miss Wiley." Cassidy said as she sat next to Ian, careful not to touch her.

"Cassidy, this is Clark Watkins. He's Miss Wiley's new assistant." Cassidy extended her hand in a friendly gesture. Ian noticed Clark hold onto her hand longer than he should have.

Hmm…watch out baby boy, you're in uncharted

Just Me

territory and the shark that swims in those waters will eat you alive! "Well, now that we're *all* here, let's get started." Ian went through the first quarter numbers in both departments. She broke each month down based on the budget, and gave them the running total for all of the departments as a whole. So far, with the first quarter behind them, they were up over ten percent. This was much higher than expected after the announcement of the inside fraud and embezzlement scam.

Ian noticed Clark staring at Cassidy off and on throughout the meeting. He seemed to smile widely each time the brunette spoke. *I'll allow you one fuck up. Let this be it. Please don't become a 'rat bastard' on me. I think I've been through enough hell for one lifetime and I'm about to board the bus to hell one more time. Who am I kidding? I'm driving the damn thing.* "Well, that seems to be all I have, how are things here? Any problems or questions I can help you with?"

"No, nothing new. How's the lawsuit going, if you don't mind my asking?"

"No Rich, not at all." She pursed her lips. "Honestly, it's going at turtle speed right now, hung up on politics. I'll let everyone know as it progresses. Just keep in mind that if we do go to trial, both of you will be asked to testify."

"I'll be glad when all of that is over." Cassidy added.

"Me too." *But it's about to get a hell of a lot worse. Is that even what you want? What if having a life with me isn't what you want or need? Then what?* Ian stood and straightened her jacket. "I'm going to leave Clark here for a few days, I'd like him to work with each of you so that he understands what you actually do here."

She handed a business card to her new assistant. "This is the car service that will be bringing you home. Just give them a call today and they'll take you over to the hotel. My butler, Giles, took your suitcase over and left everything for you with the concierge. You're in the hotel tonight and tomorrow night, so go ahead and come back late Wednesday. We'll meet Thursday morning."

"Sounds good. Have a safe trip back."

"Thank you." Ian stood and began to exit the room. "Rich, you and Clark get started. I need to speak with Cassidy alone please." As soon as the men left the room she turned her head towards the eyes that threatened to choke the life out of her.

"Can we talk?"

"Yes ma'am. What can I do for you?" Cassidy remained in employee mode. *Damn you if you think I'm that easy!*

"I'm sorry Cassidy. I never meant to hurt you." Ian tried to cover Cassidy's hand, but she pulled away.

"Don't be, Miss Wiley. It was a simple misunderstanding. I'm already passed it."

"Cut the professional shit Cassidy, talk to me."

"I can't, I'm sorry. You're my boss and I will treat you as my boss and *only* my boss."

"Fine, if that's how you want it to be. I never meant for things to end up this way between us. I don't regret anything that happened. I… I'm sorry." Ian stood up and walked out of the room without looking back. *Well that went well.*

~ ~ ~

"You should talk to her honey," Trina said as she

waved to get the waiters attention.

"I agree with Trina. You're heartbroken. I don't think I've ever seen you like this." Wendi held back from slapping the shirtless muscle-bound waiters' ass as he walked away. "Mm, I swear the men are to die for in here."

"Yeah but they're all waiters," Trina added.

"Perks of coming on ladies night, great drink specials and hot waiters, but no single patrons." Wendi laughed. Cassidy ordered another round for herself before the strapping young man left their table.

"He's not a piece of meat, ladies." Cassidy finally spoke.

"So, he's still a fine looking specimen." Wendi added with a twist of her head and a grin from hell.

"God I wish one of you would fall in love. This side of the fence sucks major ass." She knocked her drink back as soon as the glass hit the table.

"Whoa, drunky monkey, slow down! I don't know how you drink that shit." Wendi cringed.

"Why don't you call her, Cass?"

"And say what?"

"I don't know, try I love you." Trina tried the straightforward attempt. The brunette laughed, just about spitting the last of her bourbon all over the table.

"Yeah, that'll go over well! She left in the middle of the night and never bothered to contact me until she walked into the office. What the hell am I suppose to think? On top of that she sat there trying to apologize. Who the fuck knows how she feels about me? Besides all of that, I'm her god damn employee! I slept with my boss. How stupid am I?" She whistled loudly to get the waiters attention again. *Round three baby!*

"You can't drown her or the memory of her in that nasty shit you drink. Slow down, Cass." She could hear the concern in Wendi's voice.

"Look, I know what you guys are trying to do. I'll get over this. I was the idiot that slept with her boss and fell in love."

"I've seen the way she looks at you, Cass. She can't deny it. Besides, I'm sure you could feel it when you two were together." That brought the images and feelings right back to the surface. The brunette closed her eyes and smiled.

I can still feel her skin against me. Her fingers inside me. Her tongue on me. Oh my god, I want her again.

"Hello? Earth to Cassidy!" Wendi and Trina both noticed their friend go off into another world. Her tight face loosened and an endearing smile crossed her face.

"Huh? What? I'm fine."

"Sure you are."

~ ~ ~

Three weeks since her meeting at the plant, the snow was finally gone. No more salting the roads meant no more riding in the Land Rover. Of course Ian would still be chauffeured to and from the office in the Bentley, but *YLESGRL* was about to roll out of the garage.

"Be careful in that thing Ian Leland."

She turned around and shot a look at the older man behind her. He'd never called her by her name unless he was trying to get her attention.

"I'm sorry…Miss Wiley."

"No, don't be. You just sounded like my mother.

Just Me

She's the only one that ever called me Ian Leland. But, she only did it when I was in trouble or she was worried about me." She walked over and gave him a tiny reassuring hug. "I'll be fine, Giles. I'm only going to the lodge to have a drink or two. I need to air out the cobwebs in the Lotus." *In myself too, but I'm not in the mood for company, unless she's a beautiful brunette with unstoppable gray eyes.*

The sleek black car rolled out of the garage and crept toward the Iron Gates. Once she was through, Ian barked the tires for a good two hundred yards. "Woo hoo!" She yelled into the darkness. The open top caused her short hair to blow around wildly. *Free at last, thank god, I'm free at last!* The Lotus pulled into one of the many open spots in front of the *Snow Drift*.

"Evening." Ian parked her tight little but on the corner bar stool. The regular bartender with thinning dark hair slowly made his way down to her. He was probably only her height, which was short for a guy, and his tight white tee shirt clung to his muscles. She knew he thought she was arrogant and treated her like she was no one special. She always liked that about him. She also figured he'd seen her pick up more women than he ever could have imagined for himself and that made her smile. *'Shrimp dick', hmm…that's a good name for you.*

"What can I get for you?" He spoke without looking at her.

"Southern Comfort on the rocks." He made the glass and slid it down to her. *Way to go 'shrimp dick', you didn't spill it. I'm so impressed.* She rolled her eyes and shook her head. As soon as Ian finished her glass she tossed a ten on the bar and walked out.

Two and a half hours later she found herself

parked in front of Cassidy's apartment. She'd only decided to go for a ride to clear her head, not drive to the problem. *I shouldn't be here. What the hell am I thinking? I'm definitely not drunk. I'm stone sober and sitting in front of her apartment at midnight. I'm hopeless. This is pitiful.* She stepped out of the tiny car and walked towards the door. *Get back in the car and drive off. This is stupid, she hates you.* She knocked softly. *See she's asleep, just go home, no one will ever have to know you were here*…the door opened.

"What are you doing here?" Cassidy stood at the door in a tiny pair of blue shorts and a thin white tank top that revealed everything since it clung to the skin with nothing under it.

"I…uh…can we talk?" Ian fumbled for words. She wasn't expecting her to answer the door and especially not half dressed. That sent an ember to the already heated flesh between her legs.

"You show up at my house at midnight on a Friday night to talk? You could've called me at the office, unless it can't wait until Monday."

"Damn it Cassidy, this has nothing to do with Wiley Steel!" Ian tried not to raise her voice, but it still went up an octave or two.

"Then why are you here?" Cassidy's voice also went up.

"I want to talk to you. Can I come in?"

"No. I don't know…" She stepped back and let the taller woman inside. "What do you want to talk about that couldn't wait?"

"Us." Ian hoped Cassidy didn't notice her trembling in the dim light.

"Us? There is no us. You're my boss and I'm

your employee. We may have had a lousy attempt at a friendship once, but…"

"Look at me Cassidy." Ian stood a few feet away, Cassidy stared at the ground.

"I can't."

"Damn it, I'm not your boss when I'm outside of that office."

"Who are you then? Who's the woman that was in my bed? Who's the woman standing here now?" Cassidy looked up to meet sparkling blue eyes. *God you tear me up just looking at me.*

"I've always told you Cassidy, it's me, *just me*, when we're together." Ian stepped closer but didn't dare touch her.

"Why did you run away and not even call me?" A tear escaped her eye, she cursed it as it ran down her cheek. Ian reached out then, stroking soft skin to wipe it away.

"I'm so sorry Cassidy. I was scared. Everything changed for me that night."

"It changed for me to you know."

"I know. I hate myself for reacting the way I did. It's so hard. I've had to live my life backstage in the closet for so long. Now I'm the center of attention day in and day out. I'm still not sure how to deal with that, much less bringing you into it." She cupped Cassidy's jaw with both of her hands tenderly. "But, I want to try."

"What's that suppose to mean?"

"It means I'm ready to have a relationship and I don't care who knows about it."

"You mean come out of the closet?"

"I mean I'm going to live my life the way I want to, no matter what the consequences are. Wiley Steel is my legacy, but you...Cassidy I'm in love with you." A few tears finally fell from her deep blue eyes.

"Oh Ian." Cassidy threw her arms around Ian's neck. Ian reciprocated by threading her arms around Cassidy's waist and pulling the smaller woman tightly against her. "I love you too."

"You don't know how good it is to here you say that. Can you repeat it? I just want to be sure…"

"I love you, Ian Wiley."

Ian smiled from ear to ear and leaned back, still holding the other woman. "I love you so much." She pressed her lips against Cassidy's softly at first. Cassidy's lips parted and Ian probed deeper. They frantically undressed in the middle of the living room as their lips barely separated, tongues jousted for position.

Their lovemaking began quickly, both of them ferociously meeting the intoxicating high with the rush of the first orgasms. Then, they slowed down to feel each other. Ian ran her hands over Cassidy's body and rolled the brunette on top of her. She sat up to claim a piercing nipple between her lips and flick it with her tongue. Cassidy cried out for more and pressed Ian's head to her chest. She alternated back and forth between succulent, firm breasts teasing and sucking her nipples until Cassidy was sliding her swollen center full of wetness all over Ian's stomach.

"Please take me baby… I can't wait any longer…God I want you!"

Cassidy begged for release. Ian gave in and rolled Cassidy onto her back, laid herself halfway on top of her, and stroked the wet folds behind the dark curls. She could feel her lovers body quiver with each caress. She took her time, losing herself in the feel of this beautiful woman underneath her. Finally, she pushed two fingers deep inside. Cassidy jerked and stared deeply into Ian's blue eyes. Their lips met passionately, their tongues tangled with each thrust of Ian's fingers deep inside of her as the first wave of orgasm crashed over them. Ian continued to slide her fingers in and out, staying inside as Cassidy's body relaxed.

"I love the way you feel. I love everything about you."

"Mm, I love you too, all of you." Cassidy ran her hand over Ian's firm body, down the silky smooth skin of her hip to the inside of her thigh, careful not to touch the hot wet center.

"I almost came with you… I'm so close." Ian panted.

The corner of Cassidy's mouth turned up into a sexy, seductive grin. She spread the folds and slowly massaged the center. Ian's breaths were ragged and hazy.

"Go inside me."

As soon as Cassidy slid her fingers in Ian began to release the powerful orgasm that she'd been holding onto. Cassidy teased, sliding her fingers in and out slowly, going deeper with every stroke until Ian's body bucked. The hot, wet muscles tightened around her fingers, pulling her further inside as the orgasm peaked. Minutes later she removed her fingers as Ian whimpered. Slowly, Ian gathered Cassidy into her arms.

"God I want you again, over and over, but I'm so tired. You wear me out." Ian whispered into Cassidy's ear.

"Me too, I'm scared to go to sleep." Cassidy choked back the sadness in her voice.

"I promise I'll be here in your arms when you

wake up." Ian bent and placed a tender kiss on Cassidy's lips. "I do need to make a call really quick though." Ian stumbled around in the dark until she found her cell phone.

"Giles, I'm sorry to wake you...yeah I'm okay...I'm in Grand Junction...uh huh...yes...thank you...okay...goodnight." Ian set the phone on the night stand and climbed back into the bed. Cassidy curled up around her, with her head on Ian's chest they fell asleep.

Their lovemaking continued all weekend until they threatened to starve to death from lack of actual food. Ian looked across the table at Cassidy with hungry blue eyes. Sure enough, as soon as their meal was finished, they were back in bed begging each other for release.

~ ~ ~

Monday morning arrived with Cassidy and Ian wrapped loosely together, tangled in the cotton sheets on Cassidy's bed. The alarm clock next to the bed blasted Madonna's *Like a Virgin* loudly at six a.m.

"What the hell, turn it off!" Ian screeched. Cassidy laughed and reached out to shut the obnoxiously loud music off.

"That would be my wake up call, sweetie." Cassidy smiled as she peeled herself away from the blond. Ian rolled over and pulled the covers over her head.

"Call in sick, I know the boss." She mumbled from under the covers.

"Honey, I can't call in sick. Besides, don't you have to be at the office today?"

Just Me

"Yeah, actually..." She sat up. "What time is it?"
"Six. Why?"
"Damn. I'm usually in the office at eight, I guess I'll be fashionably late today."
"You think so!" Cassidy tossed a pillow at the nude blond sitting in the middle of her bed. Ian ducked the flying object and freed herself from the twisted sheets. She walked up behind Cassidy who was now getting ready for a shower. Ian wrapped her arms around her and placed gentle kisses along her shoulder, brushing her long black hair to the side. She continued the kisses along her neck up to her ear, following the same path back down with her tongue.
"If you don't stop that I'll be late too!"
"Like I said, I know the boss."
"Yes well that might work for you miss 'high and mighty', but..."
"How would you feel if they knew?" Ian asked seriously.
"What do you mean?" Cassidy turned in Ian's arms and placed an innocent kiss on her lips.
"I mean if everyone knew about us, would that bother you?"
"Are you serious Ian? You know what would happen if anyone found out."
"Yes, I've thought about it for a while. I want a relationship with you, Cassidy, and I don't care who knows."
"Wow! Uh...this is news to me. I thought you had to live in the closet and..."
"Well, technically I do, but I love you and I'm not going to hide myself anymore."
"I love you too, Ian, but this is something major

we are talking about. Are you sure you want to face the scrutiny of your employees and the rest of the world?" *Oh my god, what's gotten into her? I don't care who knows about me, but I don't think she realizes how bad this can be for her and me.* Cassidy backed away slightly, but ran her fingers through Ian's short blond hair before she broke contact. "I think this is something you should really think about. I need to take a shower, I'm already running late." She smiled bright enough to light up the room.

"I've thought about it, trust me, Cassidy. Why do you think it's taken me so long to tell you how I feel?" *Don't push me away, not now, I've come too far to get hurt.* "I want to be with you and only you."

"I only want to be with you too."

Ian smiled. "That's good to know." She joked. "I want to make an announcement…"

"A what?!" Cassidy turned on the shower water and turned back to face Ian, who stood in the doorway.

"We should tell the company."

"Why?" Cassidy's gray eyes were searching every inch of Ian's face.

"I would rather go ahead and tell them now, instead of waiting until they find out that we've been sneaking around to be together. That could seriously hurt both of us and my company. If we are honest up front, yes we'll have to deal with bullshit, but it'll be better for us in the long run."

"Okay…" Cassidy hesitated. "And how long is this run?"

"Forever I hope. I've never been like this with anyone, Cassidy. I mean I've dated and obviously you know I've been with a few women, but I've never been in love. At least, not until I met you." The corners of Ian's mouth turned up into the most adorable grin. Cassidy couldn't resist crossing the ten or so feet between them to kiss that irresistible mouth.

"I love you." Cassidy said as she broke the kiss and wrapped her arms around Ian's neck.

"Mm, I love you too."

"I would be honored to have the world know that I'm the woman that stole your heart, but I think you should talk to Mr. Guthrey about it first. It's better if we know the legalities of me working for you before you leap out of the closet blindfolded with me on your arm."

"I talked to Giles about it. He made me see through the corporate world that I live in."

"He's such a nice man."

"He's my family." She smiled. "Anyway, I'll call Max today when I get into the office." Ian pulled Cassidy tightly against her. "I should probably get going before I make love to you right now on the bathroom floor." She grinned seductively.

Cassidy answered with a raised eyebrow. "Don't tempt me. God I can't keep my hands off you." She tugged on Ian's short blond hair, pulling her head closer she claimed Ian's lips with a passionate kiss. When Ian's lips parted Cassidy's tongue probed further. Their hands wandered over each others body as their mouths bruised against each other. Cassidy pulled away panting.

"Come on, Wiley. You need to go home and I need to get my ass moving if I want to make it to work on time." She put on a thin gray colored silk robe that was hanging on the back of the bathroom door and cut the water off to the shower.

"You're so beautiful, Cassidy. That robe makes

you elegant, with a touch of 'come and get me'." Ian leaned in for another kiss.

"Ugh…what am I going to do with you?"

Ian wiggled an eyebrow and shot her a rousing grin. "I could think of lots of things!" Ian laughed when Cassidy shook her head and handed her clothes to her. "Fine, I'm going."

The blond quickly dressed in her clothes that she hadn't seen since Friday night when she arrived on impulse. "At least walk me to the door."

As soon as Cassidy opened the door she noticed the sleek black sports car parked next to her small SUV. "Now I see why you've been so wild."

"What's that suppose to mean?" Ian said as she hit the button for the keyless entry. The lights flashed when the horned beeped.

"This car brings out your wild side." She winked. "I like it!"

"The car?" Ian looked at her quizzically.

"No, your wild side! But the car is hot too!" She leaned forward and kissed Ian one last time, careful not to show the world her half-naked body. "God, Wendi would kill me if she knew you were here all weekend with that thing. I swear she's crazy for fast cars."

"What about you?"

"Yeah, what girl isn't? But I'm not crazy about fast women." She straightened.

"Good, because I'm not either, besides I use to be one. It's not all it's cracked up to be."

Cassidy smacked Ian's jean covered butt as she stepped through the doorway. "Call me later so I know you made it home 'speed racer'."

"Yes ma'am. I love you." Ian winked. She opened

the car door and slid down into the leather seat. Cassidy waited until the sports car roared to life before she shut the door.

Life as I know it has taken a one hundred and eighty degree turn practically over night. Cassidy grinned and walked back to the shower.

Chapter 16

"Are you serious about this, Miss Wiley?" The deep voice on the other end of line was trustworthy. Maxwell Guthrey tried to sound as friendly as he could.

"Yes. We love each other, Max, that's why I'm doing this now. I don't need any political noise. I'll handle the questions and concerns from my own employees. It's anticipated, society is not in agreement on gay rights, but they are my employees and I expect them to be professional."

"I understand that, but this could turn very ugly, for both of you."

"We know, basically I need you to tell me if we're breaking the law, Max."

"In that case, Miss Wiley, no you're not. There are no laws against same sex couples in the workplace. And as far as harassment goes, again everything points to heterosexual couples and fraternizing only. So no, you're not breaking any laws."

"Thank you."

"Your welcome and if it's any consolation to you, I'm happy for you both."

~ ~ ~

A week later, Ian draped her charcoal gray jacket

Just Me

over the staircase banister and walked into the dining room. She was wearing a white button down blouse with very fine charcoal colored pin-stripes and pants that matched her suit jacket. Her feet were comfortably covered with the black dress shoes that she always wore.

"I like that top, is it new, Miss Wiley?" Giles appeared as soon as she was seated.

"Yes actually, I bought it last week when I was in Grand Junction. I stopped at the mall on my way home. I would've picked you up one, but I didn't think it would go with anything you wear." She laughed, knowing that the man always dressed like a typical English butler, either a dark gray or black tuxedo complete with a matching vest and an ascot. His jackets always had short tails.

He smiled. "Can I get you anything?"

"Mimosa and a piece of wheat toast," she said with a touch of humor. The salt and pepper man returned to the table with blueberry waffles and a large glass of chocolate milk.

"You seem very cheery today."

"Hmm…is that so? Maybe it's because I'm calling a corporate meeting for this Friday to announce my relationship with Cassidy Harland." Giles dropped the newspaper that he was holding.

"I'm happy for you." He smiled tenderly as he picked up the paper and went back to his duties. He was doing flips inside. Giles always looked as Ian like she was his child or at least his niece and he wanted nothing more than happiness for her.

~ ~ ~

"Did you see her this past weekend?" Wendi sat comfortably on the small tan colored sofa. Trina sat in the matching recliner just to the left of the sofa.

"No. She's had a hectic few weeks, training her new assistant and then hiring the two new directors. We try to talk everyday though." Cassidy called out from the kitchen. She returned to the living room with a bottle of Chardonnay in the wine chiller and three glasses. Trina poured the wine and turned the stereo on while Cassidy answered the phone. Elton John played softly over the speakers.

"Speak of the devil." Wendi announced when she noticed the smile light up on Cassidy's face. She leaned closer to Trina to whisper. "I hope she doesn't get hurt. I've never seen her this crazy for someone. She's head over heels in love with that woman."

"What do you have against Ian Wiley?" Trina asked as she sipped her wine.

"Nothing, I enjoyed spending time with her. She's a very nice woman and she treats Cass like a princess. I guess I'm just worried because everything between them happened so fast you know."

"Yeah."

"Hey you two, stop gossiping about me, I can still hear you." Cassidy laughed as she hung up the phone and returned to the living room.

"We're just saying how happy we are for you." Trina said with a smile.

"Good." She took deep breath. "So I have to go to Aspen this Friday. Tomorrow morning Ian's calling a corporate meeting for Friday afternoon. She called me just now to give me a heads up."

"Oh, what kind of meeting is this?" Wendi ran a

hand through her shoulder length red hair.

"She's announcing our relationship to the directors." The brunette sipped her wine casually.

"Wow. Are you ready for that?" Trina questioned.

"Yeah, we've already talked about it and she discussed everything with her lawyer. We won't have any legal problems at all, but she doesn't want to be secretive about it. Ian trusts her employees and expects them to trust her. Wiley Steel runs like a family, it always has, I guess that's one of the reasons I took the job."

"I still can't believe you guys are together and now you're 'coming out'. Time damn sure flies."

"I've been out for years Wendi." She playfully smacked her. "But yeah, I guess I am sort of 'coming out' at work and with the boss as my lover on top of it. I'm sure everything will be okay."

"Have you told Ian about her assistant?" Trina took on a more serious tone. Cassidy poured herself another glass of wine.

"No."

"Cass, don't you think you should've said something? I mean they guy asked you out a dozen times, then called your office."

"He's not stalking me. Clark likes me and wants me to go on a date with him. I told him no. I finally did tell him I was in a serious relationship. After that he backed off an apologized."

"You never told him you were a lesbian?"

"No, of course not. Trina no one knows about my sexuality at work."

"You're nervous about this, aren't you?"

"Yeah, I've never cared who knew about me, but now, this is my workplace you know."

"How does Ian feel about it?"

"She's scared to death. I can hear it in her voice, but she's a strong woman and we'll get through this together." She raised her glass. "Hey, I didn't invite you guys over to analyze my lesbianism." She laughed. "Let's drink to friendship, happiness…" Wendi cut off her off mid sentence.

"And most of all…"

"Hot sex!" All three of them finished in perfect harmony, clinked glasses and drank between laughs.

~ ~ ~

Ian buttoned her black suit jacket over her baby blue colored blouse and proceeded down the hallway towards the conference room. She stretched her neck and took a deep breath. All of the directors were gathered around the rectangle shaped table. Her assistant sat to the right at the head of the table and Cassidy sat to the left. Everyone stood as the blond walked through the door and made her way to the head seat. As soon as she began to sit, everyone followed in unison.

"Thank you all for being here. I know this meeting is a little out of the ordinary, but traditions are capable of being adjusted every now and then." She grinned. "I want to start off by introducing the new faces at the table. Clark Watkins," She waved towards him. "All of you know he's my new assistant. Next to him is Kenneth Latrey." The red-haired man had a very thin mustache and goatee combination. He nodded and smiled. "He's the Director for our newest department, the Construction Industry. I believe this new department will play a major role in the Wiley Steel future. As I'm sure you know, I have not filled the Locomotive Services Director position yet. I do have a few candidates in mind, so hopefully I'll have a new face for you soon. Anyway, let's welcome Clark and Kenneth to the Wiley Steel Corporation." Everyone clapped their hands.

"Clark and Kenneth let me introduce you to the rest of the staff. Kenneth to your right is William Goody, Director of Railway Services. Across from him is Carey Stewart, Director of Metro Services. Last but not least, we have the two people that work behind the scenes at the plant. This is Richard Masters, Production Director, and Cassidy Harland, Logistics Director." Everyone said 'nice to meet you' to each other before Ian went on. "Clark has had the opportunity to work with everyone so far. Kenneth, you've been working here with Carey and William all week, but next week you'll go to the plant for a few days to learn the ropes." She smiled, and let them converse for a few minutes.

"This brings me to my next topic, we all know about the ever-present lawsuit on the company's front lawn. So far I have nothing new. We'll probably be dealing with this for the rest of year. If you are questioned by anyone at all please refer them to the law firm of Guthrey and Meyers. Have any of you heard anything?"

"I had a young man ask me if I was employed here and what my job was." Carey spoke up.

"What did you say to him?"

"Nothing, I ignored the little twerp."

She laughed. "Nice going Stewart. Next time this happens or if it happens to anyone else, please contact me directly." *Breathe Wiley breathe.* She shifted slightly in her chair and unbuttoned her jacket. "This brings me to my final topic. Obviously, all of you know that I am a single woman that tends to lead my life in privacy. I want to thank you for respecting my privacy over the past nine months, as well as my entire family's privacy over the years. I've never been one to live in the spotlight, and don't plan on doing so anytime in the future. Now, there is a part of my life that involves an employee of Wiley Steel, therefore I have decided to go public with…my sexuality."

She took a deep breath. No one dare said a word. "I am a lesbian and I'm in a serious relationship with Cassidy Harland." She paused to see the look on everyone's face. Cassidy looked over at her and smiled. Clark starred back and forth at the two women. Rich smiled. Carey and William looked at each other in shock. Kenneth stared at the table. "Let me continue by saying that there has never been and never will be inequity in the company. No one receives preferential treatment for any matter. Miss Harland is well respected in the company, and like all of you, she is an asset to Wiley Steel. Our life outside of the office is our own personal business. I have always been impartial when it comes to my employees, I plan to continue my beliefs and trust in all of you, that's why I offered this information as a courtesy." She looked around the room. "Are there any questions or comments regarding this issue?" She waited patiently. *Here we go.*

"I'm happy for both of you." Rich smiled. Cassidy smiled, Ian nodded and waited a few more minutes.

"Well then, if we seem to have no comments or concerns I'll consider this matter closed. Therefore, we won't hear about it 'around the water cooler'." She added edge to her voice for the last statement.

Just Me

Ian meant to put a touch of fear in everyone at that table. Her life was not open for discussion and neither was Cassidy's. She smiled inside when she saw that her point was made perfectly clear. She reached out and squeezed the brunette's hand gently, then let go as she stood up. She glanced at her watch. The meeting had taken longer than she anticipated. It was close to five thirty pm.

"I'd like to take everyone to dinner at Framaggio's. Is Italian okay with everyone?" Cassidy smiled, trying desperately not to laugh.

"That sounds good to me, Miss Wiley." Carey added. Rich was right behind him.

"I'm not in any hurry, we can drive back tomorrow if you want to Cassidy." Ian figured they might ride together.

"Sure." She answered.

"Good, let me make a few calls. I'll meet you all in the lobby in ten minutes." Ian said before she walked down the hall to her office. She went inside alone and shut the door. Cassidy didn't expect to get invited inside and continued walking with the guys. Ian quickly sat down and called Giles. She let him know her plans for dinner. She told him to be out front of the restaurant at eight p.m. to pick her up. Then she called the most elegant Italian Restaurant in town to reserve a table for six. Her last call was to the car service.

A few minutes later she appeared behind Cassidy, who was engrossed in conversation with Rich. "Are we ready?" The brunette turned around, almost into her arms.

"I believe we are."

~ ~ ~

Two hours of amazing food and three bottles of wine later, everyone was conversing about the steel industry. No one had brought up the topic on the back of everyone's mind. Ian and Cassidy were happy about that. As soon as Ian paid the seven-hundred dollar bill for the table, everyone walked outside. The Bentley was parked in front of the black limo at the curb. Ian instructed the driver to take anyone home that wasn't comfortable driving their own vehicle from the office. Cassidy was standing beside Clark outside.

"So that's why you wouldn't go out with me." He stated dryly.

"Yeah, I'm sorry."

"Don't be. I would've never pegged you for a lesbian though, her neither, to be honest." Cassidy only smiled. "You two look good together." She couldn't help but hear a touch of sarcasm in his voice. At that moment Ian walked up and grabbed Cassidy's hand, their fingers locked together.

"Good night, everyone. Please be careful driving home." Both women walked towards the waiting car. Giles opened the door and smiled at both women.

"Good evening, Miss Harland."

"Hi Giles, it's nice to see you again."

As soon as the door was shut Cassidy leaned over, their lips met passionately. Tongues tasted the remnants of pasta and wine mixed with arousal. Both women pulled away breathless.

"So that went well." Ian grinned.

"Yeah."

"What's wrong?" Ian could hear the hesitation in Cassidy's voice.

Just Me

"Ian..." Cassidy looked down at their hands that were still interlocked together. *God I love her so much.* "I need to tell you something."

"Okay? I love you Cassidy, honey you can tell me anything."

"Clark Watkins..." She stopped to stare into deep blues looking back at her.

"Uh huh, what about him?"

"He asked me out."

Ian laughed and squeezed the hand that she was holding. "I don't blame him, you're gorgeous." She smiled brightly.

"Ian." Cassidy's voice was very serious. "He was persistent."

"What did he say to you?" Now Ian straightened up. *I'll kill him!*

"He kept asking me until I told him I was involved with someone. Then, just now he congratulated me for being with you, but he seemed very sarcastic about it."

"Hmm...I'm sure he was just upset that you wouldn't go out with him. Either way, I can guarantee you he won't ask you out anymore."

"Yeah, you're right. I guess I'm just surprised that no one said anything."

"I'm not. They're scared to death of me. That's not to say that they won't be talking to each other, but you can bet they won't say it in front of me or you. Come here." She pulled the smaller woman into her arms. "I love you, that's all that matters to me."

"I love you too. I'm glad you did that today. I feel a lot better."

"Me too.

Graysen Morgen

Chapter 17

In the month after Ian came out to her employees about her relationship with Cassidy, she didn't hear any gossip through the grapevine about her sexuality and not producing the next Wiley heir. Hinkley was doing everything he could to make her life miserable, instead all it did was piss her off. The lawsuit was starting to finally take off since a settlement looked impossible. Guthrey let her know that she needed to appear with him in court for the preliminary hearing in a week. Clark Watkins backed off of Cassidy completely and settled into his position. Kenneth Latrey was already working on new deals for his department. Ian still hadn't hired a Locomotive Services Director.

~ ~ ~

Her face had finally dried from the tears she shed that morning. As soon as she awoke Giles drove her to the cemetery. This was her first birthday waking up without hearing her parents' voices. She leaned against the marble statue and talked to her parents as she always did when she went to their resting place. This time she knew they were looking down on her. She received the answer she was looking for when she felt the cool gust of wind. Giles stood next to the car watching her softly out of the corner of his eye.

Two hours later they drove back to the estate. Giles gave her the present that he had for her, a pair of cuff-links that her father had given him on his twenty-seventh birthday. They were silver with onyx gems on each end. She remembered seeing Giles wear them for years when she was a kid. This brought tears to her eyes once again.

She finally retired to her room to rest for a while. Ian was as happy as a little kid when she heard the doorbell ring, she came running down the stairs to meet the woman that Giles had just let into the house.

"Hey!" Ian threw her arms around the smaller woman and pulled her into a tight embrace. Cassidy returned the enthusiastic hug.

"I missed you so much." Cassidy said as she pressed her lips to Ian's. Giles taking that as his cue, grabbed the small suitcase and turned towards the staircase. Cassidy broke away long enough to say hi to him before he started up the stairs.

"Might I make a suggestion, Miss Wiley?" He spoke while standing on the second step.

"Sure." She turned around, still holding Cassidy in one arm.

"The next time you anticipate the arrival of Miss Harland, try not to run down the stairs like a giddy elephant. I believe you're no longer at that age." He turned and continued up, hiding a small smile.

Ian laughed and shook her head.

"So you ran down the stairs huh." Cassidy smiled and threw her arms around the taller woman's neck.

"Uh huh, and apparently I'm too *old* to run down the stairs in my own house." She pouted.

Just Me

"Aw, come on birthday girl. I don't think you're that old. Besides, I'm older than you remember?" It was Cassidy's turn to pout, she ran her fingers through the hair at the back of Ian's head.

"How could I forget?" Ian joked. Cassidy playfully smacked her shoulder and kissed her again. Ian's lips parted long enough for Cassidy's tongue to enter. As the kiss heated up Giles was making his way back down stairs.

"Miss Harland is all settled in your room, Miss Wiley." He shook his head and walked towards the kitchen. "I do believe you're too old for heavy petting in the foyer as well!" He laughed to himself. *She's so happy, Leland and Lorraine would be thrilled, I hope you both can see her from up there.*

The women prolonged the kiss and ignored the salt and pepper haired man when he walked past them.

"I'm sorry I couldn't drive in last night. I was working with William on a locomotive deal. I never thought we'd finish it, but it finally went through around nine p.m. Then, of course Wendi and Trina wanted to go to breakfast this morning. I think they just wanted to see your present. Hey, by the way, when are you going to hire someone for that position?"

"I don't know. I'm sorry you had to work so late, honey." She said with the most apologetic blue eyes that Cassidy had ever seen. "And thank you for the roses, they're beautiful." She pointed to the array of pink flowers that were on the table by the doorway to the living room.

"You're welcome. Besides, you can make it up to me later." Cassidy wiggled an eyebrow seductively. *God how does she do that? She makes me want to rip her clothes and have my way with her right here, just by looking at me.*

"Oh I intend to." Ian bent her head slightly to claim soft lips once again. "So when do I get my birthday present?"

"I can't very well parade around in front of Giles in the nude now can I?" She laughed.

"Mm, I'm sure he won't mind." Ian teasingly bit Cassidy's bottom lip and provoked another kiss. *I sure as hell won't mind!*

"Miss Wiley, you should kindly move out of the foyer. Miss Harland has been here all of twenty minutes and you've yet to let her step into the house. Tsk-tsk, shall I remind you of your manners?" Giles bit back a grin. "Dinner is on the table."

"Dinner already? It's only four."

"Yes ma'am, I am aware of the time. I am also aware of your plans for the evening. Therefore I have prepared dinner a bit early." He straightened his jacket and walked back towards the kitchen.

When the women finished their homemade Manicotti that Giles made specifically for Ian's birthday, he appeared holding a small ice cream cake with twenty-seven candles glowing on top of it.

"My god, look at the fire! Giles those candles are liable to melt that thing. I didn't know you were ancient honey." Cassidy laughed loudly. Ian made a quick wish, blew out the candles and shot her lover a look with raised eyebrows. Cassidy could've sworn she heard a growl too.

"I'm not that old." Ian grumbled.

~ ~ ~

Just Me

Cassidy slid down into the black leather seat and buckled her safety belt. Ian reached up and folded the canvas convertible top back, before starting the sleek machine.

"Wendi is going to be so pissed at me. She loves this damn car." Cassidy laughed.

"So do I!" Ian grinned and shoved the gear shift into reverse.

Cassidy was impressed with the handling and power of the tiny car as they maneuvered down the winding roads of the mountain, going much faster than Cassidy would have ever driven herself. But, considering Ian grew up on those roads she felt safe on the thrill ride down the mountain.

"Where are we going?"

"It's classified." *God I love her!*

"As in you'll have to kill me if you tell me?"

"Yeah, I'd have to tickle you to death." One blond eyebrow rose up and a sheepish grin crossed her face. Even in the darkness of the night Cassidy could see her face.

"I see. Well, in that case I guess I'll just be surprised. I wouldn't want to cause you to crash." She laughed.

A few minutes later the Lotus stopped in front of a small building. Cassidy noticed a few women standing together outside. The miniature neon sign above the door read: *Sally & Susie's*.

"Have you ever been here?" Cassidy asked as she shut the door. Ian caught up with her and grabbed her hand.

"Yes, but it was about two years ago. I was home from college one summer. Anyway, I haven't been anywhere except the *Snow Drift* since my parents died. I've sort of been in the spotlight since they announced that I was now the head of the company. And, well, I couldn't afford to be outed. Plus my picture was all over the newspaper in the entire state. I have to...*had* to be careful."

"Are you sure you want to do this? We can go somewhere else, or stay at the house. You know I don't care as long as I'm with you."

Ian leaned over and pressed her lips to Cassidy's in a soft, endearing kiss with a touch of unrequited love in her eyes, on top of the smoldering passion between her legs. "I love you and I don't care who knows anymore."

"Mm, that's good because I love you too." Cassidy winked playfully.

They made their way through the small crowd of women. Some were sitting at tables, some were dancing in each others arms, some were kissing in the corner, Cassidy figured at least thirty women were in there. The bar ran along the entire back wall. Two pool tables were across from the door where the tables and chairs were. The dance floor took up the entire middle and a small stage was on the other side of the dance floor, opposite the bar. The place was fairly dark and smelled of stale smoke and beer.

""What can I get you ladies?" The bartender was a little shorter than Ian with short curly red-hair.

"Southern Comfort on the rocks." Ian turned to Cassidy with a questioning look.

"Oh I'll have the same thanks." Ian cocked her head to the side. "I've been drinking that since the night we met." She shrugged.

"Can I see your ID's please?" Cassidy laughed,

Just Me

but deep down it felt nice to still be carded at thirty. The older woman handed Cassidy's back to her, but continued to study Ian's.

"Is there a problem? I'm well over twenty-one." Ian tried to hide her annoyance.

"No. No problem. I haven't seen you in here in a while, Miss Wiley. I'm sorry to hear about your parents." She handed the plastic card back to the blond.

"Thanks." As soon as the woman walked away to pour their drinks Ian let out a long sigh.

"I'm sorry, honey." Cassidy squeezed the warm hand that she was holding.

"Don't be. I've come along way since the accident, but I haven't really been out around town you know. It's like going through it all over again when the people in town recognize me and want to give their condolences. My parent's were well liked in this community." She took a sip of her drink when the red-haired woman set it on the bar. "I just hope my coming out doesn't ruin their reputation."

"Let's let the world run its course. Ian, you've already taken the biggest step of all, you came out to the company and then told them about us."

"Yeah, but I can control the company and what gets said." She took another sip. "Here's to us and who gives a shit who finds out. I love you, Cassidy." They clinked glasses.

"I love you too, Ian."

Cassidy took a long swallow of the bourbon. The DJ slowed the dance floor down with 'How do I live without you." Cassidy leaned against her lover.

"Dance with me."

Ian sat her glass down and tugged on the tiny

hand she was holding.

Cassidy thread her arms around Ian's neck, her fingers teased the short neck hair. Ian wrapped her arms around the brunette's waist with her hands caressing the small of her back. Half of the crowd was watching the adorable couple swaying in the center of the room. Anyone with a pair of eyes could tell they were in love. Ian leaned her head slightly forward to claim sweet lips with a heated kiss. Their tongues explored one another as the dance continued.

Another drink and a few songs later, the loving couple paid the tab and headed towards the door. A woman with shoulder length brown hair in a pony tail, wearing a black polo shirt and tight jeans grinned from ear to ear as they walked towards her.

"Do you know her?" Cassidy said when they stepped outside.

"No." Ian shook her head.

"She sure was staring at us."

"I know, with an 'eat shit' grin too. Who knows, maybe she's in lust with one of us."

"It looked like both of us." Cassidy shook her head.

"Oh well." Ian opened Cassidy's door for her and walked around to the driver's side of the black sports car. She started it up and shifted the gears smoothly, driving them back up the mountain.

"I had a good time. You're a good dancer." Cassidy looked over at Ian. She could see her deep blue eyes glowing in the dark.

"Thank you. I've had a lot of practice. My family always went to large business parties. When I got older they started taking me with them. The last one I went to

Just Me

was probably my junior year of college, the Mayor had a huge Christmas party and I was home for the holiday."

"Wow that must've been fun."

"Yeah, after a while I was tired of schmoozing, but I had to do it for the family. As a matter of fact I was invited to quite a few parties over the holidays, but it felt weird going without my parents." She sighed. "But next year, I have big plans for those parties."

"Oh you do huh. What would those be?"

"I'll have someone with me."

"And who would that be?"

"A gorgeous brunette, with smoky gray eyes, and a smile that melts the ice."

"What's her name? I'm gonna kick her ass!" Cassidy laughed. "If anyone had asked me about you six months ago I would've said you were the old bat that signs my paycheck. God look at me now, I'm hopelessly in love with you."

"OLD BAT! Excuse me?!"

"Oh yeah, I um…well…I…sort of thought you were much older and a hermit."

"Geez, that was my image?" Ian spoke nervously.

"Yeah, I was floored when I found out you were the girl in the bar. I heard from the gossip pool that you were much, much older and a very unattractive hermit."

"My god! Cassidy you met my father at least once and spoke to him many times. He was only fifty two and my mother was forty nine. Hell Giles is only forty eight."

"I never sat down and thought about it, Ian. I was told about the accident and that you were taking over. A few days later someone said something about you being old as hell and ugly, that's why you hadn't been to the plant in years. I could care less. I went back to working as usual."

"Man." Ian shook her head. "I was in college. I'd been to the corporate office a few times a year and to the plant at least once a year if I could make it. I hadn't been out on the production floor in probably six years, until I was there the day I saw you."

"Well, trust me, after that visit everyone's mind changed." Cassidy laughed.

"What's that suppose to mean?" The car twisted up the driveway and straight into the garage.

"Let's just say after that day, you were one hell of a good-looking boss and any one of them wouldn't mind going a round or two with you up against the steel press."

"What! Oh my god!"

"I'm serious. They were set straight really quickly though when Rich found out. Boy was he pissed!"

"Yeah, he's been there close to twenty years. He worked on the floor for my grandfather just before he died and my father took over." Both women made their way into the massive house through the side door into the kitchen. A small light was on in the kitchen, indicating Giles had already gone to bed.

Ian went into the refrigerator and grabbed the chilling bottle of champagne. She snagged the two glasses from the counter and raised an eyebrow with a seductive grin. "Come on, I want my birthday present!" She leaned forward and kissed Cassidy, playfully biting her lower lip as she pulled away.

"God, I want you!" Cassidy pushed the blond back against the counter and kissed her back.

"Not here. I don't want to give Giles a heart attack. Come on."

Ian set the bottle and the glasses down on the little

table by the couch across from her king-sized bed. Clothes were peeled and tossed in every direction as the two women frantically undressed between kisses and caresses. Ian moved away long enough to pour the two bubbling glasses. She handed Cassidy her glass.

"Happy birthday, to the love of my life." Cassidy smiled and tapped her glass against Ian's.

"I love you," Ian said as she returned the toast.

"Good because I love you too, and I plan on making love to you until the sun comes up." Cassidy said as she downed her glass and slowly eased Ian towards the bed when she finished her glass.

As soon as they lay on the bed their bodies tangled together, hands explored and tongues tasted as they gradually began making love to each other. Cassidy rolled Ian onto her back and straddled her stomach, rubbing her wetness all over her. She leaned down to claim soft lips as Ian ran her hands across Cassidy's breasts, teasing taut nipples and working further south. When Cassidy straightened up Ian kept one hand on a breast and her other hand massaged the pulsing folds pressed against her own stomach. Ian pushed her thumb hard against the center as she felt Cassidy's body tighten.

"Oh Ian…" Cassidy leaned backed giving Ian full access to her throbbing clit. "I'm going to…Ah…"

"I know baby…I know…" Ian worked her thumb faster and harder until Cassidy jerked and she felt the warm liquid coat her stomach.

"Oh my god, Ian." Cassidy leaned down and kissed the blond deeply. "I love you so much. I can't believe you made me…." She started to move off of Ian. "It's all over you." She laughed.

"Good." She stopped Cassidy from moving.

"Come up here, let me taste you."

"Huh uh, it's your birthday, I want to make you come for me." Before Cassidy could move away Ian slid down the bed so that her lips met the hot flesh that her thumb had just been on. "Hey!"

"Ssshh, you'll wake Giles." Ian teased. Cassidy's gray eyes lit up and her body stiffened. "Aww, I'm only kidding. He couldn't hear you if you were screaming. This house was built in the early nineteen hundreds, honey. It's solid and its walls are concrete." She stuck her tongue out and tasted the warm flesh covered with the same liquid that was on her stomach. It still surprised her how sweet Cassidy tasted. She ignored the protest of the woman above her and continued to tease the swollen folds deliberately staying away from the center.

"I can't …hold on …" Cassidy tried to make sense of her words as her body trembled with every stroke of Ian's tongue. Ian ran her hands up Cassidy's body, tenderly touching both breasts. Cassidy grabbed one of Ian's hands and kissed her fingers, sucking on them seductively one at a time. When Ian's tongue finally made its way across her clit her body jerked and she bit down on the finger she was sucking. Ian pressed her tongue hard against her clit then slipped it inside of the warmth as deep as she could go. She moved her tongue back across the center as fast and hard as she could.

Cassidy let go of the hand she was holding and pulled away, she turned herself around before she lowered back against Ian's mouth. She leaned forward to claim the mound between the blond curls with her tongue. Ian's body shuddered with the first touch of Cassidy's tongue against her clit. She was already on the edge and knew it wouldn't be long. Cassidy licked the folds and teased her entrance until she felt Ian's body go rigged under her. She was doing everything she could to hold back and release with her lover. Two strokes across the throbbing clit and a thrust inside with a warm slippery tongue was all it took. Ian's orgasm set Cassidy off, both women held each other tightly riding the wave of pleasure with their tongues inside of each other. Slowly Ian continued soft caresses with her tongue until Cassidy moved off of her shakily. Cassidy turned back around and kissed Ian intensely. They tasted themselves on the tongues of each other.

"You destroyed me!" Cassidy sighed happily as she laid her head on Ian's shoulder.

"I love you so much, Cassidy. That was the best birthday present I could've received." She pulled her lover to her chest.

"Actually, that wasn't really your birthday present." She snickered and kissed Ian's forehead before climbing out of the bed. She walked over to her small suitcase that was lying on the floor next to the couch. She reached in making a rustling noise, pulled out a thin black box out, and walked back over to the bed.

"Here. This is your birthday present, sweetheart." She smiled.

"Hmm." One of Ian's eyebrows went up quizzically as she opened the box. "Wow, this is beautiful Cassidy. Thank you." She pulled the tiny sapphire bracelet out to examine it further.

"It matches your eyes."

"I love it. I've never really worn bracelets. I guess I never thought about it since no one's every really bought me one, until now."

She leaned over and kissed Cassidy gently at first,

then deeper as she traced the brunette's tongue with her own. Somehow the bracelet managed to make its way back into the box safely and out of the way of the two passionate lovers as they explored each others body once more.

Chapter 18

"I don't care what he's saying about me or my life. He has no god damn right!" Ian screamed into the speaker phone. "That son of a bitch has crossed the line this time, Max!" She stood up and paced the floor, running a hand through her hair and still yelling at the phone. She'd shed her jacket moments before she received the phone call about the cover story in the business section of the newspaper.

"Listen, Miss Wiley, we can handle Hinkley in more ways than one. He's sour about the information that was uncovered during the investigation into his company."

"I understand that, but I'm not the one buying people out from under their nose now am I? And I damn sure didn't take it to the press. My god damn personal life has nothing to do with this lawsuit Max. Cassidy's name shouldn't be anywhere near any of this! Instead, my god damn sex life is plastered across the front of the business section with a huge picture of me and her leaving a bar together! Who gives a shit who I sleep with? It has nothing to do with the fact that this fucking piece of dog shit was paying off two of my employees to screw me over!"

"I know, Miss Wiley. You have to trust me. He's

playing dirty because he's about to lose millions of dollars, and I'm sure his attorney's know that your employees know about your personal life. I wouldn't be surprised if it doesn't come up during the questioning. You need to be prepared and trust me."

"Prepared? How the hell do I prepare for this? My employees deserve better than this. I don't want them drug through the mud because of that asshole!" Ian was surely wearing a path into the thick Berber carpet covering the floor of her office as she continued to pace.

"I've talked with my law partner and we believe the easiest way to handle the situation is to address it head on."

"What do you mean, Max? You're talking in riddles."

"You need to make a statement to the press…a…uh…you need to be truthful about your relationship and move past it like it's nothing out of the ordinary."

"You want me to come out to the entire world! Are you nuts!"

"Miss Wiley, I told you to trust me."

"I do trust you, Maxwell, but this is a little much don't you think?"

"No. Listen to me, if you acknowledge his little accusation like it's nothing then the newspaper will eat it up and move on to something new. We both know the business section has been all over this lawsuit for the past few months, with it finally going to trial in four days they will be hiding in the bushes to talk to you whenever and wherever they can. Especially, after they tear apart your staff with questions about you and Miss Harland's relationship."

"God damn it all to hell!" She drew in a deep breath. "I need to talk to Cassidy about this. I'm not making any decision until I speak with her first."

"I understand that, but, we need to act fast. I'm going to need an answer within the hour so that I can set up a meeting with the reporters this afternoon."

"How exactly is this going to go?"

"Well, I want you to make a brief statement about the allegations and your relationship. Don't mention the trial or Hinkley."

"What about questions?"

"We're not allowing any questions. I'll be right next to you. We will also not allow any photo's to be taken."

"That's going to cause them to hound after Cassidy for a picture."

"That's fine, we'll deal with that. Besides, they will get all the photos that they want at the courthouse I'm sure."

"Fine. I'll call you in an hour." She slammed the phone down then balled up her fist and sunk down into her leather desk chair. *God damn it, everything is falling apart.* She picked up the receiver to the phone sitting on her desk and dialed the number.

"Cassidy Harland." The sweet, innocent voice answered.

"Hey you." Ian's demeanor quickly changed.

"Hey, I was just thinking about you." The smile was evident through the phone.

"You were huh? Good or bad?" Ian twisted the shiny platinum and sapphire bracelet on her wrist.

"It depends on how you look at it." She spoke seductively.

"Mm, I see."

"So what do I owe the pleasure of a mid morning phone call?"

"Well, I need to talk to you about something." *I guess she doesn't read the newspaper or it didn't make it that far.*

"Okay?"

"I wish I could be there in person, but this can't wait."

"Honey what's wrong?"

"Did you happen to read the paper today?"

"No, I hate the newspaper. Why?"

"We're on the front page of the business section here today."

"Huh? We, as in you and me?"

"Yeah, coming out of the bar we were in the night of my birthday."

"That was two months ago. Why are we in there?"

"Hinkley has decided to out me to the world as some huge scandal since the trial starts Monday."

"Oh my god!"

"Yeah, the headline reads: Ian Wiley, heir to the multimillion dollar Wiley Steel Corporation spends wild night on the town with her lesbian lover and employee Cassidy Harland. Then it goes on about the upcoming lawsuit and about me being gay and how that affects my company."

"Holy shit, Ian! What are we going to do about this asshole?"

"Maxwell Guthrey, my company lawyer, wants me to make a statement to the press in a few hours."

"Are you going to do it?"

"I wanted to talk to you first. Max wants me to

tell the truth about our relationship and leave it at that. No questions and no photos. This is about to get very ugly, Cassidy. I feel terrible that you're right in the middle of it."

"Don't worry about me, honey, I'm a big girl. I can deal with a few reporters taking my picture, besides I'm pretty much out to everyone I know, including my family."

"I know, but it's going to look bad because I'm your boss."

"We kind of expected this, didn't we?"

"No. Well, I guess I never thought it would come to this. I could choke the life out of that stupid son of a bitch!"

"Whoa, calm down. Do you want me to drive down there?"

"Nah, you're needed there. Besides, this isn't going to take long. I'm going to talk quickly and leave."

"I know we decided to be apart this weekend, but I can still come there if you need me."

"I do need you. I need you every day of my life, Cassidy. I love you so much."

"I love you too."

Ian smiled. "That's why you should just stay there this weekend. Once the Grand Junction newspaper gets word of this they'll be all over you. Besides, you'll be here to testify on Tuesday and Wednesday. I think those are the days Max wants you and Rich here. Monday will be me first, then my directors, starting with William and Carey because they were here during that time. After you and Rich he'll move on to Clark and Kenneth last since they're both new."

"Are you sure you don't want me there with you

this weekend?"

"Yeah, I'm going to lock myself in the study and work all weekend. I'm sure my statement today is going to stir up the hornet's nest of reporters so they'll be sniffing around the estate and the office building. Luckily, they can't come within five hundred yards of my property or the corporate building. Max made sure of that first thing this morning."

"That's good. I miss you."

"I miss you too. I need to call Max and get this over with."

"Let me know how it goes."

~ ~ ~

Ian straightened her black suit jacket as she sat down in the chair at the head of the table in the conference room at Guthrey and Meyers. Maxwell Guthrey sat next to her in a starched gray suit. A black man sat across from them with a blond woman next to him.

Max pushed the button on the recorder in front of him. "This is going to be very simple. I am Maxwell Guthrey, of Guthrey and Meyers. I'm here with my client Miss Ian Wiley and two reporters from the Aspen Times. Miss Wiley is going to give you a statement to record and quote in your newspaper. She will not be answering any questions and will not allow any photos to be taken of her. Do you both understand?" When the man and the woman acknowledged he continued. "Okay, please state your names for my records."

"My name is Marcus Witherton. I'm a reporter for the Aspen Times."

"My name is Christie Barron. I'm a reporter for the Aspen Times."

"Thank you. Miss Wiley, you may begin at any time."

Ian took a deep breath and held it as long as she could, willing her body to relax. Her hands were wrapped tightly around the arms of the chair under the table. She could feel the sweat dripping from her palms. After a loud swallow she began to open the door of the closet that had been hiding her from the world for the past twenty seven years. "As you know, an article came out this morning regarding myself and one of my employees. I would like to resolve this issue by first saying that I am a lesbian and I am in a monogamous relationship with a woman by the name of Cassidy Harland. This woman is an employee of Wiley Steel. Miss Harland was an employee long before I ever met her and she has not received any preferential treatment from me or any of the other staff members. The entire group of directors for Wiley Steel Corporation are aware of my relationship with Miss Harland, as she is one of the directors herself. In regards to my producing another Wiley heir, there are no plans of children in my life at this time. I cannot tell you what may come in the future. Also, I do believe that my private life and personal relationship should not be laid out for the entire public to scrutinize. Privacy use to be a word with a meaning. Thank you for your time." She stood up and Max walked her out of the building to the waiting Bentley.

"You did a good job, very smooth and professional."

"Yeah, tell that to the thousands of readers in the morning." She ducked her head and slid into the car with a solemn look on her face. As soon as Giles shut the door Ian flipped open her cell phone and hit speed dial.

"Hey honey."

"It's over."

"Are you okay?" Cassidy sat back in her office chair and ran a hand through her thick black hair.

"I guess. I was to the point quickly and then it was over."

"I guess I'll call Trina and Wendi tonight and let them know. What are the chances of it showing up in my paper?"

"Since the plant is located there and you live there, probably a hundred percent. Be careful going to work tomorrow. I'm sure they'll stake out your place. Max went ahead and added your name to the restraining order for the press so you may not see them up close, but they'll be around."

"God I can't believe this is happening."

"I know. I'm really sorry."

"Why? Because we went out for your birthday? Give me a break Ian. Hinkley's a dick and he'll do whatever he has to."

"I swear if I ever see him on the street he's a dead bastard. I'll snatch his arms off and beat him to death with them!"

Cassidy laughed. "Now that I'd like to see." She stretched her legs under the desk and yawned. "I love you and damn it, I miss you like crazy."

"That goes both ways."

Just Me
Chapter 19

"All rise for the honorable Judge Roland Wynn."

Everyone in the small brown paneled room stood up. The tiny door to the left of the large desk opened and a short bald man with no facial hair walked out and stepped up the couple of stairs. He sat down and opened the file in front of him.

"You may be seated."

Ian took her seat behind the table between Maxwell Guthrey and Daniel Meyers. J. R. Hinkley with thinning gray hair and a matching beard sat with his attorney Fred Fleming at the table to the right.

"Case number eighty-one thousand, seven hundred and sixty-two, Wiley versus Hinkley, is now in session."

"Mr. Guthrey you may begin your opening statement."

"Thank you."

Max buttoned the jacket of his black Armani suit as he walked up in front of the judge and the jury. "During the course of the week I am going to explain to you how the defendant, J. R. Hinkley, paid two former employees of Wiley Steel Corporation to mishandle sales deals in order for them to be given to Hinkley Metals. These deals add up to millions of dollars lost in profit due to the negligence of the two former employees. These two men are now employed by J. R. Hinkley." He walked back to the table and sat down.

"Mr. Fleming, you may now begin your opening statement."

"Thank you." The fairly short man had thick white hair. "As you will soon find out, the accusations against my client are fairly true, except for the fact that the plaintiff has no proof that these so called deals were locked in with her company. There also is no proof that the two men in question were paid to mismanage these deals on purpose. My client simply paid them to give him inside information on his competition." He went back to his table and sat down.

"Mr. Guthrey, call your first witness."

"Thank you." He stood up.

"I'd like to call Ian Wiley to the stand."

Ian stood and walked over to the small table with the microphone attached next to the large desk the judge was sitting at. A heavyset black man walked over to her with a bible. She'd watched enough law shows on TV to know what she was supposed to do. She placed her right hand on the book.

"I, Ian Leland Wiley, do swear to tell the truth and nothing but the truth so help me god." She sat down and watched Max make his way over to her.

"Since your parents' tragic death, almost one year ago, you, as sole heir, took over as President of the Wiley Steel Corporation, is that correct?"

"Yes."

"In doing so, you worked closely with Frasier Higginbotham as your assistant as he was your fathers, is that correct?"

"Yes."

Just Me

"You also worked as Benjamin Bradford's superior, is that correct?"

"Yes."

"Benjamin Bradford was the Locomotive Services Director for Wiley Steel, is that correct?"

"Yes."

"How did you come about the botched deals, Miss Wiley?"

"When I took over the company I asked to see the books and records so that I could catch up on the company. Since I was away at college I only made it to the corporate office or the plant once a year. My father talked about the business with me, but I needed to know the exact figures since I was now responsible for the company."

"That makes sense. Please continue."

"It was during this careful examination that I discovered we bid on deals that were locked in, yet the sale didn't show in the bank statements. So, I pulled all of the records for the production plant. I also hired an auditor to go through the records in case I was missing anything, that's when I put everything together."

"And what is that you found, Miss Wiley?"

"Benjamin Bradford was bidding on deals that were never going to production."

"What happened when you asked him about this?" Max stood directly in front of her.

"He denied it at first, but I figured out that Frasier Higginbotham was helping him and I called Benjamin Bradford into my office again. That's when he confessed everything."

"Please see evidence exhibit A, a tape recording of the office confession, my law firm was present on the speaker phone."

"Objection! The two men were unaware of themselves being recorded." Mr. Fleming stood up.

"Overruled. Taped conversation doesn't need an announcement in this situation. Mr. Guthrey, you may continue."

"Thank you, your honor. If we could, please play the tape for the court."

Max turned to the bailiff, who then turned the tape recorder on. Everyone listened to Benjamin Bradford and Frasier Higginbotham both confess to the botched deals. Both men said that Hinkley was paying them a cut of the money he was making off of the deals. "I believe that is all that I have for this witness."

"Mr. Fleming, your witness." The white-haired man stood up and walked over to Ian.

"Miss Wiley, is it true that you are involved in an office affair with a female subordinate?"

"It's not an affair, Mr. Fleming. Yes, I am in a relationship with one of my female employees."

"This alleged employee was mixed up in this supposed scandal, is that true?"

"No."

"You're involved with Cassidy Harland, correct?"

"Yes."

"Is she not the Director of Logistics for Wiley Steel?"

"Yes she is."

"Wasn't part of the mix up with these deals blamed on logistics?"

"Yes it was."

"Objection!" Max stood up. "We just heard the evidence proving the stories about the botched deals were lies."

"Move on with your line of questioning, Mr. Fleming."

"I'm simply stating Miss Wiley may have let her relationship cloud her vision when logistics became involved."

"Actually Mr. Fleming, I had only just met Miss Harland the day I went to the Production Plant to go through the records. Therefore, I wasn't involved with her then. As a matter of fact, I didn't become involved with Miss Harland until after I terminated Mister Higginbotham and Mr. Bradford."

"Fine. Who was it that told you the bids on these deals were locked in?"

"Not all of them were, some of them were purposely overbid."

"Okay, first, again who told you they were locked in?"

"I called the companies behind the deals in question after Mister Bradford kept claiming that they were locked in but production and logistics had slowed him down until we lost the deals."

"So these so called companies told you they were going to buy from you, but your company was too slow with shipping and manufacturing so they went elsewhere. Is that correct?"

"Yes."

"And you believed these companies?"

"Yes."

"What made you believe these companies, but not your own?"

"I believe in everything at my company, including the records that indicated this problem to start with. I was merely trying to get to the bottom of it. Frankly, I wanted to know why we were losing millions of dollars, therefore I did some checking up on my sales staff. Is there a problem with that?"

"I'm the one that is supposed to ask the questions, Miss Wiley." He walked over towards the jury, giving his best intimidating smirk. Then he walked back over to her. "How did you find out about the overbid deals?"

"Did you not just hear the tape?" *You stupid jackass!*

"Again, Miss Wiley. Your honor?"

The judge looked over at her. "Please answer his line of questioning, Miss Wiley."

"All right. When the companies told me about the deals a few of them didn't make sense to me, on further investigation I discovered the overbids. When I asked both Frasier Higginbotham and Benjamin Bradford, they confessed to purposely overbidding in some cases, as you just heard on the evidence tape."

"How did you learn that Hinkley Metals was involved?"

"I simply asked the companies. Every single deal was picked up by Hinkley Metals. So again, during the office confession both of my former employees confessed that they were being paid by J. R. Hinkley to miscalculate deals in order for them to be picked up by his company. He then cut them in on part of the profit."

"That's all of the questioning that I have."

"You may step down." The judge spoke to Ian. She immediately stood up and walked back over to her seat.

"What an idiot." She whispered to Max.

"I know."

Just Me

"Mr. Guthrey, call your next witness."

"I call William Goody."

He went through his line of questioning, making sure William knew nothing of the dealings between Higginbotham, Bradford, and Hinkley. He also touched on the subject of Ian's relationship with Cassidy. William admitted to knowing about it, as all of the directors do. He honestly said he knew nothing of it until Ian held a meeting to announce it. Fred Fleming did his best to break William down, but there was no reason for the man to lie about something he knew nothing about.

Max moved on to his next witness, Carey Stewart. Carey was just as honest about the dealings. He knew nothing of them or the relationship until Ian announced it. Again Fleming did everything he could, but got no where with his questioning.

"I'm calling recess until tomorrow morning at nine a.m." The judge spoke.

"All rise." Everyone stood as the bald man in the black robe made his way back through the small doorway.

Once they were headed out of the courtroom Ian turned to Max. "So we're doing well so far, yes?"

"Most definitely, apparently the only thing this fool has to go on is your relationship. As you can see that's taken him nowhere. I know we're going to run into some press out here. Let me talk for you."

Max pushed through the doors. Ian stood between him and his partner Daniel Meyers. "Dan, try to shield her on that side. There's her car." Giles was waiting on the curb with the Bentley.

Flashes began going off and at least ten people jumped in her face.

"Miss Wiley? Miss Wiley?! Did your parents know you were gay? Miss Wiley, what does your company think of you sleeping with an employee? Miss Wiley, how long has the affair been going on? Do you plan on adopting children? What will happen to the Wiley bloodline? Have you ever had sex with a man? Is Miss Harland getting promoted? When is Miss Harland moving to the corporate office?"

They finally made it to the car, Ian slid in and Giles slammed the door shut. *God damn bunch of stupid as a soup sandwich no good pieces of dog shit people!* She pulled her cell phone from her belt and flipped it open.

~ ~ ~

Cassidy was out on the production floor going over the plans on a new deal when she felt her phone vibrate on her belt. "Excuse me a second, Rich, Darren." She stepped out of the production floor office. "Hey."

"We just finished for the day. I needed to hear your voice."

"Aww. How did it go?"

"Surprisingly good. Of course, our relationship was brought up every time, but Hinkley's lawyers have nothing. It's almost like a bad joke watching his stupid slimy ass fumble through his questions."

"I see. Well, I'm glad it's not as bad as you thought it would be."

"The press tried to eat me alive when we came out of there though."

"Yeah, I had a few reporters corner me with questions this morning. I just told them no comment and walked inside."

"That's good. What time are you guys leaving?"

"I was just in a meeting with Rich and Darren about this deal that they need me to go out on a limb for–"

"I'm sorry. You could've sent the call to your voicemail baby."

"No, don't be ridiculous. You're the head honcho. When you call, everything stops, whether it's personal or not."

"That's good, because it's not all personal. I need you guys to be ready to go. We start again at nine a.m. and I want you both rested. Trust me, this thing will drain you, I feel like I've been run over by a runaway freight liner on a deserted railway."

"Aww. I wish I was there to make you feel better."

"You will be soon. Hey listen, Cassidy, I want Rich to go to the hotel, but as soon as you guys pull up Giles will be there to pick you up. Hopefully, there will be no press there."

"Sounds good. I can't wait to put my arms around you. I miss you. I love you so much, Ian."

"I love you too and miss you like crazy." *Tonight.* Ian thought with a smile as she hung up the phone.

~ ~ ~

"So the drama continues huh. I figured they'd have nothing to go on. No one knew what those idiots were up to until she told us. What do they expect us to do? Go up there and say yes we were all involved." Rich vented his frustration as he drove through the afternoon traffic.

"I know, the whole thing is really stupid. I don't see why that asshole Hinkley didn't just pay back all the money he basically laundered from Wiley Steel."

"His little stunt in the newspaper is a real low blow too. I'm surprised Ian didn't rip his dick off and smack him with it. Excuse me, I'm sorry." He blushed.

"Don't be. Trust me, she wants to."

"I still treat you like one of the guys. I think that's why we get along so well, Cassidy."

"Me too. Don't ever change Rich. That would be scary."

"Yeah. Funny thing is, I never could tell when you guys started dating. You didn't change one bit."

"I don't plan on changing. At work Ian Wiley is my boss and she forever will be unless I no longer work for the company. Nothing will change that."

The crew cab pick up pulled into the hotel parking lot. Cassidy could see the black car with the salt and pepper haired man waiting for her in his perfectly starched tux.

"That's my ride."

Rich got out of the truck to make sure Cassidy got her suitcase out okay.

"I guess I'll see you in the morning. Nine a.m. right?"

"Yeah, you know where the courthouse is don't you?" She asked hesitantly.

"Yeah. Have a good night."

"You too." She called back as she slid into the black leather back seat.

"Good evening, Miss Harland."

"Hello, Giles." She smiled.

~ ~ ~

Ian sat on the couch in the formal living room with Cassidy wrapped in her arms. "I'm so glad you're here."

"Me too. I think this is where I feel the most comfortable. I mean I know this is your house and everything, but I just feel so different when I'm in your arms."

"Good."

"Dinner was fantastic, I forgot to thank Giles."

"I'm sure he's around here somewhere, it's still early. Hey, there's somewhere I want to take you before the sun goes down. Come on." Ian walked out into the garage and pulled the Polaris side-by-side four-wheeler out.

"Whoa, where'd this thing come from?"

"It's been here. You guys didn't see it because it was covered for the winter. Hop in." Cassidy stepped up into the little cart and Ian took off over the hill towards the back of the property that climbed up the mountain.

"Where are we going?"

"It's a surprise."

As soon as they rounded the last corner Cassidy recognized the drop off to the valley that she had seen during the winter when she was visiting with her friends. "Oh my god Ian, this is where I fell in love with you."

"I know." She stopped the four-wheeler and both women walked over to the ledge.

"How?"

"I could see it in your eyes. That's why I decided to bring you back here."

She grabbed both of Cassidy's hands with her own. "Cassidy I love you so much, you complete me. I've never experienced anything close to this in all of my life." She fought back a tear and bent down on one knee. She pulled a small black velvet box out of her pocket. "I was going to wait to do this, but I can't wait any longer. Cassidy Harland, I want to spend the rest of my life with you."

She could see the tears falling from the gray eyes looking down at her as she opened the box. A large oval shaped diamond was in the center of the platinum band with one matching smaller diamond on both sides of it.

"Will you marry me?"

"Oh my god…I…oh yes…Ian yes, I love you so much."

Ian stood and placed the ring on Cassidy's left hand. She then picked the smaller woman up against her and held her tightly. When she set Cassidy down they shared a deep kiss, lingering against each others lips with tiny nibbles. Cassidy pulled her head back long enough to examine the giant rock that stood out on her left hand.

"This ring is beautiful, Ian."

"I'm glad you like it. After the hearing tomorrow there's one more place I want to take you."

"I'll go anywhere with you, for the rest of my life. I love you."

"That's good because you're now engaged to me and I love you with all of my heart Cassidy."

~ ~ ~

The next day went as planned in the courtroom. Rich was the first one on the stand. He spent two hours explaining how he knew nothing about the deals or the relationship of the two women. He was even asked in depth whether or not the involvement bothered him or affected the workplace. At one point he asked Fred Fleming what the relationship had to do with the court case. This got a snicker out both of Ian's attorney's.

"Mr. Guthrey, please call your next witness."

"Thank you. I call Cassidy Harland to the stand."

The brunette stood up and walked down the small aisle. She stopped to put her hand on the book as the others had done before she took her seat next to the judge.

"Miss Harland, how long have you been working for Wiley Steel Corporation?"

"Four years next week."

"And how long have you been the Director of Logistics?"

"Almost three years."

"When did you meet Miss Ian Wiley?"

"When she came to the plant to pull the records, shortly after her parents passed away and she became the President of the company."

"So you had no prior knowledge of her?"

"No."

"Did you speak to her at all during the investigation into these deals?"

"Yes."

"When?"

"Only the two or three times that she came to the plant asking questions and meeting with me and Richard Masters."

"Were you friendly with her during this time?"

"Not beyond professional, no. We started dating

long after the two guys were terminated."

"Good. That's all I have for you." He winked and smiled before taking his seat.

"Mr. Fleming, your witness."

"Thank you." He stood and walked over to her. "Does your affair with Miss Wiley affect your performance at work, Miss Harland?"

"Objection! Your honor, I think we have established that the relationship is not relevant to this case."

"I'll allow it. Please answer the question, Miss Harland." The judge spoke with a deep voice.

Ian could see the anger in the gray eyes across the room as Cassidy replied. "First of all, it's not an affair we're…" She looked over at Ian, when the blond nodded she continued. "We're in a loving relationship and no, I keep my job separate from my private life."

"So you've stated that you had nothing to do with any of the deals or the investigation, is that true?"

"Yes."

"Do you know Katrina Sylvan?"

"Yes."

"How well do you know her?"

"We're best friends."

"Have you ever been involved with her?"

"NO. Of course not."

"Are you aware that she works for the firm that audited the Wiley Steel records?"

"Yes."

"When did you become aware of this?"

"After the two men were terminated."

"So your best friend of shall we say years, kept the secret from you that she was evaluating your job?"

Just Me

"Yes. As I have said before, my private life and my job are two different things. My friends and I don't sit around and talk about our jobs. Frankly there's more to talk about in the world than work."

"I noticed you're wearing a diamond ring on your left hand, who gave–"

"Objection! Your honor her jewelry has nothing to do with this case."

"Sustained. Counselor move on."

"I have nothing more for this witness."

"You may step down."

Cassidy walked back towards her seat next to Rich. She exchanged heartfelt glances and quick smiles with Ian as she moved past them. The hearing continued with them calling the two newest additions to the Wiley Steel Corporation, Clark Watkins and then Kenneth Latrey. Finally, they were at recess until the next day. Ian waved for Cassidy to wait up for her, Max, and Dan.

"Hey, you did good up there." Ian hugged her.

"I wanted to kick his teeth in," Cassidy growled.

"Don't we all," Max retorted.

"Hey, Maxwell, I want you to know that Cassidy and I are engaged."

"Congratulations. Although, I figured as much when he called you on the ring."

"I was about to tell him, but he didn't deserve to know."

"Here we go. Stay close and let me do the talking." Max pushed through the door and he and Dan escorted the women to the waiting car. Giles slammed the door and drove away from the downtown area.

Ian grabbed Cassidy's hand. Minutes later the car turned into the cemetery and circled around to the back.

Giles opened the door and handed a small bouquet of yellow orchids and pink carnations to Ian. She turned around and stuck her hand out to Cassidy as she stepped away from the vehicle. Ian led the way as they walked hand in hand through the grass. She stopped in front of a large marble statue of 'Apollo and Daphne'.

"Cassidy, this is the resting place of my mother and father, Leland and Lorraine Wiley. Mom and Dad, this is Cassidy." Ian bent over and laid the flowers against the stone angels.

"Oh Ian this is beautiful."

"Thank you. It's Bernini, my Mom loved him, hence all the statues in the house." She smiled.

"Wow."

"I wanted them to see you since you'll be part of the family soon. This is a part of me that I have never shared with anyone and will never share with anyone else. Unless, I have a child of course." Cassidy squeezed the hand she was holding.

"I understand. I'm glad you brought me here. I love you so much, Ian." She backed away as the tears fell from the blonde's eyes.

"I love you Mom and Dad." Ian bent over and kissed the marble statue as she usually did when she visited her parents. She stood back up and turned towards the car.

As soon as they were settled back in the car Ian smiled and took a deep breath. She felt a large weight lifted from her shoulders. Deep down she knew her parents approved, maybe they did know all along.

"So, do you want a long engagement or–"

"No. Well, not if it can be helped. I want to get married whenever you do."

Just Me

"It's up to you. I would like to have it at the house though. My parents were married there. I believe my grandparents were too if I'm not mistaken."

"Sure, that sounds wonderful."

"Well, we should probably set a date so we can send out the invitations."

"Yes. How about six weeks? The trial should be over by then and we can celebrate more than one thing."

"That's a good idea."

"I want you to go with me to Colorado Springs this weekend to meet my parents. Do you think you can manage that?"

"Sure. I'll call for the plane when we get to the house."

"Plane?"

"Of course, we have a private jet readily available. My parents always took the tra…um…they believed in the…railway system. I…uh…I don't…not anymore. So I fly when it's too far of a drive. I don't own the plane. I rent it when I need it."

"Okay. I'm going to wait until I get back home to tell Trina and Wendi."

"As soon as this mess is over with we'll make a statement to the press together. After that we should be clear of them for a while."

"That'll be great. I'm definitely not one for the limelight."

"There is one thing we need to discuss. I…well…I guess I should've done this before proposing. How do you feel about children, Cassidy?"

"I don't know, I mean I like kids, I always thought I'd have one, I just never gave it much thought after I came out, you know."

231

"Yeah. Uh…I…I'm a Wiley, the last Wiley and I need a blood heir to take my place one day. I'm not saying tomorrow, but I've given it a lot of thought this past year and I do want a child. Only one, my great grandfather, grandfather, and father all had only one child."

"I would love to have a child with you, Ian. You are the most wonderful, loving person that I've ever met."

"That's good, I guess we can still get married then." They both laughed. "I promise not to knock you up on our wedding night."

"IAN! Giles can hear you."

She shrugged and laughed. "So, you think he can't hear you in the house?"

"Oh my god!" She smacked the blonde's arm. "You said he couldn't." She whispered harshly.

"I'm only kidding, honey. He couldn't hear anything that goes on upstairs, he never could. That's why he put a baby monitor in my room when I was a kid so he could keep an eye on me."

Just Me
Chapter 20

Rich and Cassidy drove back to Grand Junction late Wednesday night. Thursday morning Cassidy was at the plant bright and early as usual. Rich stopped her at the coffee machine.

"That's a beautiful rock your sportin' there tiger." He winked at her. "Guess your trip went better than mine. All I got out off her was a hundred dollar dinner." Cassidy smiled and smacked his arm. "Congratulations Cassidy, you deserve to be happy, even if it is the boss."

"You know coming from you, Rich, I wouldn't expect anything less. Thank you."

"Good, you're one of the guys, remember?"

"Oh yeah, I'll never forget." She laughed and went back to her office and dialed a number on her cell phone.

"Wendi Blanchert."

"Hey Wendi, doing anything tonight?"

"No why? By the way how did the hearing go?"

"Not bad, stop by my place about seven. Let's have a girl's night. I'm going to call Trina and make sure she's there too. I'll tell you guys all about it over a bottle of wine."

"Sounds like a plan."

Cassidy closed her phone, opened it again, and

dialed another number.

~ ~ ~

"Mom?"

"Hey Cassidy darling, how are you?"

"Good. Have you heard anything about the hearing?"

"No, our news people aren't the sharpest sticks in the woods."

"Don't we know. I don't think they can spell news. Anyway, I was hoping you and dad would be home this weekend."

"Yes. Why?"

"I'm coming to town. Actually, Ian and I are coming to town. We're flying out Saturday afternoon so we should be there by two. We'll be flying back Sunday morning."

"Oh, I can't wait to meet her. It seems like forever since we've seen you darling."

"I know. Anyway, I'm at work so I need to go, but I wanted to make sure it was okay. We'll be on a private plane so you and dad can pick us up at the hangar. I'll call you with the details Friday night when I get into Aspen after work."

~ ~ ~

"So, tell us all about the hearing." Wendi spoke as Cassidy poured the white wine into three glasses. The three women sat lazily in Cassidy's living room.

"Well, your name came up Trina, that jackass drilled me for an hour about you. He even asked if we had an affair. I was about to knock him out when Ian's lawyer changed his line of questioning. What a dickhead."

"Man, that sucks. I actually figured I'd get subpoenaed, I usually do when it comes to a lawsuit."

"Nah, they knew you didn't have anything. They just wanted to drive a wedge between me and Ian."

"I'm so glad I don't have to deal with that kind of shit at work." Wendi sipped her wine.

"Hell, I never thought I would either, are you kidding? Who falls in love with their boss, has the perfect relationship, and lives happily ever after?"

"I don't know, you're the only one I can think of."

"Me too."

"See, I was taken by surprise." Cassidy leaned forward to pour herself another glass of wine, that's when the light caught the rock on her hand. Trina's eyebrows disappeared into her hair and Wendi spit wine all over the table.

"What the fuck is that?" Wendi spat, still choking on her wine.

"Ian asked me to marry her Tuesday night."

"Oh my god!" Trina grabbed Cassidy's hand. "That thing is huge!"

"No shit!" Wendi examined the diamonds just as closely. "I could hock that and pay off my car and buy a house! It's beautiful."

"I don't know what to say, Cass. Congratulations."

"Yeah, congrats, girlfriend."

"Thanks guys. I love you both dearly."

"Wow, I can't believe our little Cassidy is getting married." Wendi looked at Trina. "The first of the musketeers."

Cassidy laughed as she ran her hand through her hair. "What can I say? That adorable blue eyed blond swept me off my feet the night I met her."

"So when's the big day?"

"Six weeks from this Saturday."

"What! Excuse me?"

"Yeah, it's a little sudden, but we're just ready to be together. It was actually my idea to do it so soon. The trial should be over before then, so we'll have a lot to celebrate."

"Holy shit! This means we'll need to start planning immediately." Wendi was about to blow a gasket.

"Have you told your parents?" Trina asked as she poured herself another glass of wine.

"No, we're flying out there this weekend to tell them and so they can meet Ian."

"My god, this is happening so sudden."

"Yeah. I know it's a shock. I think I'm still in that phase. Reality will hit me two months after the wedding I'm sure."

"So where will you do it?"

"We're going to have the ceremony and reception at the estate. It's a big family tradition."

The three women clinked their glasses together. "Here's to love, life, and lots of hot sex!" They all laughed and took a sip of their wine. "Again, congrats, Cass. We're both really happy for you. Ian is an amazing woman. You two are perfect together," Trina finished.

"Thanks."

~ ~ ~

The plane landed smoothly on the concrete runway and taxied slowly to the private hangar on the side of the main airport terminal. Cassidy took a deep breath. She smiled when she looked down at the glistening ring on her left hand.

"Shall we?" Ian's blue eyes sparkled in the sunlight coming through the cabin window.

"Now is as good a time as any." She stood up and led the way to the door. Ian stopped behind her to speak to the pilot quickly. Both women made their way down the small staircase. Cassidy's father was average build and a few inches taller than her mother, who was taller than Cassidy. He had brown hair that seemed to be going gray rather quickly. It matched his thick mustache. Her mother was thin with jet black hair and gray eyes. Cassidy's mother looked like a slightly older version of herself.

"Hello darling." The mother hugged her daughter and kissed her cheek, followed by her father.

"Mom, Dad, this is Ian Wiley, my boss." Cassidy smiled, then remembered she forgot to take her ring off before they got off the plane. *Oh shit.* "Ian these are my parents, David and Eileen Harland." Ian stepped forward to shake their hands.

"It's a pleasure to meet you both."

"You too. Cassidy has told us so much about you." Eileen spoke first.

"She never told me that she looks so much like you Mrs. Harland."

The older woman smiled. "Please, call me Eileen."

"Thank you."

Everyone climbed into the large SUV and David drove them towards the house that Cassidy grew up in. On the flight Cassidy had explained how her mother was a high school history teacher and her father worked as a supervisor at the coffee plant downtown.

"This is a beautiful house you have Mrs., I mean Eileen."

Eileen smiled at Ian and winked at her daughter. "Thank you."

"Come on Ian, let me show you around." Cassidy grabbed her hand and started up the stairs. The house was two stories with hardwood floors throughout, partially covered by various oriental rugs. They passed by one large bedroom, followed by two smaller ones. "This was my room." They walked inside one of the smaller rooms. The walls were white with lavender trim. A full-size bed took up most of the space. The white-wash oak dresser and tiny matching desk filled up the rest of the room.

"This is cute." Ian grinned.

"Yeah, Mom never let go of her baby girl. I'm just glad she replaced the bed. It used to be a day bed. She traded it for this one when I went away to college."

"Hmm, a day bed might have been fun, if this wasn't your parents' house of course." she grinned as her eyebrow rose up seductively.

"Uh huh, let me show you where you're sleeping, come on." Cassidy tugged on Ian's hand.

"What? You mean I can't sleep in here with you?"

"No. My parents are old fashioned. I mean they're completely fine with me being gay, but I have never shared a bed with anyone under their roof." She paused. "Come to think of it, now I know why they are acting so

Just Me

strange. They know something's up. Ian I've never brought anyone home to meet them, especially a woman."

"Well this is about to get very interesting." She said dryly as Cassidy led the way into the room across the hall. It was also white, but with baby blue trim and oak colored furniture. The bed was the same size.

"The last one is my parents' room." They walked downstairs to the living room. David, was watching some old movie on TV and Eileen was in the kitchen.

"There you are, I thought you ladies were lost upstairs. Here, I made some cookies for you this morning."

Cassidy dug into the chocolate chip cookies.

"Mm, Mom these are delicious!"

"My daughter has always had a sweet tooth. She gets it from her father. He'll sit here and eat this entire batch if I let him." She shook her head.

Ian was still trying to get past the fact that Cassidy looked so much like her mother.

"Ian would you like to see Cassidy when she was in diapers? I pulled her baby books out after she called the other night."

"Absolutely."

The women joined David in the living room, Eileen sat on the couch between her husband and Ian. Cassidy sat in the reclining chair.

Ian sat there for three hours listening to stories and looking at pictures. Cassidy was involved for the first hour, before she passed out in the recliner. David was engrossed in the war movie he was watching, although he did comment on a lot of the pictures and added details to the stories.

"If you will excuse me, Ian, I need to go start dinner. Would you like a glass of wine?"

"Yes, ma'am. Thank you." Ian followed Eileen into the kitchen to retrieve the glass. "I'd offer my assistance, but I usually don't cook much."

"Yes, Cassidy tells me you have a butler that takes care of you."

She laughed. "Yes, Giles has been in my family since before I was born. He's from England, came over on a boat to seek out America. He became the butler in my parents house six months later. His mother and father were both part of the staff at the castle in Westminster Abbey. He's been like an uncle to me all of my life."

"He never married?"

"No ma'am. He did fall in love with a woman once. She broke his heart and he decided to never try again. Although, he'd never say it, but my mother and I always thought he was seeing someone in town over the years." She shrugged. "Now he just keeps me in line."

"I was very sorry to hear about your parents. What a tragedy."

"Thank you." She sipped the wine.

"What great company my daughter is? I haven't seen her butt in six months and what does she do? Comes home and passes out in the chair." She shook her head and sipped her wine. "I hope you like lamb."

"Yes, I haven't really run across anything that I don't eat, except eggs."

~ ~ ~

"I can't believe I fell asleep. I really can't believe you guys didn't wake me up." Cassidy stretched embarrassingly.

"Don't worry about it, darling, you were tired. I'm sure you guys have been through a lot lately. I can't believe those reporters are going crazy over your lawsuit Ian."

"It is a little more than we were planning for. The guy at Hinkley Metals is playing dirty, he's the one that leaked the story about our relationship."

"What a pompous ass piece of…" The brown haired man looked like a dear in the headlights. "I'm sorry. I'm just upset with that man. You don't deserve to be drug through the mud and my daughter damn sure doesn't deserve to have her face plastered all over the paper because she's in love with a woman. My god, these people need to get their heads out of there asses."

"I agree with you, Mr. Harland. It's ridiculous."

"Please call me David." She smiled at him and nodded her head. Cassidy cleared her throat and put her silverware on her now empty dinner plate.

"Uh…Mom and Dad…I, we, have something to tell you." She paused and took a deep breath. "Ian and I are getting married." She lifted her left hand that had been rested in her lap under the table.

"My word, would you look at that ring, David. Oh Cassidy, I'm so happy for you. Congratulations." She stood and walked over to her daughter to hug her.

"Wow, I'm very impressed." He stood up and hugged his daughter. "Congratulations." David and Eileen hugged Ian as well.

"There's more."

"You're not pregnant are you?" Her father asked with a grin.

"No dad! The wedding is in six weeks."

"What!" Her mother practically fell out of her chair.

"We don't want to wait and the trial will be over by then anyway. We've decided to have it in Aspen at the Wiley Estate."

"It's sort of a family tradition." Ian chimed in.

"There's so much planning that needs to be done. Oh my god Cassidy, you're pushing it."

"Nah, Ian has a lot of pull in that town. Trust me, we can get whatever we will need with no problem." Ian raised her eyebrows and cocked her head to the side. Cassidy smiled at her. "Mom, I'll get with you next week on the guest list for our side. I know you're busy with the school year just starting and everything. Besides Ian is dealing with the hearing and I'm swamped with work, so we're going to hire a wedding planner."

"A what! Oh Cassidy, you know I hate dealing with them. When you're cousin Tara got married last year they hired a wedding planner, that women couldn't find a flower if you shoved it up her nose."

"Mom, I think I have a little more commonsense than Tara, besides, Ian has to agree on the person we choose."

"I don't work with airheads, so we shouldn't have a problem." Ian assured Eileen.

"All right, just let me know what I can do to help. How often does your baby girl get married?"

"Uh once!"

They all laughed.

"I hope so! I'm only doing this once too!" Ian added.

Just Me
Chapter 21

"Good morning, young Wiley. Can I get you anything?"

Ian sat at the large dining room table. "A mimosa and a piece of honey toast."

The butler returned with a plate of French toast and a large glass of chocolate milk. "If I may say so, I'm glad you chose that woman to do your planning. She had more eggs in her basket than that man did. He seemed to be preoccupied."

"I agree. She seems to be doing a good job so far."

Chelsea Gordon was a tall African American woman with very light skin. She presented herself with professionalism and a sense of well being. Ian thought maybe she was a lesbian herself. At least, she seemed to know as much about it as the next lesbian anyway. Ian sat back and sipped her milk.

"I want you to walk me down the aisle, Giles."

"Uh...I...young Wiley, I'd be honored." He smiled and turned towards the kitchen.

Well that was easy. She thought to herself as she worked on her breakfast. The trial was dwindling down. She figured they'd go to closing arguments fairly soon. The wedding was a mere three weeks away and the planner was hard at work. She had already rented the reception tent, tables, and chairs, booked the cake, and had both women fitted for their white dresses. All that seemed to be left was the traditional tuxedo's for Giles and David. Both women had decided to allow Trina and Wendi to walk down the aisle as bridesmaids, but would take seats next to Cassidy's parents instead of standing up. That way Ian and Cassidy would be the only two standing.

Ian was definitely beginning to feel the jitters as the days went by. The hardest part seemed to be what to do about work. Cassidy would have to move to Aspen, two and a half hours one way wouldn't be worth the travel everyday. The Logistics Director would never be able to work from the corporate office. There was too much hands on with that position. *Maybe I can talk her into it…who knows.*

~ ~ ~

Ian sat behind the large mahogany desk rubbing her temples with both hands. The tiny headache she had at the beginning of the day was now a full blown migraine, undoubtedly brought on by the stress of the lawsuit and the wedding around the corner, amongst other things. Her entire body jerked when the cell phone attached to her belt vibrated.

"Ian Wiley."

"Hello, Miss Wiley, this is Chelsea Gordon."

"Who…? Oh yes the wedding planner. What can I do for you?"

"I received a call this morning from Versace, yours and Miss Harland's dresses are ready and will be delivered to your residence by the end of the week."

"Thank you, I know this has been hectic."

"Not at all, ma'am. I've seen worse." She laughed lightly.

"I guess that's a good thing. Is there anything else I can help you with?"

"Yes, you and Miss Harland will need to go to the courthouse to sign the Civil Union paperwork by the end of this week. Otherwise, we won't have the marriage certificate in time for the ceremony."

"Ah, I see." *Shit.* "Is it possible for the papers to be sent to Cassidy to sign? She's currently residing in Grand Junction?"

"Hmm…I can check on that. They need to be notarized though. I'll see what I can do and call you back."

"Thanks." She closed the phone and leaned back against the leather chair.

~ ~ ~

Cassidy spent the entire week running around like a chicken with her head cut off. It seemed that every time she cleared her logistics log another fifty shipments appeared. She enjoyed the high pressure situations day in and day out. They seemed to make her days more productive than just sitting at a computer tracking sales and routing the shipment itineraries, also known as I10's. She was certainly feeling the stress of the wedding as a heavy weight on her shoulders. If you'd asked her a year ago where she'd be, it would most likely be nothing near marrying her boss. Even now and then that thought made her chuckle. *Oh Cassidy, what have you done?*

"Hey Cassidy, can you get me the I10 for the Dwight Construction Group Account? Kenneth is on the phone razing me about the deadline. They apparently need those steel beams two weeks earlier."

"Are you kidding? Rich, I argued with that fool until I was blue in the face yesterday. I told him it was up to you guys. I can't ship until it rolls out of production."

"I know. Who does this contractor think we are Houdini?"

She laughed. "Yeah, sounds like it. I'll email you the I10, but it's not going to help you. I can reroute an I10 up until the time the damn truck arrives, we both know that. The problem is, how fast can we have those beams off of the line?"

"I don't know, I just talked to Darren. He says he can push them up, but we may not make this idiots deadline. Kenneth needs to learn the word 'no', that's all there is to it. I'll go over the I10 and talk to Darren again. At the least, we may be able to cut one week, but two is going to be cutting it very close."

"Let me know when you can have them off the line and I'll reroute the I10, maybe I can give us some room there."

"Sure thing."

As soon as Cassidy hung up her office phone, her cell phone rang as loudly as it vibrated. The caller ID made the automatic smile appear. "How do you know when I'm always thinking of you?"

"ESP or love. Who knows? Anyway, how's your day going?"

"Probably worse than yours. Are you out of court for the day?"

"Why's that? Yeah."

Just Me

"Because I doubt the head of the company knows every time someone fucks up and we all have to duck tape sticks together to make a bridge for the idiot to climb back up with."

"Huh?" Ian shook her head.

"Nothing. I'm just dealing with the day to day stresses of work. How about you?"

"Yeah."

That was a lie, she knew damn good and well she was unaware of the day to day screw ups. She was only brought in when no one else could dig them out of the hole someone dropped them all into. Usually, Clark handled it before it got to her. She was merely told of the problem and how it was already resolved.

"Hey Chelsea called me. She needs you to go to your county courthouse tomorrow and sign the Civil Union papers. They should be there before noon according to Fed Ex."

"Oh that's good. I completely forgot about that part. Did she say anything else?"

"No. Oh wait, yeah, our dresses will be here by the end of the week."

"That's good. Don't peek at mine!"

"I won't. What do you take me for?"

Cassidy laughed. "Is this a secure line?"

"Uh, it's our cell phones, why?"

"I was about to tell you what I take you for and how I plan to take it." She spoke in the most seductive voice she could muster up.

"Oh." Ian grinned. "I'm going to be out at the plant late tomorrow afternoon, when we get out of court. I need to go over the numbers for the quarter with you and Rich. Besides, I have a few things to talk to you about anyway. I was hoping to stay the night with you and drive back Thursday morning."

"That's fine. I have a few calls to make in the morning, but the afternoon should be okay. Don't you usually do these meetings in conference calls with us and the entire group?"

"Of course, but I wanted to surprise Rich. His anniversary with the company is coming up and I wanted to take his gift to him personally. I have too much going on to do it the week of our wedding."

"Ah, I see. So how long has he been with the company?"

"He's been with Wiley Steel for twenty years and he's been the production director for fifteen."

"Wow, I knew he'd been here for a while. So, what's he getting?"

"Is that something to ask your boss?"

"No." She replied professionally. "I was asking my fiancé."

"Oh, well in that case you'll see it tomorrow. I gotta go. I have a meeting with the directors here to go over the numbers with them today."

"Okay. I love you."

"I love you too."

~ ~ ~

Ian fixed herself a glass of Remy Martin and sat on the small leather couch in her father's study which was now hers. She sipped the golden liquid as she stared at the documents in her lap. Frustrated, she closed the file and tossed it on the desk across from her. A faint knock at the door caught her attention.

Just Me

"Come in."

"Young Wiley, you seem stressed. Is there anything I can get for you?"

"No, thank you, Giles." She took another sip. "Actually, have a seat."

He nodded and sat down next to her. She offered the bottle, but he refused. As far as she'd known he never drank a drop in his life. Maybe that's why he was always after her for drinking so much.

"I do believe I know what's causing all of the turmoil I see in your eyes. You hide it like your father, but your eyes could never tell a lie, neither could his for that matter."

She smiled. *Touché.* "That's my prenuptial agreement for Cassidy." She pointed to the thick blue file that she'd tossed on the desk. "I'm torn apart over it Giles. I keep thinking that it's wrong. I mean she'll legally be a Wiley in two weeks. She should have a right to everything I own. I feel absolutely awful." She took another sip.

"I figured as much. When your father married your mother…" She cut him off.

"She had to sign a prenup and my grandmother too." Another sip.

"I see."

"This is like saying 'I love you' to the person, then slapping them across the face at the end of the sentence. I've fought with myself over this for a week now. Maxwell is on my back, I need to have these papers to him by Friday. My Will and Estate documents will be changed, with her added of course."

"It makes since young Wiley. You're heir to a multi-million dollar fortune that follows a blood line, as well as a name."

"You're right Giles, I know. It's not about the money, I'll spend the rest of my life giving her everything she ever wanted. It's about telling her this is all mine and even though you're legally bound to me, you can't touch it. But if I have a blood child with you, that child will inherit everything despite your wishes. The worst part is, if something should happen to me before I have a child then the entire company will fall apart. There's not a god damn thing she could do about it because legally she'll have nothing to do with Wiley Steel Corporation."

"Yes, I suppose so." He shifted on the couch, straightening his jacket. The man never let his perfectly tailored suit falter the least bit. Ian figured it was an English Gentleman thing.

"Have you talked to her about children?"

Ian stared at the floor after emptying her glass. "We've skipped around the subject."

"So, you haven't told the person that you're about to marry in ten days that you have to produce a living heir before your twenty-ninth birthday?"

"No, Giles, I haven't." She spoke louder than she meant to. "I'm sorry."

"Young Wiley, I do believe you need to have a very serious conversation with Miss Harland, and very quickly."

"I'm going there tomorrow after the hearing."

"Good. She will be upset with you, but I know she loves you very much."

"Thanks." She gave him a halfhearted smiled.

Chapter 22

Ian sat on the couch in front of the TV while Cassidy poured two glasses of wine in the kitchen. "I still can't believe you gave Rich a Rolex." She called out.

"Why? He's spent a good amount of time with the company, more than any other employee. He deserved it. Besides, that's what the Wiley's do, especially with employees."

Cassidy joined her on the couch. "I know, but that's a lot of money for a present. Why not give him an extra week's vacation or a raise?"

"His salary is capped, has been for about five years now. And the man already gets three weeks paid vacation. He's never taken a day of it, so it gets paid out to him every year on January first, like everyone else. What's wrong with a Rolex anyway? I wear one."

"I know you do. I just don't see spending five thousand dollars on a watch."

Ian sat back against the cushion. *Oh boy.* "I guess now is as good a time as any to bring this up."

"What is it? I know something's been bothering you. You've been acting weird for the past few weeks." Cassidy sipped her wine and ran her hand through her dark tresses.

Ian downed the glass of wine and took a deep breath. "I need to tell you about me, about my family, my heritage."

"Okay."

"As you know my great-grandfather started Wiley Steel in eighteen eighty six. He had a partner, named Hinkley, which is obviously why the bastard is after me now. Anyway, in nineteen o' three they split and Wiley Steel became a sole heir corporation. My grandfather was born in the early thirties and took over the company when his father could no longer run the business. My father was born in fifty one. He took over when my grandfather passed away in the nineties. That leaves me, you know how old I am and how I came to be the head of the company. What I'm trying to get at is this company is run by bloodline, not just name."

"I understand that."

"There's more. I need to produce a blood heir before my twenty-ninth birthday. Meaning, I need to have a child soon." Ian watched Cassidy set the now empty wine glass down on the table in front of them.

"Why do you have a 'deadline' for having a child?"

"That's the family rules. You have to remember I'm the first woman. All of the men were married and had a child before twenty-nine so it never seemed to be a problem. On top of that, I can only have one child."

"Who the hell made the rules, Ian?"

"My great-grandfather and these rules have been followed for over a hundred and ten years."

"Wow... I..." She stopped to take a breath. "I mean I've thought about children, yes, but that means you'll be pregnant very soon and who would be the father?"

Ian stopped her rambling.

Just Me

"We don't need to go into the details about that right now. You just need to know what happens next in my life because you will be a part of it. I love you so much."

"I love you too, Ian. I'm sure we can figure this out. I mean you have close to two years."

"The baby has to be born before my twenty-ninth birthday. Therefore we have approximately one year and a few months, but that's pushing it close."

"This is a lot to take in. First of all, I'm getting married to you in a few days. Now you're telling me that you need to get pregnant on the honeymoon." She shook her head.

"God, not that soon. But we should start talking about it soon."

"We are talking about it, right now."

"I know, I mean the details."

She took a deep breath. "Okay, I guess that'll give me some time to let it sink in."

"That's not all."

"Ian, there's more?"

"Yeah." She grabbed Cassidy's hands. "You remember the bloodline I just told you about right?" The brunette nodded. "Well, with that bloodline comes a fortune, not just the corporation."

"Okay." Cassidy was confused.

"Meaning all of the money in the family gets passed down with the business." She held her breath. "Cassidy, I'm the heir to close to a billion dollar fortune."

Cassidy's gray eyes grew as large as saucers. She knew it was multi-millions, but didn't think it was worth anywhere near a billion dollars.

"You've seen the records, you know the kind of

money Wiley Steel produces every year. Over the years it's multiplied, a lot."

"Oh my god, Ian, I had no idea it was that large."

"No one really does. That's why I need you to do something for me."

"You want me to sign a prenup don't you?"

"Yes. Well no." *damn it.* "*I* personally wish I never had to do this, but it's part of…" Cassidy cut her off.

"The family rules?" She shook her head.

"I'm sorry."

"Why didn't you tell me all of this before now, Ian? I don't want your money, that's not why I fell in love with you and it's damn sure not why I'm marrying you. All this, the child, the money, everything, you should have talked to me before you ever asked me to marry you. Maybe I don't want all of this. Maybe it's too much."

Cassidy stood up and walked into the kitchen and poured herself another glass of wine, wishing to god she had something stronger in the cabinet. Ian didn't follow. She remained sitting on the couch dumbfounded.

I've blown it, she can't handle this. Hell I couldn't even handle it, that's why I've waited until the last minute to tell her. I'm such a coward! She ran both hands through her hair and stood up. She was headed into the small kitchen when Cassidy came back out.

"Look, I'm sorry. I'll just stay in a hotel tonight." Ian turned to walk out of the apartment.

"That's not necessary. We're getting married soon. Of course, I want you to stay here with me. I never see you as it is." She was standing less than a foot away. "That doesn't mean I can't be upset with you. I love you so damn much, Ian Wiley, you have no idea. But, you slapped me pretty damn hard tonight."

"I know. God I'm sorry, Cassidy. I've tried to tell you a hundred times."

"I expected the prenup. I don't want any part of Wiley Steel Corporation. My paycheck from them is plenty good enough. But, the child thing has thrown me for a loop." She nodded towards the couch and Ian followed her back to their original seats.

"I have to have an heir and everything that I own goes to that child the day it's born. I wish to god I could have a normal life with you and not all of this bullshit."

"You can't control your heritage, honey. I can't be mad at you for that. I can however, be mad at you for waiting until the last damn minute to tell me about it."

"You can be mad at me forever, as long as you agree to marry me in ten days."

"Of course I will. I don't think I could live without you. And I signed our Civil Union papers today, so the wedding is a go." She smiled.

"Good." Ian smiled back. "By the way, I can't live without you either."

Cassidy cleared her throat. "Let's see those papers, I want this over with."

Ian pulled two folders out of her briefcase. "This one is the prenuptial agreement, feel free to read it or have your lawyer read it."

"I don't have a lawyer, Ian." She laughed. "I trust you."

"It basically says that you are not now, and never will be entitled to the Wiley fortune, including Wiley Steel Corporation and the Wiley Estate. As well as, the Wiley assets and bank accounts. You are however, entitled to anything and everything that we put into this marriage together. As in, you have rights to everything that I purchase from our wedding day on."

"That's not bad. I don't want your business, your bank accounts, or your house. I want you and only you."

"It also says that when I produce a bloodline heir, you are no longer able to take that child from me in the case of a divorce, unless, I am abusive to you or the child."

"Oh my god. I'd never try to take your child first of all. Second of all there isn't an abusive bone in your body. Plus, I don't plan on getting a divorce."

"I actually have that planned for December third, ten years from now." She laughed and Cassidy smacked her arm. "Sorry, I wanted to see you smile, I know this is serious."

"So is this it?"

"Yeah, pretty much. I still haven't told you how happy I am that you're taking my last name."

"Well, from the looks of all of this it really has no meaning."

"You're wrong. It has every meaning in the world to me. And don't feel bad, my grandmother and mother had to sign this exact document. If I had married a man, he'd be signing it too."

'I guess that makes me feel better. So your grandma and your mom were cut off like this?"

"Yeah. Bloodline only."

"What happens if you die before you produce an heir?"

"I don't know and I don't care to find out."

"Me either." Cassidy leaned over and kissed Ian, her lips lingered playfully. Then she pulled away and signed the five pages of documents. "What's the other one?"

"My Will and a few other papers. I obviously can't leave you my family inheritance, but I am putting you in charge of my life. If something happens to me, you're my medical power of attorney. Maxwell Guthrey is in charge of the Wiley Estate if something happens to me. He'll make sure everything goes to my heir. You're also the namesake on my personal bank account. There's a little over three million dollars in it. I call it my play money, but it's now 'our' play money."

"My god!"

"I use the Wiley Accounts for the company, but my paycheck goes into my personal account since its earned money. Therefore, you have every right to it, whether I'm alive or dead. As soon as we're married your name will be added to my account.

"Wow, Ian you didn't have to do that."

"Yes I did. You'll be my wife. The least I could do is add you to my damn bank account. I'm sorry I can't do more."

"Trust me, that's plenty." She smiled and shook her head. "I guess I can definitely say this is something I wasn't expecting."

"Yeah. Sorry I have a habit of shocking you." She smiled sheepishly. "I need you to sign my Will documents too, after that, we're finished with everything. Well, not everything, not yet anyway."

Cassidy signed everything and Ian put the files back into her briefcase. "What's next?"

"You're moving in with me aren't you? I mean…"

'Well, I hope we're not going to have a once a

week marriage. But, I don't know about work. I mean that's a long haul everyday."

"Yeah, and I looked into moving you to the corporate office, but logistics really needs to stay in the plant."

"I know. It would be completely inefficient."

"Uh huh, that's why I'm offering you the Locomotive Services Director position."

"What?"

"I haven't filled that position and you'd be working in the corporate office. Who better to fill the position than someone that knows all of the divisions of the company?"

"Yeah but that's a sales position, Ian, I'm in shipping."

"I know. The money is the same for all of the directors, including my assistant. But, it depends on how long you've been with the company some people are obviously paid higher than others. Your pay won't change, but you'll be closer to home."

"That's a lot to think about. You do realize that I spend the better part of my day covering up for your sales departments that promise bullshit time frames right? That's basically what Rich and I do day in and day out. I'll miss that, we work great together."

"I know. It's going to be a challenge to replace you in logistics. It'll be a nightmare. The good thing is, having you come in as the Locomotive Services Director, maybe you can help the others learn about logistics. Maybe things between corporate and the plant will run a lot smoother." Cassidy looked at Ian questioningly. "Yes, I know everything that goes on in the company. Trust me, you guys think you pulled the wool over my eyes coming to tell me after it's been resolved. I'm very proud of my team. You are all able to work together without my help. That doesn't mean I don't know what's going on." She smiled. "I'd be a terrible company President if I didn't."

"So, big bad know-it-all company president, when are you going to make love to me?" Cassidy stated as she climbed into Ian's lap and bit her lower lip seductively. Between kisses Ian stood up with the smaller woman in her arms and walked down the hallway to the small bedroom at the back of the apartment.

Slowly, they touched and explored each others body with light kisses. Hours passed as they climaxed separately, then together, until the night's sleep finally claimed them. The two warm, nude bodies curled together under the thin sheet.

Chapter 23

Ian joined Maxwell Guthrey and Daniel Meyers at the Plaintiff's table as the judge read the jury's decision. Her palms were sweaty and her knees were weak, not because of the hearing, but because of the wedding set to take place in twenty-four hours. Ian decided to make a public statement after the wedding, announcing her marriage and her opinion of the lawsuit's ending.

"We the jury, find Mr. J. R. Hinkley guilty of aiding and abetting in the embezzlement of Wiley Steel Corporation accounts."

"So says all of you?" The judge asked.

"Yes sir." They answered.

"Thank you. Jury, you are hereby dismissed."

The twelve men and women slowly left the room as the judge folded his hands neatly on his desk. His bald head shinned brightly.

"I'm honestly appalled, Mr. Hinkley, that you yourself would allow something of this stature to take place within your company. The fact that you're the person behind the operation makes me cringe even more. Businessmen and women such as yourself and Miss Wiley hold major names in this country, I suggest you take that into consideration the next time you want extra money in your pocket. Thus, I am sentencing you to repay the seven million dollars, as well as, serve a hundred hours of community service, where I hope you shall learn what a name like yours means to the smaller man of the world. Case dismissed."

Ian stood up and shook Max's hand, then Dan's. "Thank you, guys. I know this'll be drug back through the mud when he appeals it, but for now it's over. I'm looking forward to seeing you both tomorrow." She smiled.

"Of course we'll be there, Miss Wiley." Max smiled. "As for the appeal, I doubt any judge is going to touch this once they see the transcripts of that tape. Even so, we'll be prepared until the day they hand me a seven million dollar check for you."

"Thanks."

~ ~ ~

"Well, how did it go?" Giles asked as he climbed into the driver's seat of the Bentley. Ian was already situated in the back.

"Fine, we won, but I'm sure he'll appeal it. Either way, they sentenced him to pay me all of the money that was lost and do a hundred hours of community service. I think he pissed off the judge last week when they put him on the stand. He practically denied the entire thing."

"I'm glad for you young Wiley, you deserve better than dealing with that man."

"Yeah, maybe he'll forget about the old family rivalry and move on. My father moved on a long time ago. Besides, I have a much bigger situation at hand."

"Yes, I do believe so."

"I think we should polish off that old bottle of Louis VIII that dad left in the wall safe."

"Excuse me?"

"You know which one I'm talking about."

"I don't possibly think I could drink something that's worth a few thousand dollars, young Wiley."

"Try five thousand, besides, I'm only getting married once, ol' man." She smiled.

You're just like you're father Ian Leland. "I don't take to the drink."

"Never?"

"Not since the night you were born. Your father had me share a bottle of Louis with him."

"Ah, you see, it's a family tradition." She smiled brightly. "To the house, Giles, we have a bottle to kill."

~ ~ ~

Ian woke with a splitting headache. Partly because she only ate once the day before, that being dinner, then, drinking half a bottle of very old liquor straight. She rolled out of the bed and looked at her disheveled short hair in the mirror. She had a major case of bed head with half of it pasted flat to her head. *Sexy.* She laughed.

"Wake up, Wiley, it's your big day. don't wanna be hung over do you?" She and Giles had stayed up until the morning hours drinking and trading stories of her parents. The Englishman let loose as soon as he had a few glasses in him.

"God, I wonder how Giles is feeling? He doesn't drink, oh the poor man's probably pissed at me right now."

Ian jumped in the shower to straighten herself out before going down the stairs. Her father always said, *Wiley Law-always present yourself as royalty when you walk down these stairs. Never present yourself as indisposed.* His father had told him that same thing.

As soon as Ian walked into the dining room Giles came out of the kitchen with a champagne glass full of orange liquid.

"What's this?"

She took the glass and sat down. If Giles hadn't known the woman since she was born, he'd say she faired their drinking just fine as she sat there in dark chino's and a light blue polo shirt.

"Young Wiley, if your head hurts half as bad as mine this morning, you will feel much better after actually drinking a Mimosa." He turned away from her. "I had two."

She laughed. "I'm sorry." She called out as he went back to the kitchen. When he returned the tall glass was empty, he set a large glass of chocolate milk down next to a giant plate of blueberry pancakes.

"Eat now, since I know you probably won't be eating much for the rest of the day." He picked up the empty champagne flute. "The last minute preparation has already started. Miss Gordon was here an hour ago with the florist."

"Who?"

"Miss Gordon, ma'am."

"Oh yeah, Chelsea, is she still here?"

"I don't believe so. She said she'll be in and out all day."

"Did you give her a code for the gate?"

"Yes ma'am."

"Okay, at least now she won't drive you crazy with the phone all day. Have you heard from Cassidy?"

"No ma'am. I believe she is at the hotel with Miss

Blanchert and Miss Sylvan."

"Yeah, I'm not supposed to see her or talk to her until the wedding. Wendi and Trina will make sure of that, I guarantee you. But, both of them will probably be by here sometime this morning. I'm going for a drive. I'll be back later this afternoon. Please say hello to them in case I miss them."

~ ~ ~

The black sports car pulled through the iron gates and circled the familiar path. When it came to a stop next to the curb, Ian killed the engine and stepped out into the grass. She walked the forty or so paces, until she came face to face with the large marble angels. She bent forward and placed a kiss next to her parents' names.

"Hello Mom and Dad." A tear escaped her eye as she knelt down. "So, today's the big day. God I wish you were both here. It's hard doing this without you." She didn't bother wiping the rest of the tears as they fell. "Giles is walking me down the aisle, Dad. I knew you'd be proud to have him there next to me. Mom, I'm going to wear your wedding rings as my own, I know they were grandmas. I figured Dad's was too plain for a Wiley woman." She smiled. "Besides, I wear his cufflinks every time I'm dressed for work. I'm also wearing your pearls Mom." She couldn't help the breaking of her own heart, so she let herself cry harder than usual. "I miss you both so much. I love you dearly." She stood up to walk away, but turned back towards the statue. "By the way, Dad, the lawsuit ended, we won of course. Hinkley has to pay back everything we lost and play a saint for a hundred hours of community service." She smiled when she felt the light breeze on her skin.

~ ~ ~

"No you can't call her, Cass, that's bad luck!" Wendi snatched the cell phone from the brunette's hand and tossed it to Trina. "Guard that damn thing."

"Aye, aye Captain Wendimena." Trina mocked her with a salute. Cassidy covered her mouth, but still laughed out loud. Even Wendi had to chuckle.

"Come on guys, it's only my wedding day." There was a knock on the door to their giant hotel suite. Cassidy maneuvered through the sitting area outside of the separate bedrooms. She looked through the peephole then opened the door.

"Hey, Mom, Dad."

"Wow this room is huge, darling." Her mother walked around the penthouse style hotel suite.

"Yeah, all three of us stayed in here. It has two bedrooms and the couch folds out too."

"My god, it's as big as your apartment, minus the kitchen." Her father stated. "Our room isn't quite as large." He smiled.

"Wait until you two see the Estate."

"Wendi and Trina went over this morning to make sure everything looked good. Chelsea, our wedding planner has done a fantastic job getting everything ready in basically five weeks." She shook her head. "I can't believe that I'm going to be married in a few hours."

"I know me either. David, it wasn't so long ago when she was two feet tall and getting into everything. Now look at her." Cassidy's mother had tears in her eyes. "You go on down to the bar with Calvin. You guys can get ready in our room. I'll stay here with the girls."

"Uncle Calvin's here?" Cassidy asked. Calvin Harland was her father's brother. He had a son, Calvin Junior that was a few years younger than Cassidy.

"Yeah, he and your Aunt Sherrie walked into the hotel behind us. Cal will be here soon. He had to stop and pick up his new girlfriend."

"I swear he's going to be a bachelor forever, Mom." They both laughed.

Just Me
Chapter 24

A soft Mozart Violin Concerto played on the sound system as Trina, dressed in a pale pink strapless Versace dress, made her way slowly down the flower covered, white satin aisle. Rows and rows of white folding chairs lined both sides, leading to the gorgeous arch style alter covered in white roses with candles burning all around. The Minister that performed the ceremony when Ian laid her parents to rest, was standing at the end of the long path waiting to once again perform a sacred ceremony for the Wiley family. The ceremony was outside and set up a few hundred yards from the back of the house with the giant reception tent a few hundred feet away. The sky was clear in the late afternoon and the temperature was just starting to get cooler, but the reception tent was air conditioned anyway.

Wendi's dress was identical, except the color was pale lavender. She too, walked slowly down the long runway that seemed never ending. If she had to guess, she'd say there were at least two hundred people on either side of the isle. Considering Ian had no other family except for Giles, and Cassidy's family and friends was only about a hundred people, most of the group was employees and friends of Ian's parents. Including, the Mayor, a State Senator, and a few other well known people.

~ ~ ~

"Come on, young Wiley, the music has started." As soon as the violins began Ian felt like she was going to hurl and quickly ran behind the bushes. Giles was close by to help her so she didn't puke all over her dress. As soon as she was finished he handed her a small bottle of Scope Mouthwash and she rinsed as many times as she could with the tiny travel bottle.

Ian closed her eyes and let out a long breath.

"I'm ready Giles."

He grabbed her hand and maneuvered her to the beginning of the aisle. All of the guests stood as the blond began to slowly make her way down. She wore a gorgeous halter style white Versace dress with elegant pearls and lace completing a pattern down the front and flowing back into the train. The upper part of her back and shoulders were open. She wore a light touch of make-up and a simple diamond Tiara in her hair. It was the family heirloom that her mother and grand mother both wore on their wedding days. She chose to wear only a tiny heel so that she wouldn't be much taller and Cassidy wouldn't have to wear four-inch heels to be close to eye level with her.

Halfway down the long walk Ian could feel the eyes boring into her and the camera flashes in all directions as she inched closer to the waiting Minister. Trina and Wendi were sitting by the empty seat next to Eileen Harland in the right front row so they could see Cassidy's face. The other front row was reserved for Giles, along with a picture of Ian's parents on one of the chairs. In the row behind that sat Rich and Clark with their guests and so on all the way back to the Mayor and State Senator along with their wives.

~ ~ ~

"Here we are." Giles said as they reached the end. "Your Mother and Father are so very proud of you today young Wiley. I know they are looking down on you right this moment."

Giles leaned over and kissed her check, stepped back, and took his seat. Ian let out the breath she'd been holding and turned around to see the most beautiful sight as Cassidy began to make her way down the isle with her father next to her. Cassidy's dress was also Versace, a white strapless gown with a flowing train as well as a pearl design on the front. Her jet black hair was up with small wispy pieces hanging down on her shoulders. Ian preferred her hair down, but this woman coming towards her at this moment looked like an angel sent down from the heavens. *An angel her parents sent her*, she thought as she smiled at the gray eyes staring at her.

Cassidy's father kissed the top of his daughters' head and took the seat next to his wife. Ian grabbed Cassidy's hand and stepped closer to the Minister surrounded by the candelabrums glowing on both sides of the altar. The sound system quieted down to play a soft background piano sonata.

~ ~ ~

"Good afternoon ladies and gentlemen. I thank you kindly for joining me as witnesses to this special day for Ian and Cassidy." The dark-haired Minister began the ceremony. Ian leaned close to Cassidy and whispered to her.

"I love you, my beautiful angel." A small tear fell from her big blue eyes. Cassidy felt tears falling down her face as well when she looked at Ian.

"I love you too, blue eyes." She smiled and whispered back.

The Minister continued talking briefly about both women and the powerful bond of love that they shared before asking them to recite the vows that they'd written to each other.

Cassidy began first.

"Ian Leland Wiley, I give you my love, my heart, and my soul. Since the day I met you I have felt an unconditional pull towards you. You're my strength, my weakness, my entire world. I find comfort, caring, and unrequited love when I look into your beautiful blue eyes. With this ring, I not only wed you and become your wife, I also find a life long best friend. I feel the passion and the love that flows in the Wiley tradition and I'm honored to become *your* Mrs. Wiley. I love you, Ian." Cassidy slid the ring set onto Ian's left hand as tears fell from her gray eyes.

Ian quickly grabbed the wedding band that she had made to match her own. "Cassidy Elaine Harland, you have shown me so much in our short time together. I can't begin to tell you how much I love you. When we first met I was a lost soul on the road to nowhere. You found me and helped me pick up the pieces as my life slowly came back together. For that, I will be thankful to you for the rest of my life. I have finally learned how to live, love, and to be loved in return. You are the light that leads me to our safe harbor. The day you told me you loved me was the happiest day of my life, until the day you said you'd marry me. Now as I stand here, this is the happiest day of my life, the day you become my wife, my partner, and forever my best friend. I love you, Cassidy." She slid the ring onto Cassidy's left hand. Both of them were covered in tears, their expensive make-up looked untouched.

"Now that you have both vowed to spend the rest of your lives together in sickness and in health, for better or worse, as long as you both shall live, if no one has any objections…" He paused. "Ian you may now kiss your bride."

Ian slowly pressed her soft lips against Cassidy's. The kiss was passionate, but soft and gentle. As soon as they broke away the Minister began again.

"Ladies and gentlemen, I give you Ian and Cassidy Wiley." Everyone cheered as the couple turned towards the crowd. Ian quickly kissed Cassidy again and grabbed her hand as they made their way back up the aisle and over to the reception tent.

~ ~ ~

After a very long processional line of guests congratulating them, they headed outside for an array of photos with the photographer, then back inside to begin the reception. The full bar opened up and the caterers began serving the dishes as Trina and Wendy stood up to toast the couple.

"I'll begin by saying if you'd asked me a year ago what I'd be doing today, the answer surely wouldn't be giving a speech at Cass's wedding." Wendi smiled. "But, I was there the day she met Ian and I knew something changed in her forever. There is no describing the happiness that Cassidy is glowing with, I can tell you she's been basking in it since the day they laid eyes on each other. I thought for sure it would calm down after they slept together, boy was I wrong." Everyone laughed. Cassidy felt herself turn two shades of pink. Wendi turned towards them. "I am so happy for the both of you. May your fire never burn out." She raised her glass and everyone toasted.

Trina smiled at the couple. "I won't go into as much detail as our beloved Wendi did." The group laughed again. "Although I will say that I also was a witness to the passion and powerful energy between these two women the night they met. I have never in my life seen anything like that and hope to god I do one day. Cassidy, you and Ian have taught me so much about love and honesty over the past few months. The two of you have amazing strength. Together you are an unstoppable force. I know I'll be standing here the day you have your fiftieth anniversary. I'll promise not to give the same speech, but truth be told, nothing holds a candle to the way you two love each other. I'm very happy for both of you. May your sheets never get cold." She raised her glass and cheered when the guests began laughing. Cassidy and Ian shook their heads and smiled.

"I think my parents are enjoying this." Cassidy whispered into Ian's ear.

"Wendi and Trina sure are getting a kick out of it." Ian smiled and kissed Cassidy's soft lips.

~ ~ ~

A few hours later Cassidy's parents had spoken

and even Giles stood up and said how happy he was for them. The caterers had served the most amazing Italian cuisine, although Cassidy and Ian agreed that Giles was a better cook. Most of the guests enjoyed the full bar and dancing on the large hardwood floor as Cassidy and Ian shared a few dances and made their way around talking to all of the guests. Cassidy never in her life imagined a Cinderella style wedding, complete with the Mayor and a State Senator, along with their wives. The entire event went well into the night. Cassidy and Ian made their way into the house to change clothes and prepare to leave the next day on their honeymoon. The Harland's and Giles slowly ushered the last of the guests to their cars, making sure everyone was sober enough to drive.

Graysen Morgen
Chapter 25

Ian stretched on the bed as the tiny hint of sunlight crept through the opening of the floor to ceiling drapes on the other side of her massive room. Cassidy's warm naked body was snuggled up against her. They'd spent the better part of their wedding night making love and finally dosed off together.

"What time is it, honey?" Cassidy asked as she squinted. The thin stream of light was cutting right across the bed. Ian turned her head towards the alarm clock.

"Seven a.m." She kissed the tousled dark head lying on her chest.

"Ugh! I think the morning after our wedding we should at least get to sleep in."

"Well yes, I do too. But, we need to get showered and have breakfast before we meet the press at Max's office to give a statement."

"What time does our flight leave?" Cassidy knew they were flying somewhere for their honeymoon, but that's all Ian would tell her. This was Ian's wedding gift to her. Cassidy had her gift to Ian all planned out and she was looking forward to seeing the reaction on the blonde's face.

"Ten. That's why we need to get moving, as much as I hate to get out of bed with you, Mrs. Wiley." Ian smiled and kissed her lips softly.

Just Me

"I love the way that sounds. I plan on keeping it forever."

"Good, I don't plan on ever taking it back. You're a Wiley now. It's time you learned to live like one."

"What's that suppose to mean?"

Ian winked. "You'll see soon enough my love. Go get in the shower before Giles comes barging in to wake us up. The shower's usually going by now."

~ ~ ~

Ian had arranged for Cassidy's tiny apartment to be packed up and moved to the estate while they were gone for the two week trip. Giles would see to it that everything arrived safely and was unpacked before they arrived home. The English butler was waiting in the kitchen when the happily married couple came down the stairs and sat at the dining room table.

"Good morning, young Wiley, Mrs. Wiley. May I get you anything?" He lingered for a moment.

"Yes Giles, two mimosas and a couple pieces of gingerbread toast." Cassidy answered him with a smile.

"You'll fit right in Mrs. Wiley. I see young Wiley has taught you well." He winked and disappeared into the kitchen. Ian smiled at her and picked up the funnies from the newspaper.

"Can you pass me the headlines please?" Cassidy asked. Ian looked at her sheepishly.

"Uh….I only read the funnies and the puzzles. I have Giles throw everything else out, unless it pertains to me and or my business."

Before Cassidy could make a statement, Giles appeared with the rest of the newspaper and handed it to

Cassidy.

"I thought your tastes for news might not mimic that of young Wiley." He quickly went back into the kitchen and returned with two tall glasses of chocolate milk and a stack of strawberry waffles.

"I love you, Giles." Cassidy said as she dug into the amazing looking breakfast. "You're going to make me fat."

"Tsk tsk, do you see any fat on her?" He nodded towards Ian. Cassidy's face turned three shades of red as she shook her head no. Giles smiled and went back to the kitchen.

~ ~ ~

"Max, I'd like to make this as quick and easy as possible, a small announcement of our wedding and then a picture of us." Ian sat across from the dark-haired man with her new wife Cassidy on her left side.

"No problem, I've already let them know there will be no questions."

"Good." Ian and Cassidy stood up and walked to the room where the local press was set up. Max and Dan, the Wiley attorney's spoke first and then Ian walked behind the lights with Cassidy's hand in hers. They stood with their sides touching, still holding hands.

"Good Morning ladies and gentlemen, I'll make this short and sweet." Ian smiled wryly. She hated dealing with the press and hated it even more now that her personal life had been dragged through the mud. "As I'm sure you are all aware, the lawsuit that my Corporation had against J.L. Hinkley has ended. Wiley Steel Corporation was on the winning side, but again as you should know trials almost always have the verdicts appealed. I will cross that bridge when I get to it." She squeezed Cassidy's hand. "As for my personal life, I am pleased to announce that as of four p.m. yesterday the former Miss Harland became Mrs. Wiley. We are now legally married in the eyes of Colorado. I would ask at this time that you give me and my family the same respect that you have been accustomed to over the years. Mrs. Wiley and I would gladly appreciate it. Thank you." Both women smiled for the few flashes as pictures were taken of them. They causally strode out of the office and into the back of the waiting Bentley.

"I suppose all went well?" Giles asked as he climbed into the front seat and shut the door.

Cassidy was thinking in the back of her mind about how much her life had drastically changed over night. Her Toyota SUV that she bought last year was soon to be replaced by a Mercedes, a BMW, or a Jaguar. She was given brochures to look through on the honeymoon so that Giles could have the car ready for her by the time they returned. She no longer drove herself to and from work, or even out to dinner for that matter unless she really needed to. Giles was her butler now just as much as he was Ian's. Her tiny comfortable apartment was replaced by a huge Tudor Style Mansion. Even her wardrobe would soon be replaced. Was she ready for all of this? Was she cut out for *royalty*? Her hands shook on her lap as the black car drove them behind the airport to a private hangar.

The blond felt her companion stiffen next to her. "What's wrong sweetheart?" She asked softly, her blue eyes twinkled when Cassidy looked at her.

"I…" *God, how do I tell her I'm scared to death?*

"It's nothing…I'm fine."

"I see…Cassidy we didn't start our relationship by lying to each other. Let's not start our marriage that way." She wrapped her arms around the slightly smaller woman and kissed her lips gently. "Whatever it is, you can tell me…remember when I'm with you it's *Just Me*."

"Oh Ian…I love you so much and I'm so incredibly happy with you."

"But…" Ian chimed in.

"I'm scared to death. My entire life has changed over night. I went from a single life and a regular job to being the wife of a multi-millionaire, being chauffeured around and flying in private planes and living in a mansion and driving some outrageously priced automobile." Her whole body was shaking.

"Aww honey, I know it's a lot to take in, especially overnight. And trust me I know it was literally overnight. We didn't really see each other as much as most couples that are engaged because of the lawsuit and the distance between our homes. I promise I'll do my best to make the transition easier for you." Ian leaned over and kissed Cassidy again, probing the kiss a little further and lingering a bit longer as it ended. Cassidy put her hand on the side of Ian's face.

"You're amazing," she whispered and pulled her blond wife down into another kiss.

Just Me
Chapter 26

The plane landed with a small thud on the tiny rickety single runway. Cassidy stared out the window at the surrounding palm trees and greenish blue water as the plane taxied toward a small terminal. Once the plane was stopped Ian stood up and retrieved their luggage from the overhead compartments. The small staircase descended as the door was opened. Ian grabbed Cassidy's hand and walked off of the plane as the airport staff grabbed their luggage and put it in the awaiting convertible Mercedes sports car.

"I see why you said to pack light, there's no backseat in the car and a very small trunk." Cassidy glanced slightly up at her partner. "Where are we?" *And since when do you not have a driver?*

"Welcome to the Cayman Islands, sweetheart." Ian grinned from ear to ear as Cassidy looked around at the island they were standing on.

~ ~ ~

Cassidy was highly impressed with the five star resort that they were booked at for the next two weeks. Each of the thirty suites was actually a private bungalow. None of them were connected, which left plenty of privacy. The beachfront resort had three extremely large pools, two hot tubs, and two tiki bars. As well as, a five star restaurant and nonstop entertainment with live bands every night. Cassidy stood inside of their bungalow and looked out at the ocean that was separated from them by about fifty feet of pure white sand. She felt as if she'd died and gone to heaven.

This was not her first time looking at the ocean, but definitely her most memorable. She'd never seen anything this beautiful. The windows were open letting the cool sea breeze in. Cassidy changed into the bathing suit she bought when she and Ian stopped at the upscale mall on the way to the resort. *I never knew Dolce and Gabbana made bathing suits.* She smiled to herself wondering how the hell the expensive designer could justify charging $500 for a thin piece of dental floss and a few strings. The solid black string bikini top and thong bottoms left nothing to the imagination.

"Wow!" She exclaimed to herself as she turned around in front of the mirror.

"Everything okay, honey?" Ian asked from the other side of the door. She'd already changed into her light blue Brazilian style bikini. She couldn't quite handle the thong style bottoms, but Brazilian style bottoms definitely left little to the imagination. Her string top was very similar to Cassidy's.

"What do you think?" Cassidy said as she stepped out of the bathroom and spun around in the large room. Ian's jaw hit the floor as she let out a low whistle.

"You're gorgeous!" Ian pulled her into a sexy embrace as she ran her hands down the brunette's back, stopping on her uncovered cheeks. She pressed her lips to the sensitive skin under Cassidy's ear. "I love you so much."

"Mm...I love you too. If you don't stop that we'll never get any sun while we're here. Do you want everyone to think all we did was make love during our two week long trip?" Cassidy asked playfully as she threaded her arms around Ian's neck and into the back of her hair.

"Would that be a bad thing? I mean we are married...married people do get-it-on, Cassidy." Ian bit her earlobe playfully. Cassidy tugged lightly on the hair between her fingers.

"I never want to stop making love with you, sweetheart, I'm only asking for a few hours of sunshine since we are on a beautiful sandy beach in the middle of the afternoon."

Ian pulled back slightly and kissed Cassidy softly. When her lips parted Ian's tongue probed further. Both women squeezed and caressed each other as their kiss continued to heat up. Cassidy tugged on Ian's bottom lip with her teeth and ran the tip of her tongue around the gentle lips.

Both women finally pulled away panting, their eyes were glazed over with desire. They knew if they didn't leave the room now they'd be in bed until the middle of the next day. Cassidy wrapped the black sheer sarong around her waist and tied the corner. Ian pulled on a short pair of board shorts. Both women stepped into their flip-flops and doused themselves with sunscreen even though they both had naturally tan skin.

~ ~ ~

"Oh my god the sun feels great." Cassidy lay back on a lounge chair in the sand close to the ocean and closed her eyes. Ian rolled her head to the side to look at her.

She's so incredibly sexy. "I love the cold weather, but this is nice and looking at you dressed like that is even nicer." She smiled.

Cassidy had taken off her sarong and laid it next to her chair so that she could tan evenly.

She opened her eyes to look at her lover and smiled when she saw the deep blue eyes sparkling in the sunlight.

"I have to agree, I'm a fan of the cooler weather, but this is beautiful."

Ian reached over and squeezed her hand gently. "I love you so much."

"That's good because I was beginning to wonder…" Ian cut her off and playfully smacked the brunette's flat stomach.

~ ~ ~

After a dinner filled with crab legs and lobster tail, Ian and Cassidy strolled down the beach hand in hand looking at the stars. Cassidy pointed towards a semi-secluded spot, Ian followed her lead around the palm trees and sat down next to her in the cool sand.

Cassidy leaned over and pressed her lips softly to Ian's. She backed away slightly before the kiss could go any deeper. "I brought you to this hidden little cove area because I think it's about time for me to give you your wedding present."

"Oh really…" Ian smiled.

"Yes, but I'm going to warn you now, I can't possibly top this trip. It's by far the best present I've ever been given."

"Anything you give me will be special because it's from you my love." Ian winked at her and smiled.

"Good." Cassidy took a deep breath. "Your gift doesn't involve wrapping paper or even a box. Instead, it's more of a vow or a promise if you will." Ian looked at her quizzically.

"Okay…"

"I…" Cassidy grabbed Ian's hands and held them in her own. "I've been doing a lot of thinking lately, especially, this past week. Ian I want to be the birth mother of your child." Cassidy quickly stopped Ian before she could butt in. "I spoke to my doctor a few days ago and we can do what's called Surrogate In Vitro Fertilization, meaning it's your egg and your DNA, but I carry it and have it as if it were my own."

Ian's eyes began to slowly shed the tears that she was holding back. "I love you so much, Cassidy Wiley."

Ian quickly pulled the slightly smaller woman into her arms and held her tightly as she placed tender kisses on her collarbone and then back up to her lips. She pushed back just enough to see the moonlight dancing across the gray eyes in front of her.

Cassidy spoke first. "I went with my heart on this because I believe you feel the same way. Although I have only known him a short time, I think Giles would make the perfect donor for the father."

The corners of Ian's mouth raised up as she struggled to wipe the tears from her face. "You are the most incredible, loving, beautiful woman I have ever met. I would trade everything in the world to have you in my life, I feel like the luckiest person on Earth. You make me so happy, Cassidy. I can't wait to see you pregnant with my child, that alone is a dream come true. Thank you for believing in me, in us." She forgot about wiping the tears and just let them fall as she pulled Cassidy on top of her and lay back in the sand.

Just Me
Epilogue

Cassidy finally took the Locomotive Services position at the Wiley Steel Corporate Office and they began to live their life together. Soon, they started preparing for the arrival of their child. Neither of them cared about the sex as long as it was a healthy bundle of joy. They turned one of the spare rooms in the mansion into a nursery and decorated everything in Snoopy. Ian and Giles painted the walls to look like the sky with small clouds and the sun in one corner. They also put a Snoopy border around the room at the top of the walls. The crib was against one wall with Snoopy sheets and a Snoopy blanket. Next to that was a changing table that had a Snoopy lamp clamped to one end of it. A wooden rocking chair was in the corner. Trina and Wendi made bets on whether or not the kid would grow up hating Snoopy. Of course, Ian and Cassidy had loved Snoopy as kids so they chose the theme.

~ ~ ~

Four months before her twenty ninth birthday, Ian paced the floor of Aspen General Hospital. Trina and Wendi sat in the waiting room with Mr. and Mrs. Harland. The same Minister that performed Ian and Cassidy's wedding was there to offer his prayers as the family waited for the doctors.

Cassidy Wiley was eight months pregnant and already on bed rest when she felt a sudden pain in her lower stomach. Ian called 911 and the ambulance rushed her wife to the hospital. She immediately called their close friends and family. Soon after they all arrived the doctor said that the baby was having complications and causing massive bleeding. He believed the placenta was separating from the uterine wall and would have to perform an emergency cesarean to save the baby's life. He was unsure what the chances would be for Mrs. Wiley to ever have another child since there was a very large possibility that he would need to perform a hysterectomy to save Cassidy's life as well. Ian told him to do everything that he had to do to protect her wife's health and the health of their unborn child.

Now, all Ian could do was wait and leave her faith in the hands of that young doctor. What she really wanted to do was scream at the top of her lungs and trade places with her wife on that operating table.

~ ~ ~

"I saw everyone in the waiting room young Wiley. Maybe you would like some company or would you rather pace the floor alone?" Giles asked when he put his hand on Ian's shoulder. She quickly turned into his arms and began to sob uncontrollably. It reminded him of the night her parents died. He wrapped his arms around the young woman and held her. He silently prayed for god to take her pain, just as he had done that same night two and a half years ago.

"Oh Giles…why…I don't understand why…"

Just Me

She sobbed even harder. "He can't take her from me too. I won't let him."

"Listen to me, no one is going to take that beautiful woman from you. You love her more than anything in this world. She's in good hands, and you'll both have a little life to take care of very soon. Come now. Let's go be with your family." He wrapped his arm around her as they walked down the hall. This was only the second time in her life that he'd ever physically consoled her like a father would. For those two times she would be forever grateful.

~ ~ ~

Three hours later the doctor walked through the doors to the waiting room. He looked tired. Ian could see the bags under his brown eyes. She jumped to her feet and met him face to face.

"Mrs. Wiley is going to be fine. She pulled through the procedure like a champ. I did have to do the hysterectomy. I'm sorry. She's resting now and asking to see you." He paused and Ian's heart stopped beating. "You're new baby girl also wants to see you." He smiled as Ian threw her arms around him.

"Oh thank you. Thank you so much!" She turned around to their friends and family and everyone clapped and cried at the same times. Ian said a slight prayer and hugged everyone. She wiped her face one last time before going to see her wife and newborn daughter.

~ ~ ~

The lighting was low in the large private room

and Cassidy appeared to be sleeping when Ian walked in. She quietly moved next to the bed and laid her hand on top of Cassidy's. She looked like a sleeping angel.

"Hey." She said groggily as she opened her eyes. Ian leaned over and kissed her lips.

"I love you so much." Ian smiled and brushed Cassidy's jet black hair back from her face with her free hand.

"I love you too."

"Pardon me, but there's a tiny little girl kicking and screaming out here to meet her Mothers," the blond haired nurse said as she wheeled the cart into the room. She put a small bottle on the table and left the two women to enjoy their first moments with their daughter.

"Oh my god, Cassidy, look at her!" Ian bent down and picked up the tiny infant bundled in a pink blanket and held her in her arms. "She's perfect!" Ian kissed her forehead softly and waited for the nurse to elevate the bed so that Cassidy could hold her daughter. Then Ian gently placed the baby into her arms.

"She has your eyes Ian." Cassidy pulled the little hat back to reveal a head full of blond hair. "Yep, she's a Wiley." Cassidy laughed and covered the small head back up.

"She's beautiful, just like you." Ian sat on the bed next to her wife and held the baby again.

The nurse came back a few minutes later with a thin folder. "This little angel needs a name, have you ladies come up with one yet?" She asked as she laid the file on the counter and opened it up. Cassidy looked over at Ian.

"Yes, ma'am, we have. Her name is Leland Cassidy Wiley." Ian smiled at her wife and felt the warm bundle in her arms squirm in the blanket. "I think she likes it."

"She's a Wiley, I'm sure she's going to love it." Cassidy smiled and kissed Ian's lips.

About the Author

Graysen Morgen was born and raised in North Florida with winding rivers and waterways at her back door and the white sandy beach a mile away. She has spent most of her lifetime in the sun and on the water. She enjoys reading, writing, fishing, and spending as much time as possible with her partner and their daughter.

You can contact Graysen at graysenmorgen@aol.com and like her fan page on facebook.com/graysenmorgen

CPSIA information can be obtained
at www.ICGtesting.com
Printed in the USA
LVHW051322271220
675115LV00058B/3982